W9-BHU-464

Praise for
REBECCA BRANDEWYNE

"From the prologue, it is apparent that *The Ninefold Key*
is not a simple romance...that this is a brilliant, well-planned
gothic tale much in the same vein as those of Susan Howatch.
Mesmerizing from its opening page to its very satisfying
conclusion, *The Ninefold Key* is impossible to put down.
With well-written characters and a gripping premise,
this is a not-to-be missed novel."
—Jani Brooks, for *Romance Reviews Today*

"Fans of historical romantic suspense with a touch of
Egyptology will appreciate *The Ninefold Key*, a fascinating
work that keeps reader interest starting from page one because
the audience wants to know more about the scarab and the
'nine keys.' The ensemble cast contains numerous interrelated
but unique players...readers will treasure this action-packed
thriller that has a fantastic romance as a major subplot."
—Harriet Klausner (#1 *Amazon.com* reviewer)

"Brandewyne appeals to the readership of *Across a Starlit Sea*
with a lush novel brimming with rich historical details and
written in the grand tradition of the Victorian gothic, complete
with a huge cast of characters, a stolen gem, a curse, a mystery
and a love story. More engrossing mystery than pure romance,
[The Ninefold Key] unfolds slowly, luring the reader in as
each character is brought into this carefully constructed and
intriguing tale (à la Dickens) that will captivate gothic fans."
—Kathe Robin, for *Romantic Times BOOKreviews*

REBECCA
BRANDEWYNE

PROM
Brandewy

ISBN-13: 978-0-7783-2296-2
ISBN-10:   0-7783-2296-3

THE CRYSTAL ROSE

For the Booze Brothers
and the Sweet Sisters.
May all your futures be bright and beautiful!

CONTENTS

CONTENTS

CAST OF CHARACTERS

IN INDIA:

In Delhi:

Colonel Hilary Windermere, an officer in
  Her Majesty's Army
Mrs. Violet Windermere, his wife

Their daughters:
Rose
Jasmine
Lily
Heather
Angelica
Daisy

Francis and Anamitra Drayton,
  Earl and Countess of Thornleigh
Lord Hugo Drayton, Viscount Lansdowne and their son
Mayur Singh, Indian manservant to
  Viscount Lansdowne

IN ENGLAND:

In London:

At Russell Square:

Miss Candlish, the housekeeper
Mrs. Beasley, the cook
Hannah, a housemaid
Nancy, a housemaid
Polly, the scullery maid

Professor Prosser, a university teacher

The Street Lads and Lasses:

Ashley, a flower girl
Bobby, the pickpocket
Brock, the butcher boy
Burke, the street artist
Chandon, a dock worker
Chris, the pie man
Constable Dreiling, a policeman
Jake, the livery-stable boy
Joey, the velocipede rider
Jolette, a flower girl
Jordan, the grocery boy
Leddy, the newspaper boy
Nick, the baker boy
Victor, the fish boy

In Harley Street:

Mr. Raj Khanna, an Indian gentleman
Mahout, Indian manservant to Mr. Khanna

At Lincoln's Inn Fields:

Mrs. Delphine Squasher, a widow
Onslow, a hireling
Lombard, a hireling

At Belgrave Square:

Mr. Avery Ploughell, a Member of Parliament
Mr. Douglas Delwyn, a barrister
Mrs. Lynne Ambrose, a widow
Eastlake, a butler

At Grosvenor Square:

Lord Saxon St. Giles, Marquess of Highmoor

At Southwark:

Mrs. Charlotte Blott, mother of Mr. Gerald Blott

On Dartmoor:

At Drayton Hall:

James Wormwood, Earl of Thornleigh

Mr. Gerald Blott, a rakehell
Mrs. Dora Blott, wife to Mr. Blott

THE CRYSTAL ROSE

The Crystal Rose

O, my love is like the fairest rose,
That's newly sprung in May.
O, my love in distant Delhi grows,
And sweet was that summer day

When first I spied her bonnie face
Uplifted to the sun.
Had she not a faerie's grace?
We were fated to be one.

But we must part, my only love!
So fare thee well a while!
Still, I will come again, my love,
Though it were ten thousand mile!

Trust to the gods and destiny.
A chance encounter brings
A meeting dear 'tween you and me.
Toward home, I walk on wings.

Two halves of one gold coin, we are,
United, whole again,
And I who loved you from afar
Can speak now of my pain

Stilled by the everlasting bond
The two of us e'er share,
And to my love so true and fond,
My soul's dark secrets bare.

As fair art thou, my crystal rose,
So deep in love am I,
And I will love thee still, my rose,
Till all the seas run dry.

Till all the seas run dry, my dear,
And the rocks melt with the sun!
And I will love thee still, my dear,
When the sands of life are done.*

Poem adapted from A Red, Red Rose by Robert Burns.

Prologue

In Distant Delhi

Ornament is but the guiled shore
To a most dangerous sea; the beauteous scarf
Veiling an Indian beauty.
>   *The Merchant of Venice* [1596-1597]
>   —William Shakespeare

Thieves in the Night

> Dusk faces with white silken turbans wreathed.
> > *Paradise Regained* [1671]
> > > —John Milton

Chandni Chowk, Delhi, India, 1835

It was the shouts and screams that wakened young Rose Windermere.

And the light.

Like celebratory fireworks, this last illuminated the black-velvet night sky, made all the more terrible and terrifying by the fact that despite its inherent evil, it was strangely beautiful. Its tongues of wild yellow-orange flame cast shadows that danced like unbridled revelers on her bedroom walls, and showers of bright sparks rained like tiny shooting stars through the open windows, to flicker and die upon the hardwood floor.

Her mouth forming a small O of wonder, Rose sat up in bed, momentarily mesmerized by the brilliant, blazing light and cinders, not comprehending, at first, their awful significance. Then, slowly, the shouts and screams that echoed from beyond the open windows penetrated her consciousness, just as the acrid smell of billowing smoke permeated her nostrils, and she understood that something was horribly wrong. Confirming her sudden fright was the cacophony she could now also hear ensuing in her father's *haveli* or mansion, which fronted on Chandni Chowk, the main street and marketplace of Delhi. Her mother's piercing shrieks rang through the house, panicking Rose as she made out the words through the closed door of the bedroom.

"God save us! Lord Thornleigh's *haveli* is on fire!"

At that, Rose felt a fist of even greater fear clench her heart and begin to squeeze tightly.

Hugo! What had happened to Hugo?

Abruptly scrambling from bed, she ran to one of the windows, dragging over a small stool upon which to stand, so that she could see outside. To her utter horror, the mansion next door, where her best friend, Hugo Drayton, and his family lived, was indeed consumed by a conflagration. That was the cause of the wickedly beautiful light and flying sparks that had, only an instant before, so enthralled her.

Now, they only appalled her.

From their own quarters at the rear of the burning house, the Indian servants who worked at Lord Thornleigh's *haveli* had come running. But although they had formed a bucket brigade from the old stone well in the back garden and were now attempting to douse the lethal flames, it was clear even to the eight-year-old Rose that their battle to save the mansion was futile. The fire must have taken hold swiftly, she thought, and it was now far too advanced to halt. The best that could be hoped for was to prevent it from spreading to the neighboring houses along Chandni Chowk.

Even from the window where she leaned upon the sill, Rose could feel the dreadful heat of the blaze, and every now and then, as she watched, a cinder landed upon her, singeing her. But such was her terror over what had befallen Hugo that she scarcely felt the pain, was unaware of the small holes that were being charred into her thin white cotton nightgown.

But then, startling her from her rapt fixation on Lord Thornleigh's *haveli*, the bedroom door was suddenly flung open wide, and Vina, her Indian ayah, appeared, along with several other of the Windermeres' servants.

"Little *memsahib!*" Vina cried, aghast as she spied Rose at the window. "What are you doing out of bed? You must come away from the window at once! Do you not see how the sparks have burnt you? Your nightgown could catch fire! You could go up in smoke like Lord Thornleigh's *haveli!*"

"Vina, where is Hugo? Is he all right?" Rose asked anxiously, as she allowed herself to be assisted down from the stool and led away from the window. "How did the fire start?"

"I do not know. Colonel Windermere has gone next door not only to help, but also to see what he can discover. Naturally, Mrs. Windermere is beside herself. She wishes to be assured that all her daughters are safe—so she must not see you looking like this!"

As she spoke, Vina stripped off Rose's singed, smoky nightgown, then bundled her into a fresh, clean one, along with a robe and slippers. After that, she washed Rose's face and hands, which were streaked with soot. Meanwhile, the rest of the servants who had accompanied the ayah moved to close the bedroom windows and also to rouse Rose's seven-year-old sister, Jasmine, from bed.

"Come," Vina commanded, hurrying the others along. "If the fire spreads, we must be prepared to leave Colonel Windermere's *haveli* at once!"

Rose wanted desperately to ask more questions. But Vina bade her be silent, then, taking her hand, hustled her from the bedroom and down the hall, where they were joined by more servants and the rest of Rose's younger sisters. Her slippered feet whispering along the bare wood floor as she practically skipped to keep up, Rose swallowed hard to choke back the words that threatened to tumble from her lips. She had never before seen Vina in such a stern state. Usually, the ayah was pleasant and soft-spoken. But at the moment, Vina's dark-skinned countenance looked forbidding. Her voice rasped as she urged those who trailed in her wake to even greater speed, and her grasp on Rose's small hand was positively crushing.

But still, as they descended the central staircase in the main hall to the small drawing room below, they went down the steps so quickly that Rose felt sure she would have slipped and fallen had not the ayah gripped her so tightly.

"My children! Oh, thank God, you are all safe and sound!" Mrs. Windermere cried, tears of relief streaming down her face as they entered the spacious room. To make certain, she counted heads, hugging and kissing each of her six daughters, from somber Rose, the oldest, to little Daisy, the three-year-old baby of the family, who, miraculously, still slept and had been carried downstairs by her ayah.

"Mama." Rose tugged insistently on her mother's gown. "What has happened to Hugo?"

"I don't know," Mrs. Windermere said absently, clearly distraught. "The Colonel has gone next door to try to find out, but he hasn't returned. I only hope he is all right—and Hugo, as well, of course! Indeed, we must say a prayer not only for your father and young Master Hugo, but also for Lord and Lady Thornleigh. Now, all you girls must sit here quietly and not leave the room—for if the fire cannot be contained, we shall have to evacuate the premises immediately!"

"You mean…leave our home, Mama?" Lily, Rose's six-year-old sister, asked worriedly. "But I don't want to go out into the dark!" Then, without warning, she burst into tears.

"Hush, Lily," Mrs. Windermere chided, "for I cannot think with you setting up such a wail! Oh, what must we do to prepare? Naturally, we must take my jewels and the family silver with us…."

Scurrying about the room, clutching first one highly prized object and then another, Mrs. Windermere continued alternately to talk to herself and to issue orders to the servants. The latter, long aware of their mistress's habitual fluster, now worsened in a crisis, moved swiftly and silently to do what was actually necessary. Watching mutely, Rose perched woodenly on the sofa, her heart hammering so loudly in her breast that she could hear it roaring in her ears.

What had happened to Hugo?

* * *

With his bare hands, Mayur Singh had killed a man. With his own eyes, thirteen-year-old Lord Hugo Drayton, Viscount Lansdowne and heir to his father's earldom of Thornleigh, had seen it happen. But even now, when he knew his parents, Lord and Lady Thornleigh, had been brutally murdered in their beds and that he, too, would be dead in his own if not for the quick, savage actions of his manservant, Mayur Singh, to protect him, he could scarcely believe it.

As Hugo crouched in a clump of crepe myrtle beyond his father's burning *haveli*, his only thought was that, curiously, despite the heat of both summer and the conflagration, he was cold and shivering in the clothes in which his manservant had hastily dressed him before furtively leading him from the flaming mansion. After fiercely bidding him to remain hidden and silent in the cover of the bushes, Mayur Singh had disappeared back into the house, and now, Hugo did not know what had become of him, whether he, too, was dead, had been roasted alive in the *haveli*.

Hugo did not understand why his manservant had believed it necessary to conceal him, for surely, the dacoits, the Indian bandits who had attacked the mansion, were long gone, vanished into the night after killing his parents and robbing the house of whatever could easily be carried from it. Almost, he was tempted to leave his hiding place to try to learn for himself whatever he could. Only the thought of Mayur Singh's anger at and disapproval of his disobedience dissuaded him. Still, he felt like a coward, cowering in the crepe myrtle, while the servants risked their lives to attempt to stop the raging fire from spreading.

At the thought of this last, Hugo glanced anxiously at the house next door, where his best friend, Rose Windermere, lived. Startling him, almost as though he had wished her there, her small, fairylike face suddenly appeared at one of the upstairs windows.

"Rose!" Hugo called out hoarsely, forgetting himself. "Rose!"

But much to his despair, the noise and confusion that reigned in the night were such that she did not hear him. No one did—except for Mayur Singh, who slipped up behind him and placed a hand over his mouth to silence him. At first, not realizing it was his manservant, Hugo struggled desperately, fearing he had been discovered and seized by one of the dacoits. But then Mayur Singh spoke.

"Be still, *sahib!* It is only I."

"Well, thank goodness for that!" Hugo said, with a great deal of relief, as his manservant slowly released him. "Where have you been?"

"Fetching this." Mayur Singh held up the silver strongbox that had belonged to Hugo's father. "It contains important documents you will need someday, and fortunately, the bandits did not know where it was concealed. Now, come. We must go."

"Go? Go where?"

"To your mother's people in the Punjab, of course."

"But...why?" Hugo was stricken by the very idea. "Surely, the best course of action is to go next door to the Windermeres' *haveli* and make a full report to the Colonel!"

"No." The manservant shook his head gravely. "I know the Windermeres are your friends and that you and the little *memsahib* Miss Windermere are close. But at the moment, we dare trust no one but your mother's people."

"But…why? Why, Mayur Singh? Why can we not trust the Windermeres? Oh, why has this terrible thing happened? I do not understand it at all!"

"No…no more do I, *sahib*," the manservant said gravely. "On its face, it seems nothing more than a robbery. But then, why murder your parents? I ask myself. It is troubling…that. It casts a different light on the matter, so that I do not believe that all that has occurred tonight is exactly what it appears."

"Why, whatever do you mean by that, Mayur Singh?" Hugo frowned, puzzled and perturbed.

"The dacoits evidently possessed inside knowledge about your parents, their *haveli*, and their possessions. So it may be that this was no random attack. With your parents and you out of the way, your cousin, Sir James Wormwood, stands to inherit Lord Thornleigh's title and estates, and I have never liked or trusted him."

Hugo was shocked and greatly disturbed by this last admission, for it had never occurred to him that his own cousin would wish him and his family harm.

"But…Mayur Singh, you said nothing of this before, when Sir James first came from England to India and our *haveli*."

"No, for it was not my place, *sahib*."

"But are your suspicions now not all the more reason to make a full report to Colonel Windermere?"

"No, for I have no proof—yet—to support them, and if we go to Colonel Windermere, Sir James will learn that you are still alive. If he *is* behind tonight's assault, that would endanger your life, *sahib*, and that, I cannot permit. Now, come. Hurry! We must get away while the rest of the servants are still occupied with trying to contain the fire, so that we can make good our escape unseen."

Dimly, in some dark corner of his mind, Hugo realized that he was not himself, that he was in a state of shock that had left him cold and terrified. It was difficult for him to digest the fact that his cousin might have plotted his demise. But since he hardly knew Sir James Wormwood, had been born in India, and cared for all his life by Mayur Singh, his trusted manservant, advisor, and friend, he made no further protest. Instead, swallowing hard, he nodded slowly, following Mayur Singh furtively from the bushes.

As he did so, Hugo glanced again at the upstairs window of the Windermeres' mansion, where he had spied Rose earlier. But much to his distress, she was gone now, and the window was shut up tight. He felt even sicker at heart at the sight. What if the servants could not stop the blaze from spreading? What if the Windermeres' house caught fire, and Rose was burned alive?

Sudden hot tears stung his eyes. He dashed them away covertly, hoping his manservant had not noticed them, and indeed, Mayur Singh's swarthy face was impassive in the moonlight when he spoke quietly.

"You need have no fear for the little *memsahib* Miss Windermere, *sahib*. If the flames cannot be checked, the Windermeres will have ample time and warning to escape from their *haveli*."

"Do you...do you think I'll ever see her again, Mayur Singh?"

"If you wish it."

"I *do* wish it!" Hugo insisted fiercely.

"Then, one day, it will indeed be so."

"Your more than diligent efforts to try to track down the dacoits who murdered my uncle Francis and his wife and son are to be commended, Colonel. But now that more than three months has passed, I think even you must admit it is highly unlikely the bandits shall ever be brought to justice. No...depend upon it: They have fled into the Punjab or some other wild region, where they will never be apprehended and forced to pay for their crimes. It's maddening, of course. But all the same, there it is."

After sipping from his china teacup, Sir James Wormwood replaced it in its matching saucer, then set both down on a small round table to one side. From behind the thick glass of his silver-rimmed spectacles, his pale blue eyes stared at Colonel and Mrs. Windermere unblinkingly, so that the latter was reminded of nothing so much as an odious toad, and despite the heat of the summer day, she shivered faintly.

"Really, Colonel," Sir James continued, "I'm quite

certain you've done all you can in this matter and
that you have other, more pressing duties than ferreting out the murderers of my poor, unfortunate uncle
and his family. Naturally, it is a great tragedy. But I'm
afraid that India is a harsh and unforgiving country—
filled with unexpected dangers. I wonder that concern
over the welfare of your own wife and daughters has
not caused you to resign your commission and return
home to England...."

Was there a veiled threat contained in those last
words? Mrs. Windermere rather fancied there was,
and she was glad when Sir James abruptly stood, preparing to take his leave of them. Once he had finally
departed from the small drawing room, she turned
anxiously to her husband.

"I don't like Sir James," she announced, her voice
quavering slightly and her lower lip tremulous. "He is
a devil! Truly, I hope he doesn't come here again!"

"M'dear, it's most unlike you to be so uncharitable,"
Colonel Windermere observed slowly, surprised by his
wife's uncharacteristic declaration.

"I know, but, really, I cannot help how I feel—and
if you were honest, Colonel, you would confess that
you don't like the man any more than I do!"

"No, you're right, Violet. I don't." The colonel sighed
heavily. "Worse, although I have as yet been unable to
prove it, I suspect him of having had something to do
with the murders of Lord and Lady Thornleigh and young
Master Hugo—for Sir James will now inherit the title and
estates that would otherwise have gone to Hugo."

"I knew it! Oh, dear Colonel, you have confirmed my worst fears about Sir James! I never liked him from the start! Oh, how I wish he'd never come to India! Poor Lord and Lady Thornleigh, and poor Hugo, too! His untimely, brutal death has just about killed our own poor daughter Rose, as well!" Mrs. Windermere asserted, visibly distressed by the notion. "She's always been a strange, fey child—almost like a changeling or a fairy, I've always thought. But these past several weeks since the fire and Hugo's death, she's lost so much weight that she couldn't afford to lose to begin with that she's virtually a wraith! I tell you, Colonel, I'm worried sick about her—and about the rest of us, also! For what is to become of us all in this godforsaken country? Are we to be murdered in our beds, like poor Lord and Lady Thornleigh and Hugo? If you're right and Sir James *was* somehow behind the attack on them—and I do not doubt it for a moment, since the earldom of Thornleigh is so much richer than the badly mismanaged estate Sir James inherited—why, what is to prevent him from trying to do away with us, too? It is abundantly clear that he wants your investigation to cease! And even if he is innocent, if bandits are growing so bold as to assault the *havelis* of the wealthy in Delhi, we could be their next target!"

"Yes, I know, and I've spent many a long night fretting about these same very disturbing possibilities, m'dear—and I've decided that for the safety and well-being of us all, it really *is* best if I resign my commission in Her Majesty's Army and we leave India and return home to England as soon as possible."

"Resign your commission!" Mrs. Windermere was stunned, for in all truth, she had never expected anything like this. "But—but, Colonel, how will we live?"

"Naturally, I'll be refunded the full purchase price of my commission by the army, and I've a little set aside for a rainy day, besides. We shall have to economize, of course, pinch our shillings, that sort of thing, for we won't be able to afford quite such a lavish lifestyle in England as we have enjoyed here in India. Still, I'm sure we'll manage just fine, Violet," the colonel insisted cheerfully.

Mrs. Windermere wasn't nearly as certain of this as her husband. Nevertheless, when she weighed her purse against the lives of herself and her family, she knew she would rather be poor than dead.

In the hall beyond the small drawing room, Rose, who had only moments before knelt furtively at the door, her ear pressed to the keyhole so that she could eavesdrop on her parents' conversation, at last crept away guiltily, in a state of deep dejection.

Leave India!

That thought was horrifying to her. India—not England—was her home. She had been born here, and this was all the world she had ever known. Besides, if she left India, she would never see Hugo again—for deep down in her heart, Rose held fast to the hope that no matter what anyone said, he was still alive somehow. It just couldn't be true that he was dead and buried in his grave forever. She would never believe that.

Never!

Book One

A Chance Encounter

Chance is perhaps the pseudonym of God
when He did not want to sign.
                    Le Jardin d'Épicure [1894]
                              —Anatole France
              [Jacques Anatole François Thibault]

One

To sleep: perchance to dream: ay, there's the rub;
For in that sleep of death what dreams may come
When we have shuffled off this mortal coil,
Must give us pause.

Hamlet [1600-1601]
—William Shakespeare

Rose's Dream of India…

*T*he Ancient Ones had called it Indraprastha and claimed
that it was the Kingdom of the Gods. But to the silver-blond
child who stood at the heart of its wide main road and
crowded marketplace, her small, arresting face upturned
to the bright hot sun, Delhi was simply the city of her birth
and all of the world that she had ever known. Its boundaries were marked by a great, encompassing red-sandstone

wall erected by the mighty Mughul emperor Shah Jahan nearly two hundred years before she had been born within its confines, and she had never been beyond them.

Because it was May, the stifling heat of summer already enveloped Delhi. Like a cobra, the city basked on the expansive plains along the vast River Yamuna's western bank, beneath the impassive, stony gaze of the Himalaya, Aravali, and Shivalik mountains that hove up beyond, cutting jagged-edged obliques into the sweeping azure sky. From Baluchistan to the west blew a hot, arid wind that slunk through the streets and alleys, powdering them with a fine layer of dust. Toward the end of June, the monsoons would come to flood the sandy lower plain and cool the suffocating air that hung over Delhi. But for now, the city baked in the blistering afternoon sun.

Beneath the frilly white silk parasol carried by her ayah, Vina, to protect her pale, delicate skin from the sun's harsh, unforgiving rays, the child—one Rose Windermere by name—sweltered, too. Enviously, she eyed the nearly naked, dark-skinned beggar children who splashed and waded in the cool water of the Faiz Nahar canal, which was fed by the river and ran along the center of Chandni Chowk, bisecting the length of the main road and marketplace. Rose longed to snatch off most of her own constricting English clothing and join the boisterous, unbridled youngsters at play. But that would be neither proper behavior for the eldest daughter of a colonel in Her Majesty's Army, nor setting a good example for the heathen Indian natives.

So, instead, these strictures having been inculcated in

*her since her birth by her mother, she only stood and
watched wistfully, yearning ardently for the freedom of the
other children, her face soaking up the heat of the sun,
which steamed down upon her, despite the parasol her ayah
held to shield her. Once or twice, when droplets of the canal
water stirred up by the youngsters showered like rain upon
her, she smiled with rapt pleasure.*

*Earlier that morning, as usual, the eight-year-old Rose
had been hard at work on her daily lessons in the school-
room on the upper floor of her father's haveli, the family
mansion fronting Chandni Chowk, which house he had
acquired upon having been posted by Her Majesty's Army
to Delhi. She had hurried to complete her studies so that
she could go outside before the hottest hour of the day
ensued. Then, finally, her lessons finished and Vina accom-
panying her, Rose had set out eagerly to explore Chandni
Chowk, which, despite her having been born there, she still
found endlessly fascinating.*

*Originally located in an octagonal open space beyond
Begum ka Bagh, the beautiful gardens planted by Shah
Jahan's eldest and most-favored daughter, Jahanara
Begum, Chandni Chowk had since its inception grown to
be the heart and soul of Delhi. According to the legend Rose
knew by heart, its name meant The Moonlit Square, and
it was so called because when Jahanara Begum had built
it, just as she had the gardens, she had constructed a square
pool in the center of the road, whose waters reflected the
moonlight and starlight, making it seem as though a
thousand scattered jasmine petals floated on its surface.
The pool was fed by the canal, which Jahanara Begum's*

father had ordered renovated during his reign, to provide drinking water for the people and irrigation for their crops.

To the east rose the serene Jain Temple with its pristine bird hospital and sanctuary, the great mosque Jama Masjid, and the massive, looming Lahore Gate, the latter of which gave way to the long-dead Shah's magnificent, imposing palace, Lal Qila—the Red Fort—that, like Delhi itself, sprawled along the western bank of the vast river. To the west sat the mosque Fatehpuri Masjid, in all its glorious splendor. From Chandni Chowk radiated a labyrinth of other roads and narrow, twisting alleys that housed the dozens of bazaars in the city.

East of Kalan Mahal, where the brass polishers gathered to ply their trade, caged chickens cackled and fresh-caught fish stared sightlessly in the foul, stinking poultry and fish markets. In stark contrast to that stench, air heavy with the mingled scents of aniseed, chutneys, dried mangoes, edible leaves of silver paper, ginger, lotus seeds, pickles, pomegranates, reetha nuts, saffron, sugars, and turmeric wafted from the exotically fragrant flour and spice markets of the Naya Bazaar on Khari Baoli. Shops in the Kinari Bazaar burgeoned with a profusion of brightly colored wedding finery and all its accoutrements, while at the arched windows and on the small balconies of the houses in the Chawri Bazaar, kohl-eyed "dancing girls" displayed themselves and called out to passing men to come enjoy their favors.

From all the bazaars and Chandni Chowk itself rose a cacophony of merchants hawking their wares, of buyers bartering heatedly with sellers, of servants issuing orders to clear paths for palanquins and of children shouting and laughing at play. Along the main road clattered horse-

drawn carriages and oxen-drawn carts that jostled for space alongside occasional saddled camels and howdah-topped elephants, which also served as transport in the exotic city.

"Would you like some sohanhalwa, Rose?" Hugo asked.

Lord Hugo Drayton, Viscount Lansdowne, was Rose's best friend. Although at age thirteen, he was five years older than she, since they lived next door to each other, they had grown up together and become close, sharing dreams and secrets. Earlier, Rose and her ayah had met Hugo and his manservant, Mayur Singh, on the wide main road, and companionably, the four had continued on their way together. A few minutes ago, Hugo had paused at Ghantewala, the oldest sweet shop in Chandni Chowk, where he had bought a handful of sohanhalwa, a sweet made from dry fruits, sprouts and sugar.

Nodding and smiling happily, Rose accepted one of the proffered treats, biting into it eagerly, knowing from past experience that it must be eaten quickly, before it attracted the hordes of flies that were ever-present in Delhi.

She adored Ghantewala. An old legend claimed that when the emperor's royal procession had used to pass along Chandni Chowk, it had stopped before the shop so that he could be offered its sweets, which had also been fed to his elephant. After a while, the elephant had come to know the shop so well that it had begun to halt there of its own accord, shaking its head and causing the tiny bells on its harness to ring until it received its treats. That was how Ghantewala had received its name, for the Hindi ghante meant "bell."

Now, as Rose stood there in the sun, savoring her sweet and licking her sticky fingers, she observed an elephant plodding along Chandni Chowk, and although she knew it did not belong to the long-dead emperor, still, she wondered if it, too, would pause at the shop, waiting impatiently for a treat. The beast's trappings were richly appointed, for only the wealthiest of Indians could afford the animals. Its leather harness was adorned with tall, fine plumes and little gold bells that tinkled in the sultry air, and its howdah was draped with gold-threaded silks and satins in a multitude of vibrant hues and trimmed with thick fringes and ornate braids from which hung solid-gold coins. Now and then, as the howdah's curtains swayed in the breeze, Rose could glimpse a young nobleman inside. Alongside the elephant walked its mahout.

Closing her wide green eyes, Rose imagined that the beast really did belong to the emperor and that, at any moment now, it would stop before the sweet shop. So, what startled the animal, she would never know. She knew only that, without warning, the shriek of what sounded like a woman, but that she knew from long experience was actually a peacock, rang out. Then the elephant trumpeted long and loud before suddenly knocking down its mahout and beginning to stampede along Chandni Chowk, wreaking havoc on the main road and marketplace.

As the clearly terrified beast rushed headlong down the crowded street, horrified people screamed and ran in all directions, trampling one another in their desperate haste to escape from the furiously charging animal. Ayahs and mothers hurriedly scooped up frightened, bawling children, trying to carry them to safety. But much to Rose's despair, as the throng about her scattered and fled, she was roughly jostled and pushed this way and that, and, the impetus propelling her forward, separated from her own ayah.

Glancing wildly about the road, she was petrified to observe the rampaging elephant smashing stands and carts before abruptly pelting straight toward her. Until now, she had not known that the huge, seemingly ponderous beasts could travel so fast. Fruits, vegetables, flowers, and shards of wood from the shattered stands and carts flew in all directions as a result of the animal's destruction. A pomegranate struck her hard on the cheek, making her cry out, as falling petals from broken blossoms showered like falling stars upon her.

All around her, everything seemed to move in slow motion, blurred at the edges, as though it were a scene in a vignette, frozen in time. The elephant galloped toward her, trumpeting madly. In some dim corner of her mind, she realized the young nobleman inside the howdah atop the beast was as terrified as she, for he hung on for dear life as the animal careened this way and that.

Then, the next thing Rose knew, Hugo scooped her up, snatching her from the elephant's lethal path, while Mayur Singh boldly grabbed hold of the beast's harness. For what seemed an eternity to Rose, the manservant dangled in midair, and she thought he would be crushed to death by the animal. But then gradually, much to her surprise and relief, the elephant slowed its charge and finally came to a halt, standing quietly while Mayur Singh spoke to it and calmed it.

Eventually, the beast's mahout appeared, limping forward to take charge of it, obsequiously bowing and scraping as he did so, apologizing repeatedly to his young master in the howdah and thanking the manservant profusely. The young nobleman, recovering his composure, took a small leather pouch from his belt and, opening it, threw a handful of coins into the frightened, angry crowd that had now gathered, demanding reparation for their fear and the losses they had suffered. Then he also tossed a solid-gold coin to Mayur Singh, who caught it deftly.

After that, speaking a few sharp words to his mahout, the young nobleman firmly closed the ornate curtains of the howdah, and the mahout led the elephant onward along Chandni Chowk.

As Rose's ayah, Vina, rushed forward, jabbering hysterically, Hugo set Rose down in the street, gravely inquiring if she were all right. Still trembling a little in the aftermath, she nodded.

"You saved my life," she said.

"He who saves a life is responsible for it ever after," Mayur Singh noted soberly. "Hush, Vina! The little memsahib is unharmed, and all is well."

But much to Rose's horror, as the manservant made this announcement, the elephant suddenly turned back toward them, trumpeting again savagely. Except that this time, yellow-orange flames shot from its trunk, setting Mayur Singh and Hugo ablaze, so that they became pillars of fire, running this way and that, until all of Chandni Chowk was burning, burning....

Russell Square, London, England, 1850

Rose awoke with a start from the clutches of the dream—the nightmare—that had just moments before held her fast. For an instant, dazed and disoriented, she mistakenly believed she was a child again, tucked away in her bedroom in her father's *haveli* in Chandni Chowk. But then, slowly, as the gentle pitter-patter of the rain against the mullioned windows slowly penetrated her senses, she realized she was a woman fully grown and that the bedroom in which she lay was the one she shared with her younger sister, Jasmine, in their father's London town house in Russell Square.

Rain had rarely ever come lightly in Delhi. Rather, it had come with a vengeance borne on the fierce, howling winds of the monsoons that had blown inland from the Indian Ocean to drench all in their wake. Lying in bed, the tears she had cried earlier in her sleep still trickling silently down her cheeks, Rose thought how strange it was that, after all these years, her dream should so suddenly and inexplicably have transported her back to her childhood and Delhi. It was a very long time since she had allowed either to escape from the secret place in her heart, in which she had so carefully locked them away after her family had left India forever and sailed to England.

Fifteen years had passed since then. Yet, now, as she lay with only the dim light of the hazy silver moon in the night sky, the flickering gas lamps that lined Russell Square beyond, and the glowing embers in the hearth illuminating the otherwise dark bedroom, Rose could still see the burning brightness of the sun above Delhi and feel its arid heat beating down on her, just as it had during her childhood and in the nightmare that had disrupted her slumber. Born and bred in India, she had never, as a child, imagined herself an interloper there. It was only when she had reached adulthood that she had come to fully understand that she could never truly have belonged to her birthplace, that it had been lost to her long before she and her family had ever departed from its exotic shores.

England was and had always been home. But now, without warning, for the first time since childhood, Rose wept over that, biting her lower lip hard and turning her face into her pillow to stifle her sobs, inside her an ache as raw and deep as though it were new, rather than a decade and a half old.

Beside her in the bed, Jasmine continued to sleep peacefully, her own dreams untroubled by distorted visions from the past, her own slumber unhindered by her older sister's muffled tears. Rose was inordinately grateful for that. However loving and well-meaning the concerned comfort Jasmine would offer should she awaken, Rose wanted none of it at the moment. Instead, she wished only to be alone with her thoughts and her freshly gouged grief.

After a long while, carefully, so as not to disturb her sister, Rose slipped quietly from their shared bed, donning her wrapper that lay at the foot of the bed, and curling up in a wing chair before the windows that overlooked Russell Square below. The curtains were not quite fully closed, and through the narrow opening, she could see that at this late hour, the streets encircling the old park at the heart of the square were deserted, with nary a single horse and carriage or a passerby to be seen. She was glad of that, too. Peopled streets would have reminded her of Chandni Chowk, and of much else she had tried so hard to forget, as well, but that had unaccountably crept into her dreams tonight.

Why should the past have returned to haunt her this evening? she wondered, confused and disconcerted. Her day had been much like any other, with nothing to distinguish it from all the rest.

Much to her family's disappointment and dashed hopes, still unmarried at age twenty-three, Rose lived the quiet life of a spinster, helping her mother manage the Windermere household. She felt guilty that she was as yet unwed. But sadly, she knew she had nothing beyond her pale, ethereal, silver-blond looks to recommend her to any prospective suitor. Her family, while well-bred and respectable, had neither titles nor a fortune to tempt a man into proposing marriage to any of the six Windermere daughters, and Russell Square, while still a perfectly acceptable address, was no longer a fashionable part of London. These days, its lovely, large old houses and gardens commanded only modest rents and belonged to families who could only be described as shabby genteel. Such were the Windermeres, and so, although the beauty and grace of all six of the Windermere daughters was unsurpassed, it served only to deter other matchmaking mamas from issuing invitations to the sisters. As a result, the only beau Rose had thus far managed to attract was Professor Prosser, a fussy, prosaic, balding university teacher several inches shorter and years older than she, and whom her sisters had teasingly dubbed Professor Prosy.

Rose sighed heavily at the thought, her mouth twisting wryly.

As a child, she had idyllically imagined growing up and becoming a countess. But those dreams had died in India—along with her childhood friend, Hugo Drayton. Why, after all this time, should that horrible night have returned this evening to torment her—incomprehensibly and chaotically interwoven with the day Hugo had saved her life at the marketplace? she wondered again, her breath catching on a small, ragged sob. She did not know.

Lost in the past, Rose gazed blindly out the windows trickling with rain and clouded with the mist that drifted inland from the River Thames. The London suburb of Bloomsbury, in which Russell Square was situated, lay north of the river, bounded north and south by Euston Road and New Oxford Street, and east and west by Gray's Inn Road and Tottenham Court Road. Although, earlier in the century, it had been a hub of activity, it was now a relatively quiet district, the *haut ton* having migrated to the West End. Had the Windermeres' address been in Belgravia rather than in Bloomsbury, Rose would have had no difficulty in making the kind of match of which she had once dreamed. But now, she thought her future held little in store except the continued spinsterhood to which she had gradually grown accustomed—

although never resigned. For, while she loved her family dearly, she now knew that if she were honest with herself, she yearned for more than what life at Russell Square had to offer—and always had.

Until tonight, she had simply repressed all her desires and dreams.

Of a sudden, Rose stood, tiptoeing across the bedroom to her jewelry box, which sat upon the mahogany dresser. All her jewelry was paste, except for a single piece, which, to preserve it, had long been carefully wrapped in layers of tissue paper and hidden at the very bottom of the box. Since placing the piece there, she had never removed it. But now, she did so, slowly unfolding the leaves of fragile tissue paper to reveal the necklace that lay within. Its simple but fine chain was of solid gold, from which hung suspended her half of the ancient Gupta gold coin Hugo's Indian manservant, Mayur Singh, had caught from the young nobleman in the howdah atop the rampaging elephant that day in Chandni Chowk and cut in two fifteen years ago. Rose did not know what had become of the other half, which had belonged to Hugo himself. It had disappeared the night he and his parents had been so ruthlessly murdered in their beds at the Drayton house in Chandni Chowk. But she had kept her own treasured half.

The coin was over a thousand years old and very rare, Mayur Singh had told her and Hugo. When complete, it had on its face depicted King Chandra-gupta I giving a ring to his Lichchavian Queen Kumardevi. On its reverse had been the goddess Ambika, mounted upon a lion. The Indian manservant had presented the Queen's half to Rose, and the King's half to Hugo, saying that it would forever remind them of the bond between them, born not only of their having grown up together, but also of Hugo's having saved her life. Now, with a sharp, wistful pang, Rose recognized that Mayur Singh had either hoped or intended that the coin would someday be whole again, that she and Hugo would eventually be joined in marriage. Otherwise, the Indian manservant would surely never have cut something so precious in two.

A small, poignant sigh once more escaping from her lips, her fingers trembling with both cold and sorrow, Rose slipped the necklace over her head, arranging the chain so that her half of the coin lay between her breasts. As she did so, she realized how her memory had played tricks on her, for the necklace was much lighter than she recalled. To the child who had received it, it had seemed inordinately ponderous, its coin weighty. But although the necklace was, in fact, substantial, it was still not nearly as heavy as she had remembered.

Rose closed her jewelry box. Then, turning to the hearth, she added a few lumps of coal to the blackened grate and, with the brass poker, stoked the small fire until it burned brightly, radiating heat to warm the chilly bedroom. Then she returned to the wing chair before the windows, again curling her feet beneath her.

"You'll catch your death of cold, sitting there without even a shawl or a blanket to cover you, Rose."

Jasmine's voice penetrated the semidarkness of the bedroom before she herself got out of bed. From the heavily carved wooden Indian coffer at the foot of the bed, she withdrew two fringed silk shawls, handing one to Rose and wrapping the other around herself. Then she settled into the wing chair opposite the one occupied by her older sister. "What's wrong? Why are you awake at this wee hour?"

"I don't know. I couldn't sleep." Rose sighed again tremulously. Then she confessed, "I had a nightmare."

"About what?"

"That day...that long-ago day in Chandni Chowk, at the marketplace, when that poor young nobleman's elephant stampeded—except that it was all horribly mixed up somehow with that night...that terrible night in India...when Hugo and his parents were killed."

"No wonder you couldn't sleep, then. That must indeed have been an awful dream for you."

"Yes, it was."

Distressed by her sister's obvious upset, but not knowing what else to say, Jasmine soon fell silent. Unlike Rose, she had loathed India, her birthplace, and she had never known Hugo Drayton well, either. So his murder and that of his parents during her childhood had not affected her in the same way as it had her sister. So although she truly wanted to offer Rose what solace she could, she was uncertain how to proceed. Besides which, she felt uncomfortably as though she had intruded on her sister's privacy and grief. For, despite how she tried to hide it, Rose had plainly been crying.

"I'll fetch some tea, shall I?" Jasmine suggested at last.

"I tried to tend the fire quietly...our room was chilly.... Even so, I've already succeeded in waking you. I don't want to be any further trouble—"

"I don't mind, and it's no bother, Rose, really. Besides, a cuppa will warm us both—and perhaps prove soporific." Jasmine stood and, with mild relief, exited the bedroom, hoping that her brief absence would give her sister time to collect herself.

While Jasmine was gone, Rose did indeed do her best to compose herself. She deeply regretted having inadvertently woken her sister. But it was done now—and perhaps it would do her good to talk to Jasmine, after all, Rose thought. Maybe she had kept far too much bottled up inside her for far too long. She didn't know.

She knew only that after fifteen long years, she must somehow force herself to face the fact that despite all her youthful hopes and beliefs to the contrary, Hugo Drayton was long dead and buried in his grave, and that she would never see him or India again. She must stop living in limbo, accept Professor Prosser's offer of marriage, and get on with her own life.

That she would rather be lying in a tomb herself was craven and not to be borne.

TWO

To Market, to Market

> To market, to market, to buy a plum bun,
> Home again, home again, market is done.
>
> *To Market* [Traditional]
> —Mother Goose

*Russell Square and Covent Garden, London,
England, 1850*

"Good mornin', Miss Windermere."

"Good morning, Leddy," Rose greeted the newspaper boy, who gazed at her worshipfully as, across the short, ornamental black wrought-iron fence that separated the forecourt and small porch of Colonel Windermere's town house from the sidewalk, he handed her the latest edition of the *Times*. "How are you this fine day?"

"Much better now that I've seen you, Miss Windermere." Leddy smiled shyly, touching the brim of his cap politely.

Rose colored faintly. Leddy had been delivering the *Times* to her father's town house for the past few years now, during which time she had realized that although far too young for her, the newspaper boy had nevertheless built up a romantic attachment between them in his mind. Rose had done nothing to encourage this and did not know how to discourage it, either, particularly since she liked Leddy and didn't want to hurt his feelings.

"Thank you, Leddy. Have a good day."

"Yes, miss. You, too, miss."

Turning, Rose went back up the short flight of steps into the town house, firmly closing the front door behind her. From past experience, she knew that if she looked through the peephole, she would spy Leddy still standing outside, staring reverently at the town house. For a moment, unable to resist the sudden temptation, she peeked through the peephole. Yes, it was just as she had known that it would be. Leddy was indeed still there, his feet seemingly glued to the sidewalk, his eyes riveted on the front door, his young face hopeful that she would reappear.

Shaking her head gently, Rose smiled ruefully to herself. Despite her dismay, there really was something sweet and touching about his simple regard for her that always brightened her day. Then, giving herself a mental shake, she chided herself sternly for giving in to her schoolgirlish urge to glance through the peephole. She should be doing her best to dampen poor Leddy's adulation—not wondering whether he was still mooning over her!

Squaring her shoulders determinedly, she continued to the morning room, carefully placing the neatly folded copy of the *Times* to one side of her father's place at the breakfast table.

Having spent most of his life in Her Majesty's Army, Colonel Windermere had very specific ideas about how the household under his aegis should be run, and in his mind, breakfast trays were a luxury to be indulged in only by the sick or the infirm. Therefore, the entire Windermere family always gathered for breakfast in the morning room. Today was no exception.

"How are the kidneys this morning, Rose?" her mother asked, bustling into the room, her starched crinolines crackling about her. "Oh, I do hope that Mrs. Beasley has got them grilled to perfection this time. You know how the Colonel hates it when they are either too pale or too brown."

"Yes, Mama. But Mrs. Beasley seems to have got them just right today."

Having obediently checked to ensure that this was indeed so, Rose replaced the lid on the chafing dish that contained the kidneys under discussion. Other crockery arrayed on the sideboard held rashers of crisp bacon, slices of fatty gammon, boiled eggs, fried eggs, and scrambled eggs, steaming porridge, sautéed tomatoes, fresh fruit, hot buns, toast and an assortment of jams and jellies that Mrs. Beasley had put up last summer. Hot pots of coffee and tea, as well as a cold pitcher of milk, sat to one side. It was the good, hearty breakfast with which the portly colonel liked to start off his day.

"Well, thank goodness for that." Mrs. Windermere breathed a sigh of relief. "Breakfast is always so much more pleasant when the Colonel isn't grumbling about the food!"

"Yes, Mama," Rose answered dutifully.

She had long ago learned that it was useless to argue with her mother. Mrs. Windermere, while kind and well-meaning, was one of those flighty, flustered women who are invariably in a dither about something. Her entire life was her family, whom she needed to feel couldn't manage without her. So, from her husband, the colonel, to her youngest daughter, Daisy, her family, well aware of this, had long been engaged in a benevolent conspiracy to keep her from learning that, in reality, it was the combined talents of Rose; the Windermeres' housekeeper, Miss Candlish; and their cook, Mrs. Beasley, that kept the town house in Russell Square operating smoothly.

"Oh, where are your sisters, Rose?" Mrs. Windermere now asked, her hands fluttering as she, too, turned from the sideboard, where her own investigation of the dishes had left several lids askew. "You know how the Colonel feels about being punctual for meals!"

"We're all here, Mama," Jasmine replied, with a soothing ease born of long practice, as she entered the room in time to hear her mother's last question. In her wake trailed the rest of the Windermere daughters: Lily, Heather, Angelica and Daisy. "So you need not fret."

"Well, I *do* fret, Jasmine," Mrs. Windermere insisted, sighing again. "For if I didn't, who would? It's not as though the household runs itself, you know."

"No, m'dear. Of course, it doesn't." Colonel Hilary Windermere's bright blue eyes twinkled merrily as he gazed at them all from where he now stood in the doorway. "So where we would all be without your admirable administration, Mrs. Windermere, I'm loath to imagine." He paused while his wife beamed at his praise. Then he inquired, "How is my flower garden this morning?"

The colonel always referred to his wife and daughters as his "flower garden." He was an inveterate gardener and having, in his youth, succeeded in wooing and winning the lovely Violet Mayfield as his bride, he had subsequently declared that all his daughters would be named after flowers, too— "Although none can compare with you, the fairest blossom of them all, m'dear," he was fond of telling his wife.

What would have occurred in the blessed event of a son, no one knew, for no male heir had ever been produced by Mrs. Windermere—although not from want of trying. But if Colonel Windermere lamented the lack of a son to carry on the family name and to follow in his footsteps, he seldom said so, seemingly content with his bouquet of beautiful daughters. In fact, as, chattering gaily, they gathered around to greet him good morning and to lead him to the sideboard, he counted himself among the most fortunate of fellows, and his only regret was that, being only the younger son of a baronet, he had neither a title nor great wealth with which to secure good marriages for his girls.

It grieved him sorely to see his eldest daughters, particularly, quietly resigning themselves to spinsterhood. The colonel felt he could have borne it better if they had ever reproached him. But they never had. Instead, for the most part, they were a cheerful lot, with rarely a cross word among themselves or to him.

"Be sure to remark on the kidneys, Papa," Rose whispered, interrupting his reverie. "For Mama worries that if they are either too pale or too brown, you will grumble."

"A veritable ogre at the breakfast table, then, am I?" The corners of Colonel Windermere's mouth twitched as he glanced at her conspiratorially.

"Quite, Papa!"

"Well, then, I'd best mind my manners in the future and make more compliments about meals to your mother and Mrs. Beasley—for in truth, I can think of nothing more disagreeable than an ogre amid a flower garden!"

"You're not really an ogre, dear Papa. You're our lucky garden gnome, as well you know."

"Humph! Not so lucky as that, or you and your sisters would be wed by now. I've not done nearly as well by you girls as I would have wished. No, Rose, none of your platitudes, for I hope I am big enough and old enough to shoulder my own burdens, and I know that the truth is that as a military man, I've got on as well as I might and far better than most. Still, it hasn't been nearly as much for my girls as it would have been were I not just a younger son, and for that, I'm most heartily sorry. You ought to be married and in charge of your own household by now, not over-seeing mine. And of course, your mother and I had hoped for grandchildren.... You look tired this morning, Rose. You work too hard."

"No, it's not that, Papa. I...I had a restless night, that's all, and I have a bit of a headache today as a result. But after breakfast, I shall go to the market, and the fresh air and the walk will clear away the cobwebs, and then, presently, I'll feel much better, I'm sure. So you're not to bother yourself about me."

"You're never a bother, Rose. But if that's really all it is, then..." The colonel patted his daughter's arm awkwardly but kindly.

The truth was that despite his being a household of women, he was much more comfortable in an army barracks filled with men. The male of the human species was fairly straightforward and easily under-stood, he had always thought. But the female gender was a complete mystery, with as many layers as a budding flower. Far better simply to cherish and care-fully tend them rather than to probe too deeply and risk bruising their fragile petals or, worse, destroying their roots.

So thinking, Colonel Windermere assumed his place at the head of the table, while his wife seated herself at the foot, their daughters arranging themselves three on each side. Breakfast commenced, with the colonel, in between bites, reading choice tidbits from the *Times* aloud to his family.

"Oh, who gives a fig about that old stock exchange!" Daisy finally chirruped impatiently. "Get to the good parts, Papa! Please! What news about Prince Albert's Industry of All Nations Exhibition and the Crystal Palace that is to house it?"

Five years ago, in 1845, Prince Albert, Queen Victoria's husband, had become president of the Society of Arts, located in John Adam Street, below The Strand. The purpose of the society was to stimulate technology and manufacturing, which, prior to Prince Albert's assumption of the presidency, had been accomplished primarily by awarding a few prizes. Once in charge of the society, Prince Albert, however, had suggested a much grander tack: that an exhibition be held in the attractive edifice that housed the society.

Much to London's huge surprise, over twenty thousand people had shown up for the original exposition, which, in light of its great success, had subsequently become an annual event. In June of 1849, Prince Albert had summoned the society to Buckingham Palace to discuss a far more ambitious proposal— the Industry of All Nations Exhibition, in which more than a hundred other countries would participate. Following approval of the idea, Queen Victoria had earlier this year appointed a full Royal Commission to oversee its execution, and a design by architect Joseph

Paxton for a huge "Crystal Palace" to house the Exhibition had been chosen.

"I'll have you know that I've got a bit of money invested in that 'old stock exchange,' as you call it, miss," the colonel informed his youngest daughter wryly. "I've got to try and find some way to secure the futures of my daughters, don't I? Especially yours, Daisy, since your mother tells me that you *will* go outside without your sunbonnet, causing freckles to appear across your upturned nose, and whilst I've got nothing against freckles myself, mind you, your mother assures me they spell absolute disaster for any young woman wishing to make her mark in today's society!"

"It's quite true, Colonel," Mrs. Windermere declared stoutly, favoring her youngest daughter with an exasperated glance, "as I've told Daisy myself on more than one occasion. Why, Lydia Collingwood is so spotted that she might as well be one of those big cats at the zoo. She will never catch a husband with those freckles of hers—and neither will you, Daisy!"

"I shall—for I shan't have any husband who doesn't like my freckles, but, rather, one like Papa, who does!" Daisy insisted impertinently, unabashed. "So you are just wasting all those mashed strawberries and cucumbers on me, Mama. I don't think they work to get rid of freckles, anyhow! Oh, please, Papa! Does the *Times* have anything to report today about Prince Albert's Exhibition or not?"

"Yes, do tell, Papa!" Angelica chimed in excitedly, nearly knocking over her egg cup as she reached for the salt.

"Yes, Papa, do," Jasmine urged dryly. "Or we shall surely never hear the end of Daisy's incessant chatter about it!"

"That is the truth—for she has talked of little else since learning about it," Heather observed, as she spread marmalade on a piece of toast. "I can't imagine why. It will consist of nothing but a bunch of old artifacts and new machines, as usual, no matter how many countries are taking part in the Exhibition."

"Maybe so. Still, it will undoubtedly prove to be the event of next year—and everybody who is anybody will be present at the opening ceremony in May!" Lily cried. "So we must all go, of course. The tickets are to be quite cheap, I understand," she added hastily. "So attendance shouldn't be beyond our means—and we've some months yet to save up for them, besides."

"Rose, you're awfully silent. Do you have no opinion about Prince Albert's Exhibition to add to those of your sisters?" Colonel Windermere queried.

"None, Papa—except that if the Crystal Palace is to be constructed in Hyde Park, as proposed, I most earnestly hope that the domed roof the Commissioners have insisted on will indeed result in the preserving of all the old trees there, and that the vibrations produced by all the attendees will not cause the building to collapse, either, as some fear. For the Exhibition will not last forever, and if the trees must be cut down or even trimmed, then Hyde Park would be much the worse for wear afterward, and of course, if the Crystal Palace were to fall upon the attendees, that would be a tragedy of unimaginable proportions."

"Hmm. Well, from what the *Times* has to say this morning, it would appear that you are not the only person in London to continue to voice those concerns, Rose." The colonel peered through his silver-rimmed spectacles at the newspaper he held before him. "The politicians and all the property owners surrounding Hyde Park are still up in arms, stating that the Exhibition will permanently defile the area, even though the Royal Commission has vowed to preserve all the trees, to remove the Crystal Palace afterward, and to restore Hyde Park to all its former glory. Others remain afraid that despite all the testing, the structure will not be safe, that the iron girders that are to support it will break from the resonance created by all the attendees. It also seems that several opponents still don't want the Exhibition to take place in London at all. They continue to fear that after all the unrest on the Continent two years ago and the overthrowing of various of its regimes, such as the French monarchy, revolutionaries and radicals will pour into London for the purpose of fomenting rebellion, assassinating Queen Victoria and Prince Albert and proclaiming a new republic!"

"Murder the Queen!" Mrs. Windermere was so aghast at the very notion that she shuddered. "In that case, we most definitely will *not* attend the Exhibition! Why, it wouldn't be at all safe—for you know that more than one attempt has been made on the Queen's life in the past, and we might be killed in the uprising! Only think of all those poor people who were mistakenly massacred by soldiers in Paris when King Louis-Philippe was compelled to abdicate!"

"Papa!" Lily chided accusingly.

Even Daisy's normally sunny disposition was visibly dampened as she eyed her father askance.

"Now, now, there's no need for my own daughters to take up arms against *me*," Colonel Windermere asserted hurriedly. "Nor for you to be alarmed about attending Prince Albert's Exhibition, m'dear." This latter remark was directed to his wife. "England is not like the Continent. Here, we are entirely civilized— and have no interest in doing away with our sovereigns, violently or otherwise. Mark my words, Mrs. Windermere, two hundred years from now, there will still be a monarch sitting on the throne of England!"

"I should certainly hope so, Colonel. For Queen Victoria, Prince Albert and their family are a fine example to us all."

Mrs. Windermere had a great deal more to say on this particular subject, but since Rose could tell that her mother was tuning up for a monologue about social morals in this day and age, she begged to be excused from the table, murmuring about the marketing and a list of other chores she needed to take care of.

"I've finished with my breakfast, as well," Jasmine announced, also rising from her chair. "Shall I accompany you to the market, then, Rose?"

"Yes, if you like."

Going upstairs to their bedroom, the two sisters fetched their bonnets, spencers, and reticules. Then, after retrieving generous baskets from the kitchen with which to hold their purchases, they set out companionably together for Covent Garden Market.

It was a bright, sunny day, and the walk was less than a mile—Russell Square, for all that its address was the kiss of death socially nowadays, still being ideally situated. As Rose descended the steps from the front door to the black wrought-iron fence beyond and its single gate set between two sandstone pillars capped with heavy stone orbs, she glanced in passing around the large square, realizing of a sudden that despite the elegant Georgian architecture of the imposing redbrick-and-sandstone buildings surrounding the lovely green park at its heart, the neighborhood had declined from its heyday.

Streaked with London's inevitable chimney soot, which had run repeatedly in the sprawling city's equally inevitable rain, many of the edifices had developed a worn, grimy, seen-better-days appearance, including the town house of her own family. Because of Russell Square's close proximity to the University of London, where Professor Prosser taught classes, the British Museum, and the courts of Gray's Inn Lane, the rows of sizable terrace houses still belonged to respectable people, and several were now occupied by academics, artists, barristers and solicitors and the like. The *haut ton* had gradually migrated west, to districts like Piccadilly, Mayfair, Belgravia and Tyburnia.

"I wish we could move away from here," Jasmine remarked, as though reading her older sister's mind.

"You know that's not possible, Jasmine," Rose pointed out quietly as she pushed open the gate, which creaked on its sturdy hinges. She made a mental note that those needed oiling and that the gate and fence themselves needed cleaning and painting, being encrusted with white blotches of pigeon droppings and red patches of rust. "There's nowhere else in London that we could get so big and fine a house and garden for such a reasonable rent. Papa has done his best—bless him—and I know it troubles him deeply that he has proved unable to do any more. He speaks very little about it, but he did say as much to me this morning."

"Poor Papa! Oh, what I need is a knight in shining armor to sweep me away from it all!" Jasmine sighed heavily. "Don't you ever just want to escape, Rose?"

"Yes, sometimes. But how I would manage it, I'm sure I don't know."

No more was said on the subject—because, indeed, there was nothing left to say. Both sisters were well aware of their family's circumstances, and neither no longer held out much hope of being able to improve them.

So, shutting the gate firmly behind them, they turned their conversation elsewhere and their footsteps south toward Great Russell Street and the smaller Bloomsbury Square. As they walked along together, they kept their eyes open and their purses near, highly conscious of the fact that the closer they got to the main thoroughfare of High Holborn and the area surrounding Lincoln's Inn Field, the more likely they were to be accosted by pickpockets. One of these young scamps, Bobby, they were actually acquainted with, as, once, while learning his so-called trade, he had made such a mess of cutting the strings of Jasmine's reticule that she had caught him in the act. As a result, much to Rose's shock, Jasmine had boldly seized hold of the lad by the collar, bent on marching him off to the nearest constable.

But Rose herself had been struck by Bobby's thinness and, despite all his bravado, his suddenly scared eyes. Recognizing what kind of life he must lead on the streets, she had taken pity on him and persuaded Jasmine to release him, rather than pressing charges. Because of this, the lad had solemnly sworn to be forever in their debt, and occasionally, on their way to the market, they glimpsed him and thought he must be as good as his word, for now and then, they had seen him intercept other boys, warning them off. So, despite themselves, they always relaxed a little whenever they spied him, as they did now.

"Mornin', Miss Windermere, Miss Jasmine." Bobby spoke from where he nonchalantly leaned against one of the lampposts lining the street, his shock of sandy hair in need of a good combing, a half-smoked cigarette dangling from one corner of his mouth. "'Eaded toward t' market, are you?" He motioned toward the baskets they carried.

"Yes, Bobby," Rose replied. "Have you found a job yet?"

"I'm workin' on it, Miss Windermere. I'm workin' on it," the lad insisted.

"A likely story," Jasmine observed censuringly, frowning at him. "Still robbing poor, unsuspecting passersby, you are, if the truth be told!"

"Well, you was 'ardly unsuspectin', Miss Jasmine, since you cotched me red-'anded!" Bobby grinned impudently.

"Yes—and you're lucky my sister isn't made of quite such stern stuff as I am, or else you'd be sitting in prison!"

"I know, I know—an' I'll be fore'er grateful ta Miss Windermere for intervenin' on me be'alf an' ta yerself, o' course, Miss Jasmine, for listenin' ta 'er."

"I'll tell you what, Bobby," Rose said slowly, "if you'd like to earn a few honest pence, I'll pay you to clean and paint our front fence. I noticed only this morning how shabby it's looking. The gate's hinges need oiling, as well."

"Rose!" Jasmine remonstrated sharply. "What are you thinking of? The lad's a pickpocket!"

"That may be so, Miss Jasmine," Bobby conceded, nodding. "But I got me pride, same as everybody else, an' I keep me word an' pay me debts, too. So, aye, I *will* do that for you, Miss Windermere. Just tell me when an' where."

"Tomorrow morning," she suggested, then told him the address in Russell Square. "I'll have a wash bucket and the paint and oil ready and waiting for you."

As the sisters walked on toward the intersection of High Holborn, Broad Street, and Drury Lane, Jasmine still shook her head in disbelief.

"We'll be lucky if Bobby and whatever gang of thieves he associates with don't burglarize our house, Rose! I just can't imagine what got into you!"

"The work genuinely needs doing—you must have seen that yourself when we left the house earlier, Jasmine—and as far as I can tell, Bobby has never intended us any harm since that day we released him instead of hauling him up before a constable."

"Sometimes, I think you trust too easily, Rose. I hope you don't wind up deceived by Bobby."

"I hope so, too," Rose murmured, more to herself than to her sister.

Turning on to Drury Lane, the sisters followed it to Long Acre, which had been a main thoroughfare since Saxon times. Currently, it was principally home to coachmakers, cartwrights, tanners, metalworkers and upholsterers. But tucked in among these trades were also to be found cabinetmakers, furniture designers, fruiterers, bakers and others. Two of the more interesting shops were Merryweather, which built firefighting apparatus, and The Hobby Horse, which sold draisines, hobby horses, dalsells, velocipedes and other pedestrian curricles. In front of this latter, Joey, the proprietor's son, was sweeping the sidewalk.

"Mornin', Signorina Windermere, Signorina Jasmine," he greeted them cheerfully, politely doffing his cap and smiling broadly, his white teeth gleaming against his dark skin. Joey's family were Italians who had immigrated to England.

"Good morning, Joey," the sisters chorused as one.

They were long acquainted with him because Daisy was inexplicably fascinated with all the contraptions for sale in The Hobby Horse, as well as with other modern inventions. It was that which had prompted her enthusiasm for Prince Albert's Industry of All Nations Exhibition.

From Long Acre, it was only a short distance down James Street to Covent Garden.

Covent Garden had originally begun life as the convent or herb garden of Westminster Priory. But in 1552, the site, along with seven acres of ground known as Long Acre, whence the street had taken its name, had been bestowed upon John Russell, Earl of Bedford. In 1634, one of his descendants, Earl Francis, had demolished all the old stalls and sheds that had sprung up at the back of the garden wall of Bedford House on the south side of the square and, from the designs of architect Inigo Jones, had begun work on a new plaza. Jones himself had erected the colonnade on the north and east sides.

Twenty years ago, the late Duke of Bedford had finally funded construction of an attractive market house to replace the once-grand residences and other buildings that had long since fallen into decay when the *haut ton* had moved elsewhere to escape from the cacophony of the burgeoning market. Created by architect Charles Fowler, the new edifice consisted of a large, lofty, central avenue, which was home to merchants of expensive fruits and vegetables like strawberries and peaches; a number of small shops that were primarily occupied by dealers of cheap fruit and vegetables, such as apples, pears, and greengages; a space for sellers of cabbages, as well as potatoes, onions, turnips, carrots, and other roots; and an arcade supporting a capacious terrace that boasted two conservatories filled with exotic flowers and a fountain operated by mechanical means regulated by the wind.

Amid the whole were generous walkways with room for individual stalls, wagons, carts, and barrows of all kinds, all of which spilled over into the center of the piazza. On the west side of the square, the simple but lovely St. Paul's Church, also designed by Inigo Jones, stood, keeping silent, benevolent watch over all.

As early as two o'clock in the morning on market days, the costermongers started to assemble to set out their fruits and vegetables. Vendors with wagons, carts, or barrows drawn by donkeys or ponies and filled with potatoes, broccoli, cauliflower, or peas arrived to find a good space on the plaza—many of the growers' men and boys sleeping under their vehicles, with their watchdogs to guard them; and hundreds of street hawkers, most of them Irish displaced by the potato famine, came with their baskets and trays to collect their day's supply of goods for selling. The little girls who peddled watercress—the best cultivated in Camden Town—gathered at the piazza, too, as did the older flower girls, and the street urchins who were thieves and pickpockets like Bobby, most of them half-starved and ragged, their feet bare and thrumming on the paved square as they ran from the patrolling constables and scavenged for any bit of food they could beg or steal. Here and there, musicians, mimes, artists and the like entertained passersby, as did a Punch-and-Judy show, which delighted children and adults alike.

All around, the raucous sounds of the street hawkers loudly advertising their wares, of the vocal bartering between buyers and sellers, and of the boisterous laughter of men sharing a pint, of women exchanging the latest gossip, and of children playing at hoops filled the air. It mingled unharmoniously with the strands of music from fiddles, flutes and other instruments plied by would-be troubadours, and with the neighing and stamping of donkeys and ponies, and the barking of dogs. Over the square itself hung the sweet fragrance of ripe fruit and vegetables, the sweaty odor of bodies pressed close beneath the sun, the animal scent of feed and manure, and the dank smell of the nearby River Thames.

Into all this hustle and bustle, baskets in hand, Rose and Jasmine gradually made their way, occasionally greeting merchants and flower girls with whom they had become acquainted over the years and pausing to inspect their proffered produce and nosegays. The sisters steered clear of the central avenue, for the finer fruits and vegetables and the exotic bouquets were too dear. But they spent a considerable amount of time at the cheaper stands, good-naturedly haggling over prices and filling their baskets with the best they could afford.

"You drive a 'ard bargain, Mam'selle Windermere, Mam'selle Jasmine, an' no mistake!" Jordan, the grower's son, whose family had immigrated to England from France, winked and chuckled as Rose handed him a few coins from her reticule in exchange for apples and pears.

"Not hard enough, if you ask me!" Jasmine laughed, tossing her head.

At the small cart run by their favorite flower girls, Ashley and Jolette, the sisters bought some pretty posies, tucking them in their baskets. Then they wandered on, surprised when Bobby, the pickpocket, found them in the crowd.

"What's the matter, Bobby?" Rose asked. "Have you changed your mind about tomorrow, after all?"

"No, it's not that. Miss Jasmine, I know what you think about me, but I really am grateful ta you, so I thought I should let you know that some bloke's paid me chum Burke ta draw a picture o' you. You remember Burke…'e's t' artist, miss, t' one what most often sets up 'ere in Covent Garden."

"Yes, of course…but what man, Bobby? Where?" Jasmine frowned with some confusion and dismay at this unexpected news.

"Come with me, miss. This way."

Adroitly weaving a path through the throng and glancing back over his shoulder to be certain that the sisters were following, Bobby led them to where his friend Burke sat on a stool, his head bent over the sketchbook propped on his knees and the stub of a charcoal pencil in one hand.

"Miss Windermere, Miss Jasmine, you know me mate Burke," Bobby announced, as Burke stood, nodding to them. "Tell 'em about t' fellow, Burke, what paid you ta draw a picture o' Miss Jasmine."

"I wish I could. 'E was tall an' dark, like 'e spent a lot o' time out o' doors. But 'e didn't talk like 'e was from around 'ere, an' I didn't know 'im. So maybe 'e was a grower…brought a load o' fruits an' vegetables in for market day, I expect. 'E's gone now, anyhow— took off when 'e spied you 'eading this way, even though 'e'd already paid in advance for me drawin', an' I wasn't quite finished with it yet," Burke explained. Then, seeing Jasmine's puzzlement and concern, he continued, "I really don't believe that t' bloke meant any 'arm, though. I think…I think 'e just thought Miss Jasmine was pretty—an' you are, miss, if you don't mind me sayin' so."

Jasmine flushed, but Rose could tell that her sister was pleased all the same.

"I'll give you t' drawin' if you like." Burke held his sketch out to Jasmine.

"No." Jasmine shook her head. "Thank you all the same, Burke, but since someone else paid for it, it wouldn't be right of me to take it."

"Do you want us ta let you know if t' chap comes back for it, Miss Jasmine?" Bobby queried.

"Yes…yes, please. As Burke says, there's probably

no harm in it. But still, it's...curious. Don't you think, Rose?"

"Oh, I don't know." Rose smiled gently. "You *are* very beautiful, Jasmine—and I'm not saying that just because you're my sister, either. I can understand why, even if he is someone unknown to us, a man might have paid to have a portrait sketched of you."

"Well, then, I suppose I should be flattered. But it still seems...oh, I don't know...just strange, somehow, I guess. It's a bit disconcerting to think I was being spied on!"

"Surely not so much spied on as admired," Rose suggested tactfully.

"Perhaps," Jasmine conceded reluctantly after a moment. "At any rate, it's probably neither here nor there," she insisted, as though trying to convince herself of this. "For no doubt, now that he's gone, the man won't return for the picture, anyway."

Since the morning had by now grown late, the sisters started for home, dropping by their favorite bakery, which sold flour and, in addition to its more expensive fresh-baked fare, cheap day-old breads, cakes, pies and pastries, and where Nick, the baker's jolly son, was always unfailingly cheerful and courteous when he waited on them. Then they went into the butchery next door, where Brock, the butcher's impudent apprentice, always entertained them with his antics and made them laugh. Next to the butchery was the fishmonger's shop, owned by a family of Spaniards descended from those who had washed up on

England's shores during the time of Queen Elizabeth and the Spanish Armada, and where Victor, the fishmonger's quiet son, invariably had a choice fish or two tucked away for them. After that, as they usually did when they had gone marketing together, Rose and Jasmine stopped and bought a hot pasty each from the pie cart out front, run by Chris, a young pie man, to eat on their way home.

But as they started on down High Holburn toward Southampton Street and Bloomsbury Square, Rose had scarcely taken more than a few bites from her own small meat pie when she was accidentally bumped into so violently by a man bolting pell-mell down the sidewalk that the impetus stole away her breath and almost knocked her down.

She was saved from falling only by the man's quick action in grabbing hold of her as she swayed precariously on her feet, losing her grip on her pasty and nearly sending the contents of her basket flying, as well.

"Forgive me. Please…forgive me. I'm so sorry…so very sorry," the stranger gasped out, rasping for breath and glancing over one shoulder, as though he were being hotly pursued.

For what seemed an eternity, Rose was utterly speechless. For one thing, she was wholly unaccustomed to being accosted by strangers on the street. For another, the man's slender but strong hands still grasped her arms tightly, his fingers pressing into her soft skin in a way that was almost hurtful. Yet, much to her astonishment, what she felt was not pain, but, rather, something new and strange—and so utterly intense that its unfamiliar power not only made her feel giddy, but also almost frightened her. Her mouth felt dry. Her heart pounded fast and furiously. The stranger's piercing black eyes, glinting hard and unfathomably in the sunlight, bored into her own wide green ones, as though he were searching her startled countenance for some sign of...what? Rose didn't know, couldn't ask. Her tongue was unaccountably tied up in knots.

All around her, everything seemed to move in slow motion, to be as indistinct as a vignette. For that fleeting moment in time, she was cognizant only of the man, of his hold on her, of his dark, hawkish visage so near to her own pale, finely chiseled one that she could feel his harsh breath upon her skin and smell the faint scents of sandalwood and vetiver that emanated from his being. Then, suddenly, the man's full, sensuous lips thinned, and he nodded to himself as though satisfied by what he had seen in her gaze and on her face. Reaching into his jacket, he withdrew an envelope and, to Rose's everlasting shock, shoved it into the basket she carried, deep beneath the fruit and vegetables.

"Guard that with your life!" It was both a command and an entreaty.

Then he was gone.

Three

The Envelope and the Letter

Sir, more than kisses, letters mingle souls.
> *Verse Letter to Sir Henry Wotton*
> [written before April 1598]
> —John Donne

High Holborn and Russell Square,
London, England, 1850

"Rose! Rose, are you all right?" Jasmine asked sharply, reaching out to steady her as, without warning, her knees buckled beneath her.

"I—I feel a little...dizzy."

Jasmine glanced around wildly for someplace for her sister to sit down, but there was none until Brock, the butcher's apprentice, having observed through the front windows of the butchery what had happened, hurried outside with a small wooden chair from the shop.

"'Ere, Miss Windermere. Sit 'ere," he urged, obviously concerned, setting the chair down against the front wall of the butchery, away from the pedestrian traffic that filled the sidewalk. "'Ehyup, Chris!" he shouted to the nearby pie man. "Give us a 'and 'ere! Miss Windermere's faint, an' she's lost 'er pie, too."

As Jasmine began to help Rose to the chair, two big, burly, disreputable-looking men suddenly came pelting down the sidewalk, roughly shoving aside passersby and looking about sharply, as though in search of someone.

"Did any o' you spy a tall, dark man pass by 'ere—a foreigner, 'e might o' been?" one of them inquired, eyeing both the sisters, the butcher's apprentice and the pie man suspiciously and even menacingly.

Deliberately, Brock wiped his hands on his apron stained bloody from his work, as though preparing for a fight, and Nick, the baker's son, and Victor, the fishmonger's son, also husky fellows who brooked no nonsense, having now seen from their own shops' front windows what was occurring, stepped out onto the sidewalk, deliberately flexing their muscles.

"Yes, I think you must be talking about the man who nearly knocked my sister down!" Jasmine said to the two ruffians, as Rose sank gratefully into the chair. "He went that way!" Much to Rose's amazement, Jasmine pointed toward Newton Street, an entirely different route from the one the stranger had actually taken.

Without another word, the two thugs ran off in the direction Jasmine had indicated. Her countenance strangely flinty, she watched them briefly to be certain they would not return before fumbling in her reticule to withdraw a vinaigrette, which she uncorked and wafted beneath Rose's nose.

"Oh! Oh, my, that's strong!" Rose wrinkled her nose with distaste as the ammonia fumes from the smelling salts penetrated her nostrils. But at least the vinaigrette cleared her head, so that she no longer felt as though she were going to swoon.

"Are you all right, Miss Windermere? Miss Jasmine?" Victor queried.

"Yes…yes, thank you, Victor," Rose answered, nodding her head.

"Good thing those rogues took off—or else I'd 'ave flattened them!" Brock pounded one fist into the other, to emphasize his point.

"'Ere, Miss Windermere. 'Ere's another pasty for you—on t' 'ouse." Chris handed her another meat pie to replace the one she had dropped earlier.

"Oh, how sweet! Thank you, Chris."

"Do you feel well enough to go home now, Rose?" Jasmine's face was anxious.

"Maybe we can get our mate Jake ta lend us one o' t' 'ackneys from 'is dad's livery stable, if you can't manage t' walk, Miss Windermere," Nick offered.

"No…no, there's no need to trouble Jake. I'm sure I'll be fine."

Rose stood, and after thanking all the lads again for

their assistance, she and Jasmine headed for home, keeping a wary eye out for the two sinister scoundrels who had plainly been chasing the man who had run into Rose. As the sisters walked along contemplatively together, they quietly discussed all the morning's unexpected events, wondering whether the stranger who had paid the street artist, Burke, to sketch a portrait of Jasmine might have anything to do with the tall, dark, unknown man who had bumped into Rose. At last, they reluctantly decided there was probably no connection between the two incidents. But they continued to wonder curiously about the envelope stashed at the bottom of the basket Rose carried and what it might contain.

"Whatever is in the envelope, it must be something damaging to someone…perhaps even dangerous," Rose speculated thoughtfully. "For otherwise, those two threatening rascals would not have been pursuing the first man. Clearly, had they caught him, they intended him some harm—and surely, it must have something to do with the envelope's contents, and that is why the stranger gave it to me and issued such a dire warning."

"Yes," Jasmine agreed. "That's why I sent those two ruffians off in the wrong direction. I didn't like the look of them. Do you think we should make a full report to Constable Dreiling and seek his advice?" Young Constable Dreiling patrolled the area around Russell Square.

"I don't know—for we don't know what the

envelope actually contains. What if...what if we're wrong, just allowing our imaginations to run wildly away with us, and the affair all turns out to be nothing more than a tempest in a teapot?"

"I don't believe that's likely. But...do you think we should open the envelope, then, Rose?"

"I've been giving that considerable thought, of course. But, unfortunately, I have as yet reached no conclusion. The envelope doesn't belong to us, Jasmine. Therefore, we surely have no right to open it. On the other hand, if the man who gave it to us has by his action involved us in something unsavory or perhaps even criminal, then I believe that it would be incumbent upon us to learn what that is, don't you?"

"Most assuredly!"

"Let us say nothing about any of this to the rest of the family, Jasmine." Laying one hand on her sister's arm, Rose paused on the steps leading up to the front door of the Windermeres' town house. "For it would only outrage Papa that we have been dragged into such an, at best, curious matter—and by a complete stranger, besides—and upset Mama terribly, not to mention instigating an endless barrage of questions from our sisters, all of whom we might somehow be unwittingly imperiling by informing them of this affair."

"I agree."

Thus decided, once inside the foyer of the town house, Rose furtively slipped the mysterious envelope from her basket into one pocket of her spencer. Then she and Jasmine carried their baskets through the long hallway to the kitchen, where the cook, Mrs. Beasley, took charge of the groceries, exclaiming, as she always did, over the meats, fish, and breads, the fruits and vegetables.

"I'll use some of these apples to bake a tasty pie for supper," the cook said, as she unpacked the overflowing baskets.

"That sounds wonderful, Mrs. Beasley," Rose remarked.

But her mind was scarcely on the conversation as she and Jasmine helped the cook and Polly, the scullery maid, make short work of putting away the groceries and arranging the nosegays in flower bowls to brighten the town house. When the chores were finished, the two sisters, bonnets and jackets in hand, hastened up the front stairs to their bedroom, firmly closing the door behind them.

"Now, we can finally investigate the envelope!" From the pocket of her spencer, Rose drew it forth, gazing at it curiously as she sat down on the edge of the bed. "Well, it hasn't been franked or mailed, for there's no address for either the sender or the recipient." Slowly, she turned the envelope over, and as she did so, observing on its reverse a broken red wax seal stamped with a coat-of-arms, she gasped.

"What is it, Rose?" Jasmine asked, startled, as she sat down next to her sister, peeking over her shoulder at the envelope. "What's wrong?"

"The seal...I—I think that it's the seal of the Earl of Thornleigh! Of course, we were only children in

India, so I could be remembering all wrong. But really, I believe that's the coat-of-arms used by Hugo Drayton's father, Lord Thornleigh! So whatever's inside the envelope must have something to do with Hugo's older cousin, Sir James Wormwood, the present Lord Thornleigh—for it was he who inherited the title and estates after Hugo and his parents were killed. The seal's already been broken. What do you think, Jasmine? Shall we look inside the envelope?"

"Yes," the younger sister replied, after a short contemplation. "I believe that we must—for this entire matter only grows more and more curious. The man who gave you the envelope might have been from India, Rose, for not only was he tall and dark, but he was also indeed a foreigner, as those two burly scoundrels suspected—at least half Indian, I should have said, if asked."

"Oh, Jasmine, wouldn't it be wonderful if all this has something to do with why Hugo and his parents were murdered when we lived in India! Papa and Mama always suspected Sir James of having had something to do with that terrible night at Lord Thornleigh's *haveli*, although Papa never could obtain any proof of it."

"No, I know. But still, I don't think you should get your hopes up, Rose. I doubt that after all this time, Sir James would have proved so careless as to put anything about that night in writing."

Although she knew this was unquestionably the truth, still, Rose felt her hands tremble with sudden apprehension and excitement as she opened the envelope.

"There's a letter inside, nothing more."

"What does it say?"

"Oh...oh, no. It appears...it appears to be discussing a lovers' secret rendezvous." Rose's voice sank with supreme disappointment at the realization. "'My dear, we have only some months left now for planning our assignation,'" she read aloud, "'and we must take every precaution to ensure we are not discovered. Trust no one, not even our mutual friends, for they are a volatile couple and frequently quarrel with each other. Still, they are useful to us. Sometime during this coming spring, I will travel to London, and on the day of the ceremony, we will be united in our celebration—and the woman who has stood in the way of our future will be no longer be able to trouble us. Yours faithfully, etcetera.'" The letter was unsigned. "Good grief!" Rose cried, after she had stopped reading. "Lord Thornleigh must be scheming to elope with some young lady so that her mother will not act to prevent their marriage! Oh, I always suspected that he was no good—and now, I know it must be true! For what kind of a man would induce an innocent young lady to elope with him?"

"We don't know that she actually *is* a young lady, Rose," Jasmine pointed out logically. "Perhaps she is of age and merely a timid spinster with a frightful, overbearing mother."

"I suppose that could be true," Rose answered hesitantly. "But still, knowing what I do of Lord Thornleigh, I confess I'm more inclined to believe the former—and that would explain, as well, why he didn't want his wicked plot to be discovered. For if the young lady's family learnt of it, they would most assuredly put a stop to it. He must be over fifty by now, for Hugo's father, the former Lord Thornleigh, wed very late in life, so that Hugo was much younger than his cousin. Prior to Hugo's birth, Sir James Wormwood was heir to Lord Thornleigh's title and estates, of course, and little more than a rakehell, a—a devil, I heard Mama call him once."

"I'll take your word for it, Rose, for I was never as close to Hugo and his family as you were. But if the present Lord Thornleigh were indeed the profligate you believe, how fortunate for him, then, that the Draytons were killed by those dacoits, so that he inherited the title and estates, after all."

"Yes, so it must have been." Rose paused for a long moment, remembering, her brow knitted in a faint frown. Then she continued slowly, "You know, Jasmine, I always wondered if he really did have something to do with Hugo and his parents being murdered—for as I said, Papa and Mama themselves suspected as much at the time." She sighed heavily. "Well, it's just as well that we didn't consult Constable Dreiling about the envelope, for all this is certainly no more than a lovers' elopement! The only thing I don't understand is how the man who gave me the envelope fits in."

"Oh, but, surely, he was merely some sort of messenger hired to go between Lord Thornleigh and his lady love—and no doubt, those two dubious wretches chasing him were spies set on the couple by the young lady's old dragon of a mother," Jasmine reasoned.

"In that case, the mother must truly be horrid! Perhaps I was mistaken earlier, and instead of protecting the young lady, her mother is ill treating her. For that also could explain why the young lady has been driven to escape by means of an elopement, and perhaps Lord Thornleigh is simply rescuing her and that's why the stranger told me to guard the envelope with my life, as well. It's been fifteen years since Hugo died. I suppose that during that time, no matter what he was like in his younger days, Lord Thornleigh could have changed for the better. At any rate, it's certainly none of our affair and nothing to place us in any jeopardy ourselves, I shouldn't think."

"No, I shouldn't think so," Jasmine agreed.

"Well, that's that, then." Rose stood, neatly refolding the letter and tucking it back into the envelope. "What do you think I should do with this?" She tapped the envelope lightly, idly, against the palm of her free hand.

"Put it safely away—for you know how Lily and Daisy sometimes pry. Oh, I know that Lily only likes to know everything that's happening so that she doesn't feel left out and that Daisy is simply a curious creature, but still…"

"Yes, quite." Rose smiled ruefully, understanding. Much as she loved all her sisters, it was difficult to find any privacy from them at the town house.

The secretary at which she and Jasmine wrote their own correspondence had a secret compartment, and Rose hid the envelope inside it.

The younger sister nodded with satisfaction and approval at this resolution, then exited the room, clearly dismissing the peculiar matter. As far as Rose, too, was concerned, that was indeed the end of it, and inwardly, she was relieved to be rid of it. Like the nightmare she had experienced last evening, the entire affair had opened painful memories for her. Further, once she had realized that it actually involved nothing more than an elopement, it had made her feel slightly sordid and ashamed to have played any part, however small and incongruous, in it.

The only thing that continued to trouble her was such a crazy idea that she had not even voiced it to Jasmine: For one wild, terribly emotional instant, as the tall, dark foreigner had gazed at her so searchingly, then spoken to her so softly but urgently, bidding her to guard the envelope with her life, Rose had experienced a wholly bewildering but overwhelming sensation that he was her own dear Hugo, somehow miraculously alive, grown up, and returned to her.

But now, with a sick, sinking feeling, she realized that, of course, that was not possible, that it was surely only the strange, unexpected wakening of all her memories of India that had made her think that. Logically, she knew that Hugo had been dead and buried in his grave for the past fifteen years. It was only the faint hope that still somehow incongruously survived deep in her heart that had made her believe otherwise, if only for that one fleeting moment.

Still, at the thought of it, she abruptly sat down on the bed and cried.

Four

The Game Revealed

Time reveals all things.

Adagia
—Erasmus

Harley Street, London, England, 1850

Keeping a wary eye out, lest the two beefy scoundrels who had pursued him should somehow once more pick up his trail, Hugo Drayton, the true and rightful Lord Thornleigh, turned his footsteps toward his lodgings in Harley Street. Only there did he feel safe, for it was home not only to Englishmen who had done very well for themselves in India, mostly through the auspices of the East India Company ("John Company," the English often called it), but also to Oriental nabobs and their manservants. There, as he had hoped when he had come to England from India, no one paid him the slightest bit of heed. As Raj Khanna, the alias he had adopted following his parents' murders, he was simply one more East Indian who had been "civilized" by English missionaries and Her Majesty's Army, and, having seen the Light of Progress, had sailed from his homeland to England to celebrate his good fortune.

Once he finally reached Harley Street without further incident, Hugo breathed a small sigh of relief, although a troubled frown at the morning's events continued to knit his handsome brow. Walking along the sidewalk, his ears assaulted by the sound of not only English, but also Hindi, Punjabi and other Indian languages being spoken, his nostrils permeated by the aroma of not only mulligatawny, but also curry cooking, he could almost imagine himself back in India. Briefly, homesickness assailed him. But then, sternly, he reminded himself that that part of his life was over forever. Someday, perhaps, he would return to his native India to visit. But he would never live there again.

His destiny lay here, in this land of gentle green pastures and heather-dappled moors, of long-shadowed forests and gorse-strewn hills. If he were honest with himself, Hugo knew he would admit that it was not unappealing, this place where the sun melted like sweet butter from the cloud-churned sky instead of searing like a hot poker thrust from the heavens by the hand of a vengeful god; where the rain fell in soft drizzles that kissed the earth and one's upturned visage like a lover instead of in hard torrents that drenched the ground and the very soul; and where the ethereal white mist enshrouded not only the distant craggy mountain peaks, but also cloaked the sweeping heaths that stretched to crumbling cliffs and shingled beaches before falling to the sea, and blanketed the secret, sleepy hollows that hid among leafy bowers of gnarled old trees and budding new flowers. He could—if he tried—be happy here.

But first, there was much he must do.

With his key, he let himself into the modest terrace house he had acquired upon his arrival in London. Although he had made a fortune in India, so could have afforded the best Piccadilly or Belgravia had to offer, he had wanted to be here in Harley Street instead, among his own kind, and ostentation was not his way, besides. His goal was not to impress the *haut ton*.

"Was your hunt successful, *sahib?*" his manservant greeted him impassively in the Minton-tiled foyer.

"Yes and no, Mahout." Hugo employed the name he had years ago bestowed upon Mayur Singh to conceal their real identities. "I bagged the prey, but then lost it. Now, I must get it back."

"It is unlike you, *sahib*, not to accomplish what you set out to do."

"Yes, I know," Hugo answered shortly. "Unfortunately, although my search of Mrs. Squasher's residence was thorough and uninterrupted, and, in fact, proved fruitful, she must have discovered my theft almost immediately after I had left the premises, and she raised a hue and cry, sending two of her more questionable hirelings in pursuit of me. She is evidently fashioned of even sterner stuff than I imagined to have risen so early. Given the amount of wine she consumed last evening and the wee hour at which she finally retired, I had erroneously believed she would sleep at least until noon."

"What was it you found, then, *sahib?*"

"An envelope stamped with the Thornleigh seal—and a somewhat incriminating letter. Very careless of Sir James, I should have said. But, then, whilst he's as sly and cunning as a fox, he's hardly the best and the brightest, is he? For no matter how clever he is—or thinks he is, as the case may be—he has made mistakes in the past, and he does not appear to have learnt from them. That is scarcely the mark of a truly intelligent man."

"But this envelope and its contents are now no longer in your possession?" Mayur Singh queried, for he already knew Sir James's many failings, so had no interest in them, except to exploit them to Hugo's advantage.

"No. When it seemed to me that I might actually be caught, I gave them to Rose. My God! I still can't believe it!" Hugo went on to relate what had occurred in High Holborn, so aggrieved and angry with himself that he didn't know what to do. He had never intended to involve his beautiful, beloved Rose in his determined plan to gain revenge on his mortal enemy, his cousin, Sir James Wormwood.

But now, however unwittingly, he had.

What were the odds, Hugo wondered, that it should have been Rose whom he had nearly knocked down in High Holborn, while fleeing from Delphine Squasher's henchmen?

If only the two brawny ruffians who had pursued him hadn't been so hard and close on his heels! If only he hadn't been so afraid that he might be caught—forfeiting not only the envelope and its contents, but also his very life! For the hired thugs would surely have tortured and then killed him, Hugo suspected, dumping his body into some filthy, garbage-strewn alley for the rats to find or else perhaps into the River Thames, stinking of sewage, where he would have been food for the fish. So he'd had to trust someone with the envelope and letter—for then, even if he were apprehended, those would not be found on his person, and he could deny all knowledge of them, perhaps saving his life. He had known that it was a sliver of hope at best, but still, it had been better than none at all.

But to have handed them over to Rose…

"The gods work in mysterious ways, *sahib,*" Mayur Singh declared gravely, when apprised of what had happened. "So it may be that the *memsahib* is meant to help you in some way, as you did her that day in Chandni Chowk, when the young nobleman's elephant stampeded."

"I don't want her involved, I tell you! Sir James is a very evil, dangerous man—as well you know! He murdered my parents—and would have killed me, as well, if not for you. So I have no doubt that he would not scruple to hurt Rose if he believed her to pose a threat to him."

"Be at ease, *sahib*," the manservant insisted, "for your spies have told us nothing to make us think Sir James is even aware of her existence."

At last, however reluctantly, Hugo nodded, for he knew that to be true. He had trustworthy and well-paid informants all over London, most of whom he had brought with him from India and who therefore understood the dire folly of betraying him, so there was no reason to doubt their reports. Indeed, according to these, Sir James—Hugo would never think of his cousin as Lord Thornleigh—was completely incognizant of the fact that Hugo himself still lived, had not been burned alive in his father's *haveli* that horrible night in Chandni Chowk, when his whole world had vanished, to be replaced by one that had, at the time, seemed heartrendingly alien and sometimes incredibly harsh.

No, not for Sir James were the likes of those who resided in Bloomsbury—although he associated with others of far worse means and ilk.

Delphine Squasher was one of these.

But in the end, Hugo had managed to elude her henchmen, to make good his escape. So he had got rid of the envelope and letter—and perhaps inadvertently drawn Rose into the deadly game he played—all for naught. As he dwelled on that again, the realization both sickened and infuriated him. Equally disturbing was the fact that he didn't know what Rose would do with what he had given her. Seeing the Thornleigh seal on the envelope, perhaps she would get in touch with Sir James to return it and its contents. That would prove disastrous! They were the only tangible proof Hugo had at this point of the vile scheme his cousin was hatching. He must get them back—and quickly, he thought, his carnal mouth setting grimly.

"I understand, *sahib*," Mayur Singh said, when Hugo voiced this thought. Then the manservant continued, abruptly changing the subject. "Are you hungry? I've prepared a curry."

"I'm famished, Mahout, for I've had no breakfast."

Even though Hugo dined alone—for despite the fact that it was just the two of them in the town house, his manservant usually insisted on preserving the formalities—his luncheon was served in the dining room rather than in the morning room or kitchen. It consisted not only of the curry, but also fried vegetables, rice, chutney and chapati—this last an unleavened bread fried on a griddle. It was followed by a tasty rice pudding. After he had hungrily eaten his meal, Hugo retired to his study to smoke a cheroot and ponder his next step.

But try as he might, he could seem to think of nothing but Rose's lovely, haunting eyes, as expressively wide and honest as he had remembered from their childhood, and such a soft, forest shade of green that, as he had gazed into their startled depths in High Holborn, he had thought of the northern hills of India and felt a sudden, sharp stab of homesickness. Now, he cursed himself for a fool. India was his past, and England was his future. He knew that. He had worked many long, hard years for it, starting from nothing, a mere boy in those green hills he sometimes still yearned for, despite how driven he had been to escape from them and to carve out his destiny.

That his fate had always included Rose, Hugo had never once forgotten or doubted. Once his spies had located her and the Windermeres in London, he had always intended, in his own way and time, to renew their acquaintance.

But it seemed that the damnable gods had other plans. Hugo's mouth twisted bitterly at the thought, for when did they not...?

Five

Cabbage Roses

There is a garden in her face
Where roses and white lilies grow;
A heavenly paradise is that place
Wherein all pleasant fruits do flow.
  Fourth Book of Airs, Cherry-Ripe [1617]
                                    —Thomas Campion

Russell Square, London, England, 1850

The next morning, true to his word, Bobby, the pick-pocket, arrived bright and early at the Windermeres' town house to clean and paint the ornamental front fence and to oil the gate's hinges. When she spied him through the front windows, Rose felt a sense of relief that her trust in him had not been misplaced, after all. Opening the front door, she greeted him pleasantly, then showed him where she had set out the wash bucket, paint and oil by the front steps the night before.

"How long do you think it will take you to complete the job, Bobby?"

"Oh, not more 'n two or three 'ours, I reckon, Miss Windermere. T' main thing will be ta get all those patches o' pigeon droppin's an' rust off t' fence. Otherwise, they'll make a real mess o' t' paintin'."

With a stiff wire brush Rose had also provided, Bobby set to work cleaning the fence just as Leddy, the newspaper boy, showed up to deliver the *Times*. Seeing Bobby, Leddy called out a greeting to him, for the two lads were friends, then stood chatting with him a few minutes before turning his attention to her.

"Good mornin', Miss Windermere." Reaching into the canvas bag in which he carried the stack of newspapers he delivered daily to the houses on his route, Leddy withdrew a copy of the *Times*, folding it neatly in half before handing it to her. "I didn't know you wanted your fence painted, or else I'd 'ave been 'appy ta do it for you." He gazed at her, enraptured, as usual, his face beaming with pleasure at the sight of her standing there in the morning sun, her silver-blond hair glowing like a halo around her lovely countenance.

Before Rose could reply, however, Bobby, grinning hugely, impishly snatched Leddy's cap from his head, giving him several rough cuffs with it.

"Clapper-dudgeon!" Bobby cried teasingly. "Miss Windermere don't want you standin' about moonin' o'er 'er like some cow what's just been poleaxed, Leddy!"

"I wasn't moonin' o'er 'er," Leddy protested, obviously embarrassed. "I was just bein' polite, is all. What's wrong with a little conversation an' bein' pleasant ta someone, Bobby, I'd like ta know? I always speak ta Miss Windermere when I make me mornin' rounds. Ain't that right, Miss Windermere?"

"Yes, Leddy." She smiled at the two lads, thinking they couldn't be any older and might be even younger than Daisy, who was just eighteen. "Well, I must go in now. My father will be wanting his newspaper at the breakfast table, as usual. Bobby, I'll have our cook, Mrs. Beasley, fix you a plate, and I'll bring it out when I come back to check on your progress. Leddy, have a good day."

"Thank you, Miss Windermere," the boys said.

Still smiling, Rose went back into the town house. She liked all the young lads and lasses with whom she had gradually become acquainted over the years she had lived in Russell Square. Although she would not have parted with any of her sisters, whom she loved dearly, she had still often longed wistfully for a brother or two. But that was not to be, so she must be content with what she had and be glad of the glimpse the boys gave her into what having one or more brothers would have been like.

After breakfast, Rose stepped into the kitchen, where she had Mrs. Beasley prepare a heaping plate for Bobby from the leftovers, as well as a steaming-hot mug of tea. These, she carried out front to where Bobby labored on the short wrought-iron fence. He had been working very hard, she observed with satisfaction, for already, considerable headway had been made in the cleaning, so that even before it had been painted, the fence looked better, not nearly as shabby and worn.

"Golly, Miss Windermere, I wasn't expectin' nothin' so fine as all this." Bobby stared with amazement at the plate and mug she handed him.

"Cleaning fences is hard work, so I imagine that you've got quite hungry."

That was an understatement, Rose saw, as, sitting down on the front steps, the pickpocket fell upon the food as though starving—which he no doubt was, she realized, suddenly wishing she had put even more on the plate.

"Bobby, I've got a lot of other small jobs you could do here," she told him slowly, "and of course, in addition to your being paid a small sum, you'd receive meals, too. Would you be at all interested?"

His mouth crammed full of food, Bobby nodded vigorously.

"Good."

After establishing what needed doing around the town house and determining a schedule for the pickpocket, Rose soon settled back into her complacent routine and would have continued it undisturbed had she not a few days later begun to have the oddest feeling that she was being followed and spied on wherever she went. The unnerving sensation did not start all at once, but, rather, crept up on her so gradually that, at first, she was certain that she was letting her imagination run wildly away with her.

But after a while, she could no longer dismiss the disconcerting impression, especially when, once or twice, she thought she caught a glimpse of the man, the foreigner, who had given her the enigmatic envelope and instructed her to guard it with her life. She was confused and upset by the notion that he might be following her, spying on her. If he wanted the envelope and its contents back, then, surely, all he need do was ask! They didn't belong to her, and she would be more than happy to return them.

Even more distressing to Rose was the thought that she was mistaken and that it *wasn't* actually the foreigner shadowing her every footstep, but, rather, the two burly knaves who had pursued him that morning when he had nearly knocked her down. Unlike the first man, those last two had made her distinctly uneasy, and she knew that they had frightened her sister, also. That was why Jasmine had sent them off on a wild-goose chase. But perhaps, now, recognizing how they had been misled and thus lost their quarry, they had sought out their deceivers, intent on somehow punishing them!

Rose was so disquieted by this last notion that, the following morning, although she had not intended to do any such thing, she confided her apprehensions to Leddy and Bobby, asking them both if they had seen anyone lurking around the town house.

"No, Miss Windermere, but I'll sure keep a sharp eye out," Leddy responded stoutly, clearly indignant at the thought that anyone might wish her harm.

"Me, too," Bobby insisted, equally incensed.

A few days later, her nerves so peculiarly and unfamiliarly on edge that she accidentally dropped a flower bowl and broke it, Rose decided that since the afternoon was sunny and warm, she would take her paintbox and sketchbook across the street into the park and paint awhile. That serene activity always helped her to order her thoughts and to feel better. So thinking, she went upstairs to her bedroom, where she buttoned on a spencer taken from the wardrobe, tied a pretty straw bonnet on her head, then gathered her artist's supplies.

Then, going back downstairs, she informed the housekeeper, Miss Candlish, that if anyone needed her, she would be in the park. After that, she slipped out the front door and through the front gate, inordinately cheered by the fact that it now swung smoothly at her touch instead of creaking on its hinges. She was also pleased that the freshly painted fence and other sprucing-up out front that Bobby had done, including hanging some potted primroses and filling with red geraniums the stone planters that sat on either side of the newly black-painted front door, had brightened up the appearance of the entire town house considerably.

Once on the sidewalk, Rose glanced with seeming nonchalance around Russell Square. But she saw nothing out of the ordinary: just the usual horses and carriages on the streets, the familiar passersby on the sidewalk. Although the square appeared crowded at this hour of the day, she knew that compared to other parts of London, it was actually a relatively quiet and secluded place, for Bloomsbury was home to no main thoroughfares, but, rather, simply bounded by them. Its streets, once a hub of seemingly unceasing activity and some of the most fashionable in London, now saw comparatively little traffic beyond sedate coaches and hansom cabs. Its sidewalks were peopled by the middle-class and the respectable but shabby genteel, who lived in town houses built by the architect James Burton, just like that of the Windermeres, and the elderly of whom still thought Bloomsbury was the most desirable of addresses, unaware that the *haut ton* had years ago moved on. So Rose had no difficulty in crossing the heavy old paving stones of Montague Street in front of the Windermeres' town house to the park beyond, her crinolines rustling and swaying around her Morocco slippers as she did so.

The park at the heart of Russell Square was one of the largest in all London. It had been designed by the landscape gardener Sir Humphrey Repton around the turn of the century and was populated with numerous plane trees and other trees, shrubbery, and flower beds filled with a profusion of beautiful and fragrant blossoms. An iron fence enclosed the whole park, along which, on the inside perimeter, grew a hornbeam hedge. From the various gated entrances ran loose-gravel paths that wound through the park to the reposoir at its center. Here and there were benches where one could sit and rest, enjoying the scenery. Near the south gate, looking imperiously down

Bedford Place, stood a statue of Francis, fifth Duke of Bedford, one hand reposing on a plow. An imposing sculpture by Sir Richard Westmacott, it had been erected in 1809. Facing it from the opposite end of Bedford Place, in Bloomsbury Square, stood a statue of Charles James Fox, also by Westmacott.

As it had long been one of her favorite places, Rose had often retreated to the park during the years she and her family had lived at Russell Square. Now, pushing open the gate of the nearest entrance, she stepped inside, then latched it securely behind her before finding her way along the serpentine paths to the heart of the park, the loose gravel crunching beneath her slippers. Once or twice, she suffered the anxious feeling again that she was being watched. But when she paused and gazed around suspiciously, her head tilted attentively to one side, she could see and hear no one. So, at last, deciding that she must indeed be permitting her imagination to run unbridled, she determinedly shoved the idea from her mind. She had come here to escape from her vague and, thus far, unsubstantiated fears—not to dwell on them!

Choosing a green swath of thick grass as her destination, Rose spread the light blanket she had brought with her on the ground, beneath the shade of a soaring old plane tree. Then, settling herself upon it, she opened her paintbox and sketchbook, and soon she was immersed in painting a watercolor of a cascade of pink cabbage roses.

Six

The Plot Thickens

> Ay, now the plot thickens very much upon us.
> > *The Rehearsal* [1663]
> > —George Villiers, Duke of Buckingham

Lincoln's Inn Field, London, 1850

Comprised of twelve acres, Lincoln's Inn Field was the largest square in London. Like various others of its ilk, it had been designed by the architect Inigo Jones during the seventeenth century and had once been one of the *haut ton*'s most fashionable addresses. In an earlier era, the actress Nell Gwynne, mistress to King Charles II, had lived here, and traitors, religious martyrs and duelists had met their deaths beneath the towering old plane trees that forested the park at the plaza's heart. But gradually, just like Bloomsbury, the area had declined, until, being used as a shortcut between Holborn and The Strand, it had become home to cutpurses and cutthroats of all kinds. In 1735, in an effort to curtail all the crime, the sprawling park itself had been enclosed with a stout iron fence to preserve it from the unwashed masses. Nowadays, due directly to the square's proximity to the courts of Lincoln's Inn in Chancery Lane, Lincoln's Inn Field was home chiefly to barristers and solicitors.

Delphine Squasher's late husband had been one of the former, for not being a man herself, marriage was the closest she had been able to come to the practice of law—and this fact had forever blighted her entire life. She felt unshakably certain that she would have proved far more capable before the Bar than had her less-than-dearly departed husband, Jeffrey (who, if truth be told, had been glad to leave this earth, since it had meant finally escaping from his wife). But the Bar did not call those of the fairer sex to its distinguished halls. Thus thwarted but nevertheless determined, Mrs. Squasher had eventually, by means of charitable social work, found an outlet for her ambitious aspirations. But unfortunately, she was so supremely arrogant and blindly stupid, so bent on impressing her meager education and her grand pretensions to intellect upon others, that she failed miserably at her labors, doing a great deal of harm to the luckless recipients of her pompous, overbearing manner and general ill will, and little, if any, good. Recognizing this, her superiors had increasingly ignored all her recommendations and remonstrations. At last, Mrs. Squasher had resorted to teaching at a female academy, but at this, too, she had demonstrated herself wholly unfit and unsuccessful, and in the end, she had abruptly been terminated from her post, much to the vast relief of the charges who had suffered immeasurably under her tutelage.

Now, as she restlessly paced the threadbare carpet in the drawing room of her town house in Lincoln's Inn Field, Mrs. Squasher felt herself beset by utter idiots on all sides, as usual—all of them incapable of comprehending her extraordinary brain and inestimable talents.

"What do you mean, you lost him, Onslow?" she asked yet again, staring at him as though she were fully cognizant of the fact that he was the bastard son of a tavern trollop and an itinerant sailor who had remained in port only long enough to beget him.

"Just that, missus." Onslow shifted guiltily from one foot to the other, uncomfortably aware of the fact that he had made a complete mess of the task she had set him. "For just a moment—no more 'n that, I swear!— we lost sight o' t' thief on 'Igh 'Olborn. So we inquired o' two ladies if they 'ad spied 'im runnin' by, an' they sent us off down Newton Street. But when me an' Lombard got there, 'e 'ad vanished. We figger 'e 'ad circled around ta 'Igh 'Olborn only ta throw us off t' scent an' that it was for Waterloo Bridge an' Southwark or Lambeth 'e was bound for all along—maybe even Bermondsey."

"You figure!" Mrs. Squasher mocked contemptuously, her big round face, with its narrowed brown eyes, its pug-dog nose, and its full, puffed cheeks, furious. "You aren't smart enough to figure anything! What if those two ladies misdirected you?"

"Why would they do that, missus?" Lombard asked, with seeming innocence. He was the bigger and stronger of the two men and more experienced at handling his mistress's freaks of temper. " They 'ad no good reason ta lie."

"Very well, then," Mrs. Squasher said at last. "You may go. Indeed, the sooner you are out of my sight, the better! But mind, I expect you to find that thief—wherever he may be—and to get back what he stole from me! Is that clear?"

"Yes, missus." Glad to have got off so lightly, the two men quickly made their escape.

After they had gone, Mrs. Squasher strode to the teacart to pour herself a stiff drink from the cut-glass decanter that sat on a silver-plate tray. From long habit, she downed the splash of whiskey in a single greedy swallow, then thumped down the cheap glass tumbler, cursing Onslow and Lombard for a pair of fools. You just couldn't get good help these days, she thought, incensed. Regardless, she must make do with what she had.

At all costs, the unknown thief who had so brazenly broken into her town house and robbed her must be located. Why he had taken the envelope and letter, she didn't know, although she suspected that he must have recognized the coat-of-arms stamped into the red wax seal and meant to blackmail Lord Thornleigh with it. If that were the case, then the thief was no mere robber, but a highly intelligent adversary— perhaps one who had somehow learned of the game that was afoot. If he were indeed a player... Mrs. Squasher's pursed mouth thinned grimly. Well, she would find out soon enough, and then he would wish he had never involved himself in this affair!

But first, she must retrieve what he had taken from her. That envelope and its contents were her insurance. As fond as she was of Lord Thornleigh, she sensed with a feral instinct that he was not a man to be trusted.

Seven

The Spy in the Park

> In maiden meditation, fancy-free.
> Yet marked I where the bolt of Cupid fell:
> It fell upon a little western flower,
> Before milk-white, now purple with love's wound.
> > *A Midsummer Night's Dream* [1595-1596]
> > > —William Shakespeare

Russell Square, London, England, 1850

Lost in reverie and the watercolor of pink cabbage roses swiftly taking shape on one page of her sketchbook, Rose soon left her troubles behind, as she had hoped she would. She had chosen watercolors instead of oils because the former were a medium that required not only concentration, but also quickness, since one must capture the image before the paint dried. Thus there was little room for error, so she could not permit her mind to wander.

At first, her plan worked, and her surroundings faded into the background, so that she was only absently aware of the birds twittering and the squirrels chirruping in the trees with which the park was wooded, of the toads croaking and the grasshoppers singing in the flower beds. But after twenty minutes or so, when her painting was nearly complete, she gradually grew cognizant of a sound that initially seemed to her like the wind soughing through the boughs of the trees, but that after teasing at the edges of her consciousness finally disrupted her focus. Laying her brush down on her palette and wiping her hands on a cloth, she glanced around curiously, puzzled and uneasy. A faint breeze stirred, rustling the leaves of the branches and causing the blossoms to sway gently. Yes, that must be what she had heard, she thought.

But then, of a sudden, from a tall, thick stand of nearby trees and shrubbery, there burst such an explosion of noise that Rose cried out with fright, struggling to her feet. With raucous screams, the startled birds perched in the boughs took flight, and with incredible rapidity, a rabbit bounded from the underbrush. The next thing Rose knew, amid shouts of "Get 'im! Don't let 'im get away!" and grunts and groans of pain, a group of lads flew, sprang, tumbled, and rolled from the copse, arms flailing, fists flying, and legs kicking as they pounded their stunned and grossly outnumbered opponent mercilessly—and often mistakenly belted one another, too, in their zeal.

"Oh, my God," Rose breathed, as she recognized the boys. Her eyes widened even more when she realized the man they were pummeling was none other than the stranger, the foreigner, who had given her the mysterious envelope and letter. "Stop! Oh, stop!" she exhorted then, running forward into the fray, trying to drag the lads away.

"Look out, Brock, you dolt!" yelled Burke, the street artist from Covent Garden. "You almost 'it Miss Windermere!"

"Sorry, Miss Windermere!" Brock, the butcher's apprentice, called over his shoulder before gleefully rejoining the spirited confrontation, his bloodstained apron flapping wildly.

In the end, it was only the loud shrilling of young Constable Dreiling's whistle as he appeared on the scene, wading knee-deep into the fray, and Nick, the baker's boy, and Victor, the fishmonger's son, finally coming to their senses and hauling the combatants apart, that brought a halt to the battle. After that, all the lads stood panting for air, nursing their injuries and grumbling under their breath at their sport having been terminated, while the foreigner lay still and moaning upon the ground, obviously much the worse for the zealous assault upon him, although he had defended himself remarkably well under the circumstances. Still, fearing that he was badly hurt and feeling responsible for that, knowing that Leddy and Bobby must have taken the apprehensions she had voiced to them to heart and put the rest of their chums up to this, Rose ran to the fallen man's side, kneeling to see if he were conscious.

"Gor, I think me nose is broken." Jake, whose father ran a livery stable in Long Acre, felt his bloody nose gingerly, trying to determine whether it was still straight. "Which one o' you rum curs did it, I'd like to know?"

"It was Leddy!" Bobby, the pickpocket accused, pointing a finger at the newspaper boy.

"No, it wasn't." Leddy's eyes opened wide with shock at this false charge. "It was Chandon. You know 'ow crazy 'e always gets in a fight!"

Chandon, who, Rose knew, worked on the docks, unloading barges, merely folded his arms across his chest and grinned hugely. He was a tough, wiry lad with tattoos, who loved to wrestle and who, at a relatively early age, had run away from home to make his own way in the world.

"If it's broken, Jake, it'll be an improvement," he observed cheekily, "'coz you were too pretty, any'ow."

"Why, you—" Jake doubled up his fist threateningly.

"Now, now. That'll be enough o' that, Chandon, Jake!" Although, in truth, he was scarcely any older than they, Constable Dreiling glared at both lads censuringly and authoritatively, grabbing hold of the latter boy before another brawl ensued. Warningly, the policeman shook the stout black truncheon he held in his other hand. "Be'ave yourself, or else I'll give you a crack upside t' 'ead! You know I don't like trouble on me watch…it means I got ta take notes an' fill out reports.

So what's all this about? 'Ow come you lads jumped this 'ere poor foreign bloke, beatin' 'im 'alf ta death?"

"'Coz 'e's been followin' Miss Windermere around these past few days, spyin' on 'er!" Chris, the young pie man, explained. "Leddy an' Bobby saw 'im!"

"*Oui*, that is right," Jordan, the grower's son, confirmed. "Leddy an' Bobby told us 'e meant ta do 'er some 'arm. We couldn't allow that ta 'appen, now, could we? We've all been acquainted with Mam'selle Windermere for years. She is our friend! So when Joey came 'round earlier on 'is velocipede ta let us all know about t' plan, o' course we agreed ta 'elp."

"I simply…wished to…talk to her. I assure you…I did not…intend to…hurt her, Constable," Hugo gasped out slowly, one hand cradling his ribs, which he was afraid were cracked, if not broken. In his wildest dreams, when he had set out to get back the envelope and letter he had given Rose, he had never imagined anything like this occurring. Because of that, the attack by the bunch of boys had taken him totally by surprise.

"Why, you nearly knocked 'er down just t' other day!" Victor stared down at him fiercely.

"Aye—an' caused 'er ta lose t' pasty she'd only just bought an' paid for," Brock added. "You're lucky I didn't take me meat cleaver ta you!"

"Why are you followin' 'er around an' spyin' on 'er, anyway, *signore*?" Joey, whose father ran The Hobby Horse, loomed over Hugo menacingly. "You'd better tell us t' truth, too, 'coz I warn you, I belong ta a secret society o' Italian assassins—an' we know 'ow ta deal with t' likes of you!" Gurgling dramatically, he drew one hand sharply across his throat, as though slitting it.

"If t' organization's so bloody secret, 'ow come you're always braggin' about it, Joey?" Constable Dreiling stroked his muttonchops and handlebar mustache absently as he contemplated the entire situation. "But you, sir, answer t' question, anyway," he ordered Hugo. "We don't 'old with spies 'ere in England, especially one's what's stalkin' women, like some tiger its prey!"

"Oh, can't you all see the poor man is in too much pain to be interrogated this way!" Taking a handkerchief from her pocket, Rose dabbed at Hugo's cut lip, carefully wiping away the blood. "Help me get him up and over to my father's town house."

"No, really—" Hugo started to protest.

"Please, sir, I won't hear any objections," Rose insisted stoutly. "You're injured, and it's all my fault. When I confided my fears about being watched to Leddy and Bobby, I never dreamt that it would lead to all this!"

"You are fortunate...to have a band of...such stalwart admirers, Miss...? I'm so sorry, but in all the hubbub, I'm...I'm not certain I...caught your name." Much to his dismay, Hugo was unsure whether it was the fact that his ribs were hurting him that caused him to be so strangely short of breath or whether it was the wide green eyes that gazed down at him with such gentleness and concern.

"Windermere. Rose Windermere."

Beneath his raven-wing eyebrows, the stranger's eyes were as black and fathomless as she remembered; his dark, handsome visage was hawkish, finely boned and molded. Like that of so many who came from India to England, it was a blend of European and Indian features, set beneath gleaming black hair. Staring at him, Rose felt a sudden rush of familiarity, yearning, and grief sweep through her, for he reminded her of everything she had left behind in her birthplace: the rugged mountains that hove up in the distance, keeping eternal watch over Delhi, and the sweeping plains from which the city itself rose, sprawling along the western shore of the vast River Yamuna, sacred to the god Krishna. Even now, in the middle of London, she could still smell the tang of the river's blue-green waters, fed by a glacial lake in the Himalaya Mountains, see the tall, slender golden reeds and the long, squat sandbars that had dotted its shallows, hear the piercing cries of the great flamingos that had strolled and fished among them. Somewhere beyond Delhi, she knew, the River Yamuna had intersected the River Ganges, their joining a holy place. She had always longed to see it.

"Please, sir, I truly cannot help but feel responsible for what has befallen you. So please permit me to make amends by taking you to my father's town house. It is just on the other side of Montague Street. From there, if necessary, I can summon a physician."

Finally, wordlessly, Hugo nodded. At that, Constable Dreiling and a few of the lads assisted him to his feet and across the wide street, the rest of the boys carrying Rose's paintbox and other belongings. Whereas, previously, the lads had been buoyed up by the success of their scheme, they were now appropriately subdued, recognizing that in their enthusiasm to help Rose, they had perhaps severely injured the foreigner and might be arrested by Constable Dreiling.

Once the little procession reached the front gate of the town house, Rose thanked the boys, then told them that they had best return to work so that they didn't get into trouble over their absence.

"Do you want to press charges against them, sir?" the policeman inquired.

"No." Hugo shook his head. "Their intentions were honorable. They were looking out for a friend."

When the lads had all gone, Rose, after asking Constable Dreiling if he would be good enough to fetch Dr. Haverham, led Hugo inside the town house to the drawing room—where she unwittingly drew up short at the sight of Jasmine and Professor Prosser, seated stiltedly together on the couch.

At the unexpected intrusion, both the latter stood, each, although for entirely different reasons, dismayed by the sight of the foreigner leaning for support on Rose.

"Jasmine, Professor Prosser, this gentleman was unfortunately set upon in the park and has been injured as a result. Could you help me get him on the sofa, please?"

"My dear Miss Windermere, I understand perfectly the innate kindness that prompted you to come to this gentleman's assistance," the professor declared, hurrying fussily and proprietarily toward Rose, causing her to color with embarrassment and annoyance. "But, really, do you think it wise to have brought a complete stranger into your father's household? No offense, sir."

"None taken," Hugo managed to say, through teeth gritted against pain. "However, as it happens, I do have some slight acquaintance with these ladies. Permit me to introduce myself, sir. My name is Raj Khanna, lately of India and now lodged in Harley Street."

As Hugo prudently announced himself by the alias he had assumed in India and produced his card, upon which that name was inscribed, he did not even begin to imagine how Rose's heart sank at his words. Hearing his name, seeing it written upon the calling card he handed to the professor, she felt a sudden rush of overwhelming and utter despair sweep through her entire being, and she realized that despite everything, she had, however foolishly and futilely, harbored some small, desperate hope that the foreigner was somehow her own dear Hugo miraculously come to life again.

But of course, that was not possible. She did not know why she had ever thought it was. Still, as she helped the stranger to the settee, she bent her head and blinked back tears, hoping the others did not notice.

"I must find our housekeeper, Miss Candlish," she murmured, after getting the patient settled on the couch, "so that I can inform her why I have summoned Dr. Haverham, and so that the rest of my family will not worry. I'll just be a minute. Jasmine, would you attend me, please? Professor, if you would be good enough to keep Mr. Khanna company…"

"Yes, Miss Windermere, I will. But, then, afterward, if I could be spared a few minutes of your time…? For naturally, as always, it is you whom I came to see. I was so sorry to find only Miss Jasmine at home. Of course, she is pleasant company." He bowed slightly in Jasmine's direction. "As are your other sisters and your parents, whom Miss Jasmine informed me were out, except for your dear mother, who is resting in her room, I understood. But it was really you I wished to visit with most particularly." From behind his large, horn-rimmed spectacles, the professor peered at her raptly, looking, in Rose's mind, so like an overgrown, curious owl that she didn't know whether to laugh or cry.

"Of course, sir. But first, I truly must attend to Mr. Khanna's well-being."

When the two sisters returned to the drawing room, they carried clean cloths, a basin of hot water, a bottle of antiseptic, bandages, and other supplies they had thought they might need to tend the patient's injuries. These appeared to consist of a number of cuts and bruises, but Rose had observed how he seemed to cradle one side of his torso, and she feared that perhaps he had suffered some broken ribs, as well. But Dr. Haverham would be able to determine that for certain.

"No, Mr. Khanna, please don't try to rise," she insisted, as he struggled to stand at the women's reappearance. "You're clearly not at your best at the moment, and surely, given the situation, we need not stand on ceremony! Now, let us try to determine how badly you are hurt."

It had been many years since a female had fussed over Hugo, so to now have two of them washing his face and hands, cleansing not only blood, but also dirt from the park from his cuts and scratches, was a peculiar sensation. With the sole exception of his manservant, Mayur Singh, Hugo was long accustomed to looking after himself. Under normal circumstances, following the pummeling he had received, he would have dragged himself to his feet and hired a hansom cab to convey him to his lodgings in Harley Street. He did not like being wounded. Much less did he like being seen in such a state by others. So he did not quite understand why he had allowed himself to be brought to the Windermere town house. Surely, it could only be because he had hoped to obtain the envelope and its contents without further ado.

Yet, if he were honest with himself, Hugo knew that he would admit that was not the whole truth. There were any number of reasons why he had permitted himself to be brought here—not the least of which was that he was immensely eager to learn everything he could about Rose, and he had wanted that curiosity satisfied. Now, as she bent near to him, gently exploring the gashes and bruises on his face to see how bad they actually were, he could smell the heady fragrance of the attar-of-roses perfume she wore, mingled with the sweet scent of warm sunlight in her hair, and he was transported back to their childhood and Chandi

Chowk. The memory of her, poised like a fairy in the main road and marketplace, with the hot sun over Delhi beating down upon her silver-blond tresses, was forever seared into his memory.

He could have watched her forever in the park, he thought, could have painted a portrait of her painting the cabbage roses. Yet, he knew that it would only have been a pale imitation at best, that no matter how hard he had tried, he would never quite have been able to capture the true essence of her being. She seemed as elusive and ethereal as a fairy queen from some mythical place dappled with sunlight and swept by the sea.

"You are staring at me, Mr. Khanna," Rose observed quietly. "I've tried to be as gentle as possible with my ministrations, but if I've hurt you somehow——"

"No, no, it's not that. I'm sorry. It's simply that your eyes…their color…it reminds me of the green hills of my homeland, India, that's all."

"I see." Rose smiled. "I shall take that as a compliment, Mr. Khanna. For my sisters and I were all born in India and spent our early years there before coming to England. Even now, I sometimes miss my birthplace. Are you often homesick, Mr. Khanna?"

"I, too, miss India, yes. But England is my home now."

No more was said, for just then, kindly, bewhiskered Dr. Haverham arrived and was ushered by the housekeeper, Miss Candlish, into the drawing room. Following the necessary introductions, Rose, Jasmine, and Professor Prosser tactfully withdrew to give the physician some privacy with his patient—with the professor again eagerly pressing Rose for a few minutes of her time. Not seeing how she could politely avoid granting his request, she led him into the library, hoping he had not noticed how Jasmine had wryly rolled her eyes as, stating that she was needed elsewhere in the household, she had made good her own escape.

Fortunately, it did not take much for Professor Prosser to launch himself enthusiastically into one of his lectures, as though Rose were one of his pupils at the university. So she was, as usual, able to listen with only half an ear, only occasionally compelled to interject a comment or two. Still, she was relieved to be in a position to cut today's narrative short, reminding Professor Prosser that she must check on the patient's well-being.

"Of course, my dear Miss Windermere," he agreed, somewhat peevishly. "Still, I cannot think why you should have brought Mr. Khanna here in the first place, for surely, even if you have some slight acquaintance with him, the best course of action would have been to permit Constable Dreiling to deal with the matter."

"Sir, my good conscience would have compelled me to offer assistance to any person in such an unfortunate situation, and as I am, in fact, acquainted with Mr. Khanna, however slightly, it would surely have most uncharitable to consign his care to the hands of a stranger, I'm sure you will agree."

"Well, yes…yes, when you put it that way…."

"Now, Professor, I trust you will understand, as well,

why I feel it necessary to bid you good afternoon, as I must also make arrangements for Mr. Khanna to be transported to his lodgings, if he is well enough to be moved, and there are some other matters, too, that require my attention."

"Yes, all right. I shall say *adieu*, then, and look forward to calling on you again in the future."

After she had firmly and gratefully closed the front door behind Professor Prosser, Rose nipped upstairs to the bedroom she shared with Jasmine, there to retrieve Mr. Khanna's envelope—except that it didn't really belong to Mr. Khanna, she reflected thoughtfully as she drew it from the secret compartment of the secretary, but, rather, to Lord Thornleigh's intended recipient.

For a moment, she wondered if she really ought to contact Lord Thornleigh about the entire matter. Then she reminded herself that it involved nothing more than an elopement, in which she wanted no part whatsoever, and she decided that since Mr. Khanna had originally been in possession of the envelope, it must have been with Lord Thornleigh's full knowledge and blessing.

"You're going to give Mr. Khanna the envelope, then?" Jasmine entered their bedroom in time to observe her older sister's actions.

"Yes. I think it's best, don't you?"

"Of course." Jasmine looked vaguely surprised. "He seems a proper sort of person, exactly the kind of man who could be trusted with a secret. So I'm not surprised that Lord Thornleigh employed him as a go-between."

"No...I guess not." Closing the secret compartment, Rose tucked the envelope into a pocket of the gown she wore.

Then she and Jasmine went back downstairs. Knocking tentatively upon one of the French doors that opened into the drawing room, and being told to enter, they stepped inside to see that Dr. Haverham had completed the examination of the patient. Mr. Khanna, with some difficulty, was easing himself back into the jacket he had removed for the examination.

"Ah, Miss Windermere, Miss Jasmine, you'll be happy to know that aside from the obvious cuts and bruises, Mr. Khanna has suffered no more than a few cracked ribs," the physician informed them, as he stowed the tools of his trade in the black bag he always carried with him. "But I've bound them tightly, and they'll soon mend."

"I'm relieved to hear it," Rose said.

Declaring that he would see himself out, Dr. Haverham took his leave just as Miss Candlish appeared with the tea Rose had earlier, upon arriving home from the park, instructed Mrs. Beasley to prepare.

"I thought that perhaps you might be hungry after your ordeal, Mr. Khanna." Rose poured the tea from its china pot into a matching china cup, then filled a plate for him from the assortment of small sandwiches, cakes, tarts and sweetmeats the cook had fixed. "Tea seemed the least I could do to make amends."

"You've already done more than enough as it is, Miss Windermere." Hugo's face was grave as he accepted the cup and plate she handed him. "Indeed, I cannot thank you and your sister Miss Jasmine enough for everything. I am in your debt. So should there ever prove anything I can do for you, I hope you'll let me know."

"You're very kind, Mr. Khanna." Rose took a sip of tea, then set her own cup back into its saucer. "I regret that on two occasions now, we have crossed paths under such inauspicious circumstances, but I hope we can set matters aright. So let me put your mind at ease immediately: I still have the envelope you gave me. I presume you now wish it returned to you, and I am quite happy to do that. You had only to ask, you know. You really didn't need to follow me about and spy on me."

"You have my deepest apologies for that," Hugo said stiffly, realizing how he had offended and perhaps even frightened her.

He thought, now, that he should have followed his initial instinct, after all, and properly presented himself to the Windermeres, revealing his true identity, laying all before them, and begging their assistance. Only the notion that perhaps they would doubt his story, think him an impostor, and, worse, contact Sir James, had dissuaded him from this course of action—that, and the knowledge that he did not want Rose dragged into his affairs and thereby exposed to peril. Thus, Hugo had judged it prudent before taking any action at least to observe the Windermeres, and most especially Rose, from a distance for a few days to determine for himself what he should do.

"The...envelope and the letter it contains are very valuable to me," he continued slowly, "and there was always the chance that I had...misjudged your character. I see, now, that I did not. I am most grateful to you for everything you've done, Miss Windermere. I had no right to impose on you, to involve you in my affairs to begin with. It is I who am to blame for what has occurred, not you. You are indeed fortunate to have such friends as those boys who came to your defense."

"Most people would find it not only strange, but indeed also wholly unsuitable that I have such friends as those lads, Mr. Khanna."

"I am not most people—and a single genuine friend is worth a hundred who call themselves such, but who are the first to desert one in one's time of need."

"I have always thought so." Reaching into her pocket, Rose withdrew the envelope she had taken from the secretary. "Here is your envelope. I trust you will find it in order."

"I feel quite certain I shall." Not wishing to give further affront by actually examining what he had been handed, Hugo stuck the envelope into one pocket of his jacket. "Miss Windermere, I don't mean to pry, but...may I be so bold as to inquire whether you and Miss Jasmine took it upon yourselves to read the letter the envelope contains?"

"I'm afraid we did, sir." Rose blushed faintly at the confession. "However, it was not done from any evil design, I promise you. Rather, because you were being chased by two disreputable-looking men that day in High Holborn, we feared that perhaps you had involved us in something that might prove damaging or even dangerous to us and our family. Although Jasmine misdirected the two men who pursued you, we did not know whether we would ever see you again. Thus, we felt it incumbent upon us to examine the envelope and its contents."

"Yes, of course. In your own place, I would have done the same," Hugo reluctantly admitted.

"However, once we discovered that the matter was apparently nothing more than a lovers' elopement—about which, you can, of course, be assured of our discretion—we were at ease and doubtless would never even have given it a second thought, had you not begun to follow me around," Rose explained. "Not that I actually saw you, of course—it must have been Bobby who did that, for he…he lives on the streets, so he's very wise about their ways. I know it will probably sound odd, but somehow, I…I just sensed your presence…felt as though I were being watched."

"I see." Hugo was greatly relieved to know that Rose had not actually witnessed him spying on her, that it had taken an extremely sharp-eyed lad to spot him—and to hatch the successful, however overly zealous, plot to catch him. Otherwise, he would have doubted the skills he had spent many long years acquiring in India. Still, the wheels in his brain churned as he considered the situation—how much, how little, if any, to reveal, of what he suspected, the deadly game he had begun to play.

"I didn't mean to frighten you by following you. However, as I mentioned earlier, the envelope and its letter are very valuable to me. Miss Windermere, I don't want to alarm you and Miss Jasmine. However, the...character of the two men who were chasing me that day in High Holborn was, as you say, most unsavory. Should either of you or any of those boys who are quite clearly your devoted champions spy them, should they bother you in any way, I hope you will let me know. In fact, I reiterate, should you ever require my assistance for any reason, please do not hesitate to get in touch with me." Reaching into his jacket, he withdrew one of the plain white calling cards with elegant black script that he had given Professor Prosser earlier, this time handing it to her. "As you can see from my card, I am, as I mentioned previously, lodged in Harley Street. Should the need ever arise, I also have a manservant, whom you may trust. His name is...Mahout."

This last was not exactly a lie, Hugo thought, and having already, due to Professor Prosser's earlier presence, been compelled to introduce himself as Raj Khanna, he did not believe that now was the time to suddenly reveal his true identity and explain the quest for revenge upon which he had embarked.

"Thank you, Mr. Khanna."

"Not at all, Miss Windermere. I am indebted to you. But now, since it has been rather a long day and I begin to grow weary, I shall take my leave of you." Carefully setting his empty cup and plate to one side,

Hugo stood. "Please tell your cook for me that the tea was delicious."

"Mrs. Beasley will be delighted to hear that, sir. It is...seldom that we have visitors, so I'm afraid she has few opportunities to show off her culinary talents."

Also rising, Rose and Jasmine walked Hugo to the front door, distressed to discover that he limped slightly from the beating he had received. Expressing their dismay at the sight, the sisters pressed one of their father's malacca canes upon him. Then, bidding him goodbye, Jasmine tactfully disappeared up the front stairs that wound from the Minton-tiled foyer to the landing above.

"Shall I send one of our housemaids for a hackney coach or a hansom cab, Mr. Khanna?" Rose queried, her brow knitted in a small frown of worry at the idea that, even with the cane, he might not be able to manage.

"No, I appreciate the offer. But a short walk to hail a cab myself will no doubt do me good, for if I don't get some slight exercise, my muscles shall stiffen up on me, I fear."

"As you wish, then." Rose extended one hand politely. "Good day, Mr. Khanna. Although I'm sorry for how it came about, I do not regret meeting you, for among other things, you have made me remember my birthplace and all that I treasured about it."

"Despite the circumstances, I, too, have enjoyed our time together, Miss Windermere." Taking her hand in his, Hugo bowed low over it. "I hope that we shall meet again."

Book Two

Two Halves of a Coin

I see you stand like greyhounds in the slips,
Straining upon the start. The game's afoot.
          King Henry the Fifth [1598-1600]
                    —William Shakespeare

Eight

A Story Told

> What is life? A madness. What is life? An
> illusion, a shadow, a story.
>> *Life is a Dream* [1195]
>> —Pedro Calderón de la Barca

Russell Square and Harley Street,
London, England, 1850

After the man whom she knew as Raj Khanna had
departed from the town house, Rose stood in the foyer
for a long minute, contemplating everything that had
occurred. Her hand that he had held still radiated
the warmth of his touch, and she pressed it to her
breast, folding her other hand over it. She didn't know
why, but she felt strangely, giddily, exhilarated and
scared, as though somehow after today, her life would

never again be the same. But that was a foolish notion, surely.

"Has the gentleman gone, then, Miss Windermere?" Miss Candlish asked, as she appeared in the foyer. "Shall I clear away the tea tray?"

"Yes, please, Miss Candlish."

Collecting her wits, Rose hurried upstairs to her bedroom, where, as she had expected, she found Jasmine waiting for her.

"Where is everyone, Jasmine? I could scarcely believe we had the drawing room to ourselves when Mr. Khanna was here, that we were not overrun with the rest of our sisters, poking and prying!"

"Well, it certainly wasn't for lack of curiosity, but, rather, because after you went to the park, they decided the day was so fine that they would walk to the Pantheon Bazaar. Lily wanted some new flowers and ribbons to make over a bonnet, and the others accompanied her to see what bargains they might find, as well. Papa went away to his club, and Mama was in her room, reading, but long ago fell asleep on her chaise longue. So except for us, the only ones in the house who yet know about Mr. Khanna are the servants."

In addition to Miss Candlish, Mrs. Beasley, and Polly, the scullery maid, these consisted of the two housemaids, Hannah and Nancy.

"Well, it would seem very odd if we instructed them to say nothing to the others. So, if asked, I think we should simply explain that Mr. Khanna was set upon in the park whilst I was there and not mention anything further," Rose said.

"I think so, too. Oh, you did like him, Rose, didn't you?"

"Was it that obvious?" Rose smiled ruefully.

"Only to me, who knows you so well."

"Yes, I did like him…very much. Still, the truth is that we know very little about Mr. Khanna, and although he certainly appeared respectable and well dressed, and his deportment was faultless, both looks and manners can be deceiving."

"Yet he did not hesitate to give you his card and direction," Jasmine pointed out. "Did he ask to call on you?"

"No, although he did say that he hoped we would meet again."

"Well, that is encouraging—and he offered his assistance, too, should we ever stand in need of it. I thought that spoke well of him."

"Yes." Rose nodded in agreement. "I thought so, also. Still, however much I may have enjoyed his company, I dare not hope that Mr. Khanna has any interest in me, Jasmine. The first was a chance meeting, the second the result of the neighborhood lads' ill-conceived scheme."

"They meant well, Rose."

"I know they did, but, really, what if they had hurt Mr. Khanna badly, perhaps even killed him? What if he had decided to press charges against them, to insist that Constable Dreiling arrest them? They could have wound up in prison."

"I'm sure they never thought of all that. They're simply young and impulsive. Oh, I know it's probably awful, but I found their concern for you rather sweet and touching myself. So don't be too hard on them, Rose. Had the situation turned out differently, they might have saved your life!"

Rose and Jasmine were wholly unaware that at that particular moment, Hugo was thinking the very same thing.

With the aid of Colonel Windermere's silver-knobbed walking stick, Hugo had managed to make his way up Montague Street to Upper Montague Street, where he had finally spied a hansom cab. Hailing it, he had settled himself inside, giving his direction to the driver and stoically ignoring the man's glance of disapproval at his appearance. Although Hugo had not yet glimpsed himself in a mirror, he knew he must look much the worse for wear, as though he had been engaged in some tavern brawl. But as Hugo seldom cared what others thought of him, the driver's scorn was simply beneath his notice. At its master's command and a slap of the long leather reins upon its back, the single dapple-gray gelding harnessed to the vehicle obediently started forward, and soon, the hansom cab was en route to Harley Street.

As Hugo settled back into the seat, he closed his eyes tiredly. Although his body ached more than he had let on to either Dr. Haverham or the Windermere sisters, and he wished only now to rest, he still could not seem to stop his mind from racing. It was crowded with countless thoughts, images, and memories—the foremost of which pertained to Rose.

There was a bond between them, he thought. That was why she had sensed him spying on her, even if she had not actually seen him. Now, despite the ill treatment he had suffered at their hands, Hugo was grateful for the group of lads who had served as her guardian angels this day. They could not have known he had intended her no harm, and under other circumstances, they might have saved her life. Knowing that, he felt easier in his mind—and glad, as well, that she and her sister Jasmine had not grasped the true import of either the envelope or the letter it contained. They were far better off not knowing. Further, after spending time with them, he felt certain he could indeed trust their discretion, that they would speak of the affair to no one.

Startling Hugo from his reverie, the hansom cab jolted to a halt by the curb in front of his town house. After paying the driver, he let himself inside with his key.

"By the gods, *sahib*, what has happened to you?" Mayur Singh cried, running to his master's side.

"I've had the great misfortune to have been beaten and bested by a bunch of streetwise boys, Mahout."

"A gang of footpads, do you mean, sir?"

"No, for robbery was not their aim. Only help me into the study, and I shall tell you all about it—for I promise you, my old friend, you will not wish to miss hearing this particular tale."

"Very well, sir. Lean on me. Have you dined?"

"Yes, I have had a most excellent tea, in equally excellent company. So there is no hurry about supper."

The study in Hugo's town house was handsomely appointed, filled with an elegant, harmonious blend of English and Indian furniture and accoutrements. Occupying the room were heavily carved bookcases packed with books, an armoire, a sideboard, and a desk, this latter of which was fashioned of ebonized wood that matched the mantel surrounding the fireplace. A mixture of leather chairs and upholstered chairs provided seating, and occasional tables and large potted plants were nestled throughout. An Oriental screen stood in one corner. Rich velvet curtains designed to keep out the often chilly English weather hung at the mullioned windows. A huge Oriental rug carpeted the floor, atop which lay a Bengal tiger skin. The beast had been a man-eater, which Hugo had shot and killed during a hunt in India. On the walls was an array of impressive artwork.

Gratefully, Hugo sank into one of the comfortably stuffed brown leather chairs, propping his injured leg up on a nearby ottoman. Somehow during the brawl with the lads at the park in Russell Square, he had sprained his ankle, probably while scrambling to get away. He thought the leg had sustained a few well-placed kicks, too.

"Fix us a drink, Mahout." Reaching for an ornate box that sat on a table next to his chair, Hugo opened it to remove one of the cheroots he favored. Lighting the cigar, he drew on it quietly for a moment, puffing thoughtfully. Then he said, "After that, you shall hear my story."

Nine

> People of the same trade seldom meet together,
> even for merriment and diversion, but that the
> conversation ends in a conspiracy against the
> public.
>
> *Wealth of Nations* [1776]
> —Adam Smith

Drayton Hall, Dartmoor, England, 1850

Although the now-setting sun glowed orange over
London, on distant Dartmoor, it shone with a pale,
sickly light that scarcely penetrated the storm clouds
roiling in the pewter sky. Earlier that morning, the rain
had only drizzled, but now, it fell heavily, drenching
the moors. Sodden heath, broom and bracken bowed
beneath the downpour, and even the isolated tors that

loomed like giants over the land seemed to shiver in the wet. Granite outcrops splayed like dripping fingers against the miasmal sky; among their stony knuckles, soggy green veins of gorse crept. The peat bogs, dangerous on a good day, were even more treacherous in the gray light and the rain, and it was only by instinct that the herds of wild cattle, ponies, and sheep that roamed the moors avoided the fatal mires. Here and there, trees twisted and stunted by years of weathering harsh elements grew, their gnarled branches whipping violently in the thundershower. Beyond the crumbling cliffs and shingled beaches that fell into the sea, the white-foamed waves maddened and churned.

As a serrated fork of lightning split the sky, igniting the heavens, it illuminated a manor house that rose in grim, desolate splendor in the distance. Built in the shape of an **H**, of the same stalwart granite that scarred the moors, it stood three solid, forbidding stories high and was capped with a gabled black slate roof lined with dormers. Flanking the stout oak front door were soaring twin towers that seemed to pierce the seething clouds; and the battlemented gray walls bore tall, mullioned oriels and casement windows with lozenged lead-glass panes that peered like eyes behind the slits of a mask through the rain.

This was Drayton Hall—home to the Earls of Thornleigh for centuries, and the present Earl, James Wormwood, was no exception. Long had he coveted the house that, at the deaths of his uncle, his uncle's wife and his cousin in India, had become his.

Really, it had been too bad of Uncle Francis to marry and beget an heir at such a late date, when it had been settled for years that he, his nephew, James—the only son of Francis's younger, wild sister and her dissolute husband, Sir Philip Wormwood, baronet—was to inherit the title and estates. But then, what could one expect of an Englishman who had "gone native" and wed an Indian woman, fathering a half-caste child upon her? Since the incursion of the British into India, it had become an old story. This one, however, had ended with the dacoits who had murdered Uncle Frances, his wife, Anamitra (Lord Thornleigh would never think of her as his aunt), and his son, Hugo. That was when the earl's own life had truly begun, when he had taken what he had always considered his rightful place at Drayton Hall.

"My lord, did you hear what I said? The letter we delivered from you to Mrs. Squasher has been stolen!"

Turning from the misted windows streaming with rain, Lord Thornleigh glanced around the small drawing room to where his guests, Gerald and Dora Blott, sat before the Parian hearth, in which, earlier, a fire had been lit to take the chill from the damp air. It was Mrs. Blott who had asked the question, impatiently nudging him from his reverie.

"So?" He lifted one silver eyebrow.

Although never a great beauty, Mrs. Blott might once have been passably attractive. Now, however, she was well on her way to becoming a blowsy wench. She was a big woman, being several inches taller than Mr.

Blott, her husband, and since, lately, she had put on quite a lot of weight, she appeared to the earl to have doubled in size. Her hair was an extremely unnatural shade of pale yellow, made so by whatever concoctions she used upon it, and despite the fact that she and Mr. Blott never seemed to be short of funds, she was always most vulgarly dressed—in cheaply made clothes completely inappropriate to the occasion.

Once, Lord Thornleigh had thought her somewhat amusing. Now, he merely found her tiresome. As he knew that her husband frequented a number of gaming hells and brothels, the earl suspected that Mrs. Blott's dubious charms had long ago worn thin there, as well.

"Whatever do you mean, my lord?" Tittering like a silly schoolgirl, she favored him with the kind of ruefully disapproving look one would have given to a naughty but amusing child. "The envelope was stamped with your seal—and surely, the letter it contained was rather incriminating!"

"How would you know what was in the envelope—unless, before giving it to Mrs. Squasher, you opened it, Mrs. Blott?" Through his large, thick, silver-rimmed spectacles, Lord Thornleigh stared at her unblinkingly, so that quite unbeknown to him, he momentarily reminded her of a gaping fish or toad.

"Why, my lord, I did no such thing!" Widening her own blue eyes with feigned innocence, Mrs. Blott pretended to be shocked by the very suggestion.

Of course, she *had* opened the envelope, employing a hot, thin-bladed knife and being careful not to break the red-wax seal, but only to soften it enough that she could prize it from the paper. She had needed to know what Lord Thornleigh and Mrs. Squasher were up to.

Mrs. Blott liked the earl and wanted to bed him.

But she didn't trust him.

He was perhaps cleverer than her husband, and if their scheme went awry, she didn't intend to be the one left holding the bag. That, she would leave to the others, for none of them was as smart or as well-off as she was. After all, she had quite a bit of money left to her by her late father, who had gone stark-raving mad from some brain defect before he had died in a lunatic asylum, but who, prior to that, had been sane enough to accumulate the funds he had set aside for her. Mr. Blott, however, had not a tuppence to his name, except for whatever he could beg, borrow, or steal from his frowzy old whore of a mother or some other unsuspecting person. Lord Thornleigh had inherited a fortune, of course, but Mrs. Blott knew that gambling and other rakehell habits had dissipated it considerably. Mrs. Squasher resided in Lincoln's Inn Field. What more than that needed to be said about her?

"What will you do, my lord, now that Mrs. Squasher has been robbed of the envelope and letter? Such a pity she proved so careless. Her sloppiness could threaten us all." Mrs. Blott sighed heavily. But secretly, she was delighted that Mrs. Squasher had made such a stupid mistake. "But then, one does not suppose that Lincoln's Inn Field is the most agreeable

of addresses. I imagine that there must be many un-
desirables who come across the River Thames from
their hovels in Lambeth, Southwark, Bermondsey and
the like." She did not mention the fact that Mr. Blott's
slovenly old mother lived and plied her trade in
Southwark. There was no need for the earl to know
everything.

"In that case, our thief is a very clever man indeed,"
Lord Thornleigh observed dryly. "For I doubt that
most in those districts would recognize my seal or are
able to read, besides."

"I tried to tell Mrs. Blott that." Glancing up from
his third glass of whiskey, Mr. Blott gave his wife a
withering look. Then he smiled oilily at the earl. "But
you know how women are. Once we learnt of Mrs.
Squasher's mishap, Mrs. Blott would hear of nothing
but that we must travel for Dartmoor straightaway. Of
course, I agreed, because I would not wish you to be
placed in a difficult situation through Mrs. Squasher's
carelessness, my lord."

"No, indeed." The earl, too, smiled. But behind his
spectacles, his pale blue eyes were cold and hard.
"However, there was no need for you to leave London,
I promise you. Mrs. Squasher had already informed me
by messenger of the loss of the envelope and its
contents—not that it matters, however. They were
hardly as incriminating as you and Mrs. Blott appear
to think, since the letter contained nothing of any real
consequence and was meant merely to reassure poor
Mrs. Squasher, who seemed to be wavering. No, it is

the thief himself who interests me. For if robbery were his aim, why did he take what he did—leaving behind Mrs. Squasher's jewels, for instance?"

"Perhaps because they're all paste?" Mrs. Blott suggested archly.

"Even so, they could have been sold to a pawnshop for a coin or two." Having been compelled to explain what he had thought obvious, Lord Thornleigh was annoyed by Mrs. Blott's lack of perception. "From what I have now learnt, it seems that our thief— whoever he may be—ran into two ladies on High Holborn whilst making his escape from Mrs. Squasher's town house. Although Mrs. Squasher believes neither that incident nor the ladies' subsequent misdirecting of her hirelings was deliberate, I myself am not so easily satisfied. I have since discovered the identity of the ladies, and as it happens, I have some slight knowledge of them through my deceased uncle Francis. Before your arrival, I was planning to journey to London to call upon them—or, rather, their father, Colonel Hilary Windermere, by which means I can ingratiate myself with the family and find out whether they have, in fact, involved themselves in my affairs. For a number of reasons with which you needn't be concerned, it may be that they have. Equally, they may simply be innocent bystanders, and in that case, we needn't trouble ourselves further about them. Either way, we shall see."

After some further discussion, it was arranged that Mr. and Mrs. Blott would accompany Lord Thornleigh to London, traveling in his own coach. He was not particularly enthused at the idea, but at the moment, he needed the Blotts, and because they were extremely capricious and unstable, he knew that it behooved him to keep an eye on them.

Ten

The Visitors

But they are the last people I should choose
to have a visiting acquaintance with.
                                The Rivals [1775]
                            —Richard Brinsley Sheridan

Russell Square, London, England, 1850

Much to her vague distress, following Raj Khanna's departure from the Windermeres' town house, Rose found that her days soon settled back into their usual placid routine, so that it was almost as though they had never previously been disrupted. She felt a strange sense of restlessness at the realization, as though she had expected something that had not materialized. For all that the events that had occurred had dismayed her, now, if she were honest with herself, she knew that she must admit that they had also enlivened her life, filling her with an unaccustomed excitement.

Nor could she forget Mr. Khanna himself, with whom they had all begun.

He had attracted and intrigued her. Once her family had learned that Rose had brought him to the town house after he had been set upon in the park, she had faced a barrage of questions.

"I'm sure you meant well, Rose, and naturally, it wouldn't have been Christian to leave the poor man lying prostrate in the park. But really, who is he, this Mr. Raj Khanna?" Mrs. Windermere had fretted anxiously at the dinner table. "Oh, perhaps Professor Prosser was right, and you ought to have let Constable Dreiling handle the matter, instead of bringing a stranger into our home."

"Maybe Mr. Khanna wasn't a stranger to Rose, Mama," Daisy had suggested impishly, grinning. "Maybe she's had a secret admirer all along—and just hasn't told us about it! What do you think of that?"

"I think you shouldn't be impertinent, Daisy," Mrs. Windermere had chided, frowning. "Of course, Rose would have told us if she had an admirer other than the professor! Why would she keep such a secret? I'd like to know. I, for one, would be very happy indeed to be told that any of my beautiful daughters had found a prospective suitor—not that Professor Prosser doesn't qualify on that score, but, well, one *could* hope to do far better, I'm sure! How any man can see any of you and not immediately be struck by your loveliness,

I really don't understand. Oh, if only we could move from Bloomsbury to Belgravia! I'm quite certain that all of your prospects would improve immeasurably!"

"We don't know that to be true, Mama," Rose had put in hastily, not wishing her father to be upset. "But I assure you that to the best of my own knowledge, Mr. Khanna is not my admirer and is not likely to become so, either."

"Well, I'm sorry for that, dear." Mrs. Windermere had sighed heavily. "But perhaps it's just as well, for we know nothing about him. Whilst there is a good deal to be said for Harley Street, it is not Piccadilly, after all. And for all that Mr. Khanna appears to have been well dressed and to have behaved in a most gentlemanly manner whilst here, it may be that he is in trade or something else equally undesirable. I had so hoped for more for my daughters!"

"If the man is from India and lodged in Harley Street, then it will be no bother to learn more about him," Colonel Windermere had suddenly announced, much to his family's surprise. "For there is bound to be someone at the club who knows him—or, at least, knows something about him."

The colonel belonged to the East India United Service Club, which had been established a few years ago for gentlemen who were or had been commissioned officers in either Her Majesty's or the East Indian Army or Navy. Other gentlemen connected with the administration and affairs of India were also eligible for membership. Thinking he must have someplace to go when a houseful of women proved too much for him, Colonel Windermere had applied to the club for membership, paying an entrance fee of thirty pounds. Much to his delight, he had passed muster, receiving not a single blackball. Having been accepted into the club, he maintained his membership with a home-member subscription fee of eight pounds and eight shillings, and a library donation of one pound. He considered it a small price to pay for the escape and male conversation with which the club provided him.

"Of course, Papa!" Lily had cried eagerly. "I hadn't thought of that. Now, Mama, you can be at ease. For if Mr. Khanna is anybody, Papa shall soon know of it!"

"Yes—and what a disappointment it shall be for you, Lily, if Mr. Khanna turns out to be nothing more than a mere tradesman!" Heather had smiled teasingly. "For you cannot deny that you entertain visions of Rose marrying some rich, titled lord and then finding like husbands for us all!"

"Well, what is wrong with that?" Lily had asked, coloring faintly. "Why should we not aspire to more than our own lots in life? Everyone else does."

"That may be," Rose had quietly agreed. "But for myself, if I marry, I wish it to be only for love."

"You're such a romantic, Rose," Angelica had noted, shaking her head.

"Yes. But although I wouldn't wish a loveless marriage on any of my sweet daughters—for my own to the dear Colonel was a love match, you know—you must admit, Rose, that it would help a good deal if your husband had more than two coins to rub together!" Mrs. Windermere had stoutly insisted.

"Perhaps. But then, I haven't any husband, Mama, and I do not foresee one in my future, either—for although Professor Prosser may have thoughts of our making a match, I myself do not. Further, as you say, we know nothing of Mr. Khanna, and as our paths crossed merely by chance, I think that it is most unlikely that I shall ever see him again."

"'There's no such thing as chance; and what seems to us merest accident springs from the deepest source of destiny,'" Jasmine had quoted softly. "So I would not be so certain of never seeing Mr. Khanna again as you are, Rose. For, even if for no other reason, he will surely call on us to return Papa's malacca cane!"

This pronouncement had instigated such a sudden flutter of nervousness and excitement at the dinner table that Colonel Windermere had been strictly charged with visiting his club posthaste, there to discover whatever he could about the mysterious Mr. Khanna.

In the days that followed, although the Windermeres were indeed called upon—it was not, much to Rose's disappointment, by Mr. Khanna. Instead, she was utterly stricken when the housekeeper, Miss Candlish, informed Mrs. Windermere and all six sisters that Lord Thornleigh and an associate of his, Mr. Blott, were closeted with Colonel Windermere in the study.

"Lord Thornleigh!" Mrs. Windermere cried, visibly startled and dismayed by the news. "Why, whatever business can he have with the Colonel? I simply can't imagine! But, oh, my dear daughters, what an opportunity this would be—if only his lordship were not such a—a snake! But as it is, I cannot think that we should have anything to do with him, for I never liked or trusted the man, and I always suspected—perhaps wrongly, however—that he had some hand in the murders of the late Lord and Lady Thornleigh and their son, Hugo. But I suppose your father will feel obligated by good manners to bring Lord Thornleigh and Mr. Blott here to the drawing room to meet us once they have concluded their business, and we shall have to do our best to be polite, regardless of the upset to our own sensibilities!"

"Polite?" Rose parroted lamely, so agitated that she accidentally stabbed herself with the embroidery needle she was plying. A small bubble of blood issued from the wound. "Oh! How stupid! I've pricked myself." Rising, she laid her embroidery hoop to one side, and taking a lacy white handkerchief from the pocket of her morning gown, wrapped it around her bloodied thumb. "I must see to it immediately."

"Hurry, Rose," Mrs. Windermere urged nervously. "For as much as I dislike and mistrust the current Lord Thornleigh, it would surely not behoove us to offend him and thereby earn his enmity. He is a *most* unpleasant man and, I believe, quite dangerous."

Rose did not stay to hear any more of her mother's

flustered chatter, but exited the drawing room as quickly as possible, Jasmine following hard on her heels. Their skirts flying, the two sisters hastened upstairs to their bedroom, where they closed the door firmly, gazing at each other with shock and anxiety, their breathing labored from having climbed the front stairs so fast.

"My word! What do you think it means, Jasmine?" Abruptly rushing over to the washstand, Rose splashed some water from the pitcher into the bowl, with which to clean her thumb. "In all the years we've lived in England, Lord Thornleigh has never before bestirred himself to call upon us, despite the fact that Papa and Mama were well acquainted with his predecessor. Now, he has suddenly taken it into his head to come here. Why? Oh, it must have something to do with that envelope and letter. I just know it!"

"I think so, too." With a bar of soap, Jasmine scrubbed her sister's injured thumb, then rinsed and dried it. "There. As needle pricks go, it wasn't too bad, for it has already ceased bleeding. I'll swab it with some antiseptic to guard against infection."

Her mind racing, Rose stood mutely while her sister concluded her ministrations. Rose could only remember two other occasions in her life when she had felt as frightened as she did now: that day in Chandni Chowk, when the elephant ridden by the young nobleman had gone berserk, and that night in Delhi when she had looked out her bedroom window to see the Draytons' *haveli* aflame. Her mouth had gone dry, and her heart pounded.

"You've got to calm down, Rose," Jasmine insisted softly. "Otherwise, Lord Thornleigh will know we have seen the envelope and recognized his seal upon it. He will know we have read the letter."

"How do we know he doesn't know all that already? For, if you were right about Mr. Khanna acting as a messenger for Lord Thornleigh, then perhaps he has told him everything! Oh, Jasmine, I now feel that our trust in Mr. Khanna must have been sadly misplaced!"

"I agree that's certainly one possibility. However, we really don't know that Mr. Khanna is employed by Lord Thornleigh, and perhaps Mr. Khanna had some other reason, of which we are as yet unaware, for being in possession of the envelope and its contents."

"I can't think what."

"No, nor can I," Jasmine admitted reluctantly. "But honestly, Rose, in the end, it's all just a matter of a lovers' elopement, isn't it? And since we've no interest in that or in thwarting Lord Thornleigh's designs, then I cannot see why we should have any reason even to mention the affair. Besides, even if the subject is somehow brought up, what is there to fear? We can simply assure Lord Thornleigh of our discretion—and that will surely be the end of the matter!"

"Yes, I suppose you're right," Rose said slowly. "Perhaps I am indeed worrying for naught, letting my childhood fancies run wildly away with me now. After all, I've never actually met Lord Thornleigh, but only seen him once or twice in India, when I was a child. So maybe, because of all of Mama's own uncharitable feelings toward him, I've judged him unfairly, wrongly suspected him of murder, as she freely admits that perhaps she has, when it really *was* dacoits who killed Hugo and his parents."

"Let us hope that is indeed the case. Children often have such extremely odd ideas, based on misunderstood snatches of conversations they've inadvertently overheard or else deliberately eavesdropped on. And you know how Mama is. It is possible that, hearing servants' idle gossip about Lord Thornleigh's failings, she decided that he must be a very bad person, one capable of murder, when, in fact, he was merely a reckless young man sowing his wild oats. For all we know, he may be much changed now."

"When you put it that way, it all sounds so unarguably sensible, Jasmine." Rose sighed, then smiled ruefully. "But then, you've always been much more down to earth than I have. Poor Mama. For her sake—and ours—I do hope our suspicions about Lord Thornleigh are as groundless as you've almost persuaded me they are."

"Then if you are able to compose yourself now, Rose, let us return to the drawing room before we are summoned by Mama—for if that becomes necessary, we shall never hear the end of it!"

Laughing gaily together over that, their mood considerably lightened, the sisters descended the front stairs to the foyer, their progress arrested halfway down as they spied three men standing in a jovial knot together below. One was their father, and they knew the other two gentlemen could be none other than Lord Thornleigh and Mr. Blott. At the appearance of the sisters, all three men stopped speaking to glance up at them appreciatively.

"Ah, my lord, Mr. Blott, here are my two eldest daughters now." In quite an excellent mood, Colonel Windermere beamed with visible pride at what a pretty picture and striking contrast the sisters presented standing there on the staircase together, the older so fair and ethereal, the younger so dark and earthy. Took after his side of the family, Jasmine did, he thought, although, like all her sisters, she had her own version of her mother's green eyes. "Girls, come down here! Join us! I was just escorting his lordship and Mr. Blott into the drawing room to meet Mrs. Windermere and you and your sisters." Turning to the older of the two gentlemen, the colonel said, "Lord Thornleigh, allow me to present my daughters Rose and Jasmine. Girls, this is Lord Thornleigh and his associate Mr. Blott."

"How do you do, my lord?" Politely, Rose extended her hand to the earl.

He bore only a faint resemblance to how she had remembered him from her childhood, and because of that, she now recognized that Jasmine had undoubtedly been correct in her assessment of the matter. In her mind, Rose had envisioned Lord Thornleigh as a complete ogre—the devil that her mother had once called him. Instead, the gentleman who bowed over her hand had little to distinguish him from any others of his ilk. She found him neither handsome nor ugly, but merely nondescript. Had she passed him on the street, she doubted that she would even have noticed him. He was slightly taller and a good deal heavier than his companion, and except for his rather shaggy hair, which was wholly gray, and his pale blue eyes that were magnified by his thick, silver-rimmed spectacles, there was nothing remarkable about him, let alone monstrous. He was well dressed, but not ostentatiously so, and he wore little jewelry.

"It is a pleasure to meet you, Miss Windermere." The earl's lips curved pleasantly enough, but in that moment, for the first time, Rose observed that there was something cruel about his thin mouth and that his smile did not quite reach his eyes, which glittered with a strange, hard, avaricious light. "I can see now why Colonel Windermere is so proud of his daughters."

It was all Rose could do to suppress the shiver that suddenly assailed her. In an instant, all of her sister's earlier reassurances deserted her, and her fears returned to haunt her, confusing her so that she wasn't certain what to think.

"Yes," she murmured, lowering her gaze modestly. "Papa is our greatest champion."

Withdrawing her hand from Lord Thornleigh's grasp, she then offered it to Mr. Blott. Rose thought that in his youth, Mr. Blott would perhaps have been deemed attractive by some. But now, years of ruinous living had clearly taken an enormous toll on him.

His inordinately tightly curled black hair, which revealed some foreign blood in him, was thinning—despite how he had attempted to hide it, there was a visible, large bald spot in back—and beneath his dark-brown eyes were bags that bespoke too many late nights of carousing. His plainly once-slim face was puffy, and there was an odd, pasty cast to his swarthy skin, as though he were unwell. His waist, too, had thickened with age, but he was, if anything, even more handsomely garbed than Lord Thornleigh, and wore much more and flashier jewelry. More than anything, he somehow reminded Rose uneasily of a sinuous snake bloated from swallowing its hapless prey.

Instinctively and uncharacteristically, she disliked him on sight—and as a result, all her apprehensions about Lord Thornleigh also increased, for she believed strongly that a man might be judged by the company he kept. Further, from Jasmine's own reticence and merely courteous rather than genuine smiles as she, too, greeted the two gentlemen, Rose knew that her sister had revised her own earlier opinion of the earl and now shared her fears and emotions. That realization only served to heighten Rose's trepidation.

Colonel Windermere, however, obviously sensed nothing amiss, for laughing and joking with the gentlemen, he grandly ushered them into the drawing room, there to introduce his wife and remaining daughters to them. Tea was served by Miss Candlish, and Mrs. Windermere did the honors, pouring the tea into the china cups and filling the matching china plates with an assortment of food prepared by Mrs. Beasley. By unspoken agreement, Rose and Jasmine had been careful to seat themselves in the wing chairs before the Parian fireplace, so that neither of them must sit beside either the earl or Mr. Blott.

"It is so nice to see you again, Lord Thornleigh," Mrs. Windermere said, with only a shadow of her usual smile, "and to meet your associate Mr. Blott, as well. But you have come early to town, have you not? For the Season does not start for another few weeks, of course."

"I have neglected renewing our acquaintance far too long as it is, madam, and for that, I offer you my sincerest apologies. But to answer your question, yes, as I had some pressing business matters that required my attention, I thought to spare myself an unnecessary journey and come early to London," the earl explained. "Although Drayton Hall is conveniently situated on Dartmoor, I fear I have reached the age when I begin to desire to slow down a little and to spare myself whatever discomforts I may."

"Haven't we all, my lord? Haven't we all?" Mrs. Windermere nodded. "We often spend the summers in either Derbyshire or Yorkshire ourselves. But this year, I'm afraid I just didn't feel up to making the trip. Travel is invariably so exhausting that it quite shatters my nerves. But there, it will hardly do to bore you with idle chitchat about my health! So, please, do tell us all about yourself and Drayton Hall instead. I remember that your uncle, the late Lord Thornleigh—whom we knew in India, of course—spoke of it often, and although it has been many years now since I have been to Dartmoor, I recall that it was quite a windswept and desolate place, although strangely beautiful, even so."

"You would find it relatively unchanged, madam, and Drayton Hall is as it ever was—a formidable block of granite that shall no doubt be standing long after I, too, am dead and buried in my grave."

"Well, let us hope that does not occur anytime soon, my lord." Mrs. Windermere paused to sip from her teacup. Then she continued. "Has Lady Thornleigh accompanied you to London, or does she arrive at a later date?"

"Alas, madam, I find myself in the unfortunate position of having reached my middle years without yet acquiring a wife. In my youth, I enjoyed being footloose and fancy free, traveling widely—which is perhaps why I no longer care so very much for it—and then when Uncle Francis and my cousin, Hugo, were killed in India, the burden of Thornleigh and other estates fell upon me. I had not expected that, for naturally, until then, Hugo was his father's heir."

"Yes, such a tragedy, it was, that befell the poor late Lord Thornleigh and his family," Colonel Windermere put in, his voice grave. "We left India shortly thereafter, for although I deemed it safe enough for myself, I could not bear to place Mrs. Windermere and my daughters at risk. What with the crimes committed by the dacoits, the thuggees, and other outlaws, the grumblings of the Mughuls, the sepoys, and other natives, the increasing heavy-handedness of John

Company, I came to believe that India was a virtual powder keg. I still think that, someday, it will explode."

"You may well be right, Colonel," Lord Thornleigh agreed, seemingly unconcerned, however. "But in the meanwhile, there is still money to be made, eh?"

"Yes, so it would appear." Bending forward in his chair, the colonel helped himself to another cucumber sandwich from the tray upon the teacart. "Lord Thornleigh and Mr. Blott wished to consult with me about various aspects of Indian culture and trade," he informed his family. "That is why they called on us today."

At that, alarm bells rang in Rose's mind. She remembered that her father had previously told them he had made some investments at the stock exchange, to try to secure his daughters' futures. She hoped that he was not now also thinking of going into some kind of business with Lord Thornleigh and Mr. Blott, whom she did not trust.

From beneath the thick fringe of her long sooty eyelashes, she had noticed that for all the gentlemen's apparent congeniality, they had surreptitiously surveyed the drawing room appraisingly, taking in the faded curtains at the windows, all the tired furnishings that needed refurbishing, and the carpet that was threadbare in places. She thought that all this, combined with the fact that he had six daughters to provide for, would give the gentlemen the idea that her father would prove easily drawn into any scheme that offered the promises of riches. But then, surely, any sum that her father could afford to invest would be so small as to be entirely negligible to one such as the earl, she reflected. So, no, she must be mistaken on that score.

Still, Rose was inordinately grateful when Lord Thornleigh and Mr. Blott finally took their leave of her and her family—especially as, however strange it seemed to her, no mention whatsoever had been made of the envelope and letter that she had previously returned to Mr. Khanna.

Eleven

Dark Suspicions

Suspicion all our lives shall be stuck full of eyes;
For treason is but trusted like the fox.
　　　　　King Henry the Fourth [1597-1598]
　　　　　　　　—William Shakespeare

Harley Street and Russell Square,
London, England, 1850

Hugo had dressed this morning with more than his usual care. Normally, except to ensure that his appearance was clean and neat, he paid it little heed. On some level, he knew that women found him handsome, for there were many over the years who had offered to share his bed. However, he was also contemptuously aware that, to some, he would be considered unacceptable, and even offensive, as a suitor, because he was half Indian.

Hugo himself was fiercely proud of his mixed heritage, finding it nothing of which to be ashamed. In his eyes, his Indian mother had been the equal of his English father, although he knew that London's *haut ton* would not think so. Since arriving in the city, outside of those whom he had met in Harley Street, he had found few people who had not looked down on him. Perhaps because they, too, had been born in India, Rose Windermere and her sister, Jasmine, were two of those who had not. Although he had been little more than a stranger to her, when he had been beaten, Rose—in his mind, Hugo still called her that—had not hesitated to bring him into her family's town house and to tend his injuries herself before Dr. Haverham had arrived.

When she had left him alone with the physician, Hugo had, during his examination, covertly given in to his need to drink in everything about the drawing room, to learn everything he could about Rose and her family. Having known and treated them for the past fifteen years, old Dr. Haverham had been more than happy to chatter on about the Windermeres, what lovely people they were, what a shame it was that all six daughters were as yet unmarried.

Hugo had not needed to ask why. His perusal of the pleasant but outmoded drawing room had provided the answer. The younger son of a baronet, Colonel Windermere had probably not received a large inheritance, for the price to purchase his commission (which his father or some other relative would have paid) would have been considerable, and that, the colonel would have got back in full upon his retirement from Her Majesty's Army. Had he also been able to save some of his annual pay during his years as an active officer, he would have a modest amount put by with which to support his family, but little more. Their Bloomsbury address had done the Windermere sisters no favors.

But Hugo needed neither a titled nor a wealthy wife—and Rose interested him far more than she would ever have imagined. After long and careful reflection—and goaded, as well, by the fact that Professor Prosser had most unpleasantly struck him as being bent on acquiring Rose for a wife—Hugo had decided that despite his deep reluctance to involve Rose and her family in his currently dangerous and unsavory affairs, it would be equally loathsome to continue to deceive them about his real identity and what he hoped to accomplish, now that he had come to England. He had, he reasoned, because of giving Rose the envelope and its contents that day in High Holborn, already inadvertently drawn her into the tangled web being woven, and although she was clearly ignorant of the letter's true import, that she had read it at all might have placed her in jeopardy. Thus, Hugo had finally resolved that upon recovering from his injuries sustained in the park (which, unfortunately, had proved worse than he had initially supposed), his next course of action should be to present himself properly to the Windermeres, making them privy to his real identity and the truth about his cousin, Sir James. In that way, he would be in a much better position to protect Rose, he thought, should something amiss occur; and having spent some time with her and her sister, Jasmine, he had seen no reason to believe that they would doubt his identity and the story he had to relate. Nor had his spies reported to him anything that would cause him to hesitate further to take the Windermeres into his confidence.

"You are off to see her again, then, *sahib?*" Mayur Singh inquired inscrutably, as, with one final glance at himself in the cheval mirror in his bedroom, Hugo turned to him.

Hugo did not need to ask to whom the manservant referred.

"Yes, Mahout. How do I look?"

"Very well, *sahib*. Your cuts are so healed as to be only faintly visible, and your bruises have faded. Therefore, I can see nothing objectionable about your appearance."

"Good—for I would not wish to make an even worse impression than I already have."

In the foyer, from the ornate hall tree with its heavy marble top and deeply beveled mirror, Hugo collected the borrowed silver-knobbed walking stick that belonged to Colonel Windermere. Then his manservant opened the front door for him.

"Good luck, *sahib*," Mayur Singh said.

For a moment, Hugo was certain that his manservant's dark-brown eyes twinkled.

"Thank you, Mahout."

Once out on the sidewalk in front of his town house, Hugo hailed a hansom cab, giving the driver the Windermeres' address in Russell Square, a little less than a mile away. He could have walked and, under other circumstances, would have enjoyed the stroll. But as the last of summer had finally faded into autumn, the days had turned chilly, and, like today, often brought with them a gray drizzle. While Hugo did not mind the coolness and the gentle rain, his cracked ribs still ached a little, and his sprained ankle still bothered him enough that he did not want to walk nearly a mile on it in the cold and wet.

Amid the usual hustle and bustle of the London traffic, the cab ride took approximately twenty minutes, slightly longer than it would have done had not Hugo stopped along the way to buy a pretty posy from a flower girl who dared to approach the vehicle while it was stopped at a corner. But when the hansom cab at last turned into Russell Square, Hugo saw to his surprise and sudden confusion that a large, expensive black coach, to which four fine, matching bay horses were harnessed, stood out front of the Windermere's town house. With Colonel Windermere's malacca cane, he knocked upon the box above him.

"Driver, pull up here a minute," he instructed.

Obediently, the driver tugged on the long leather reins, bringing the white gelding harnessed to the hansom cab to a stop. From his vantage point, Hugo could now see one side of the black coach clearly. Emblazoned upon the door was a coat-of-arms that he recognized as being the same as that stamped into the red-wax seal of the envelope that Rose had many days ago returned to him and that he had concealed behind a secret panel in his study.

The coach belonged to the Earl of Thornleigh!

As Hugo realized that, his black eyes narrowed with sudden suspicion, and his jaw set grimly. Colonel Windermere's walking stick, which Hugo now clutched so hard that it was a wonder that it did not snap in two, seemed to burn his hand with such a terrible heat that, without warning, he felt a wild, vicious impulse to throw it away. Instead, he abruptly hurled the nosegay from the hansom cab into a puddle alongside the curb. Then, with his fist, he pounded furiously upon the box.

"Take me back to Harley Street," he commanded the driver curtly.

As the vehicle lurched forward, its wheels splashing through the puddle and crushing the angrily discarded bouquet, Hugo did not look back.

Twelve

True Identities

> The Book of Life begins
> with a man and a woman in a garden.
> It ends with Revelations.
>> *A Woman of No Importance* [1893]
>> —Oscar Fingal O'Flahertie Wills Wilde

Russell Square and Harley Street,
London, England, 1850

During the passing days, much to Rose's bewilderment and dejection, Raj Khanna did not, as she had hoped and expected, call at the Windermeres' town house, not even to return her father's malacca cane. Instead, the silver-knobbed walking stick was delivered by a messenger, along with a note that seemed positively frigid in its excruciating politeness. Of course, that might have been due to the fact that English was perhaps a second language for Mr. Khanna. But somehow, Rose did not think so, for he had certainly spoken it fluently. She did not understand why he appeared to have so suddenly become so distant, and she was deeply hurt by it. For several reasons she had hardly even acknowledged to herself, much less to her family, she had wanted very much to have Mr. Khanna for at least a friend, if nothing more.

From his many cronies at the East Indian United Service Club, Colonel Windermere had dutifully discovered and reported to his family that the enigmatic Mr. Khanna was labeled a mystery even by those who knew and fraternized with him. Although unfailingly courteous, with faultless dress and manners, he was evidently reticent and even something of an eccentric recluse. No one seemed to know his origins, beyond the fact that he came from India. He never spoke of his parents or any other family, so nobody knew who his relations were. Even so, these were widely assumed to have been well-born, for it was extremely unlikely that an impostor would have proved so well-bred and well-educated, so well-acquainted with the social rules of the *haut ton*—into whose ranks, however, Mr. Khanna had not sought to gain admittance, despite more than one invitation issued to him by those ladies who were curious about him and his dealings with their husbands.

Outwardly, his town house was no different from any of the others in its terrace row, but its interior was said by those gentlemen who had actually seen it to be richly appointed, filled with an expensive mixture of both English and Indian furnishings. Still, despite the fact that Mr. Khanna was obviously wealthy, he employed only a single manservant, named Mahout. In addition to all this, Mr. Khanna was known to hold interests in a number of lucrative enterprises having chiefly to do with Indian trade and shipping; to be an extremely shrewd and hard but fair businessman; and, if crossed, to be a dangerous, implacable adversary.

Hearing all this, Rose had grown even more puzzled, for this description had not sounded to her at all like that of a man who would have consented to act as a furtive messenger between Lord Thornleigh and whatever young lady with whom he meant to elope. But perhaps Mr. Khanna had owed the earl a favor, Rose now conjectured, absently biting her full lower lip as, standing and staring blindly out her rain-streaked bedroom window, she contemplated the curious matter yet again.

Nor did any of it explain why, after more than a decade, Lord Thornleigh had suddenly taken it on himself to call upon her family, with his associate Mr. Blott, or why, having done so, neither of those two gentlemen had mentioned either the envelope or the letter, but, rather, had ostensibly premised their visit on the idea of consulting her father for guidance on Indian affairs. Although her father had been highly flattered, as he himself had observed, while he was certainly still highly knowledgeable about India, he had not actually resided there for fifteen years now—and surely, in that time, much had changed.

Really, it was all most peculiar, and the longer she dwelled on the matter, the stranger Rose thought it. Why, if he had genuinely required counsel, had Lord Thornleigh not sought it from his go-between, Mr. Khanna, who, as a native and having only recently immigrated to England, was intimately familiar with India? None of it made any sense.

Because of her instinctive loathing for the earl and Mr. Blott, Rose experienced a sick, gnawing feeling that something more was afoot than what either she or Jasmine had previously grasped, and she worried for her own safety and well-being and even more so for those of her family. She tried to tell herself that she was merely being foolish, that knowledge of Lord Thornleigh's intended elopement could not possibly pose any peril to her or her family. To the contrary, in fact. If Mr. Khanna had indeed apprised the earl of the fact that she and Jasmine had read the letter, Lord Thornleigh had no doubt finally called on the Windermeres as a courtesy, to tactfully signal his appreciation of their discretion, without actually mentioning it. Yes, that could satisfactorily account for everything.

But still, Rose worried, unable to shake her sinister impression of the earl and Mr. Blott, the awful sense that there was something vital, and perhaps even deadly, that she had missed somewhere along the way.

What if…what if she and Jasmine had somehow misunderstood the letter? she now wondered, for the first time. They had been very upset, apprehensive and nervously excited when they had opened the envelope, and they had read the letter through not only quickly, but also guiltily, knowing that despite all of the good reasons for their actions, they were still prying. Now, frowning, closing her eyes to concentrate, Rose tried to call up a mental image of the letter, to remember exactly what it had said, precisely how it had been worded, so that she could determine whether there was any way she and Jasmine might somehow have misconstrued its meaning.

But the attempt was useless, for they had read the letter only once before hiding it safely away in the secretary, and that had been some weeks ago now.

For her own peace of mind, Rose desperately wanted some answers, but she knew that there was only one man who might give them to her: Raj Khanna. He had said that should she ever require his assistance, she should not hesitate to get in touch with him, and that, further, should the need ever arise, she could also trust his manservant, Mahout. Had all that been an empty offer—or had Mr. Khanna really meant what he had told her?

There was only one way to find out. But still, Rose felt her heart flutter hard and fast with both fear and excitement at the idea. Surely, she should not call on Mr. Khanna by herself, but take at least Jasmine with her. No, she would go alone, Rose decided abruptly, her green eyes flashing with sudden grim determination and her small chin lifting with equal resolution. If there were indeed more to this matter than met the eye, then involving Jasmine any further might be to put her at even worse risk than perhaps she already was.

Her mind made up, Rose knew she had to act quickly, before her courage failed her. Even now, it wavered, and she was beset by qualms, assailed by doubts. Turning from the window, she crept from her bedroom to make her way furtively down the back stairs. After luncheon, her father, she knew, had gone to his club, and her mother had lain down with a book, as usual, and now no doubt napped. Bored by the drizzle that had fallen steadily all day, her four youngest sisters, learning that the colonel meant to visit his club, had begged him to take them up in his carriage as far as the Soho Bazaar, which was en route. That left only Jasmine unaccounted for, and hearing faint strains of music issuing from the distant drawing room, Rose knew that it must be her remaining younger sister at the piano. Miss Candlish and the two housemaids, Hannah and Nancy, were occupied with the linens in the airing cupboard, and Mrs. Beasley and Polly, the scullery maid, were baking bread and buns in the kitchen. As Rose did not intend to be gone long, she thought that she could safely get away without being missed.

Sneaking into the rear lobby, she took down from its peg on the wall the old mantle she wore when gardening and wrapped it snugly around her, carefully drawing its hood over her head. Then, removing an umbrella from the stand, she slipped out the back door into the large garden beyond and, by means of the rear gate, found her way to Keppel Street, where she hailed a passing hansom cab. She gave the driver the address in Harley Street, and a quarter of an hour later, the vehicle deposited her at her destination.

After paying the driver, Rose stood out front of Raj Khanna's town house uncertainly, stricken with second thoughts. Although polite, the tone of the note he had sent when he had returned the cane that he had borrowed had seemed very cold and distant. What if he slammed the door in her face? Then, highly conscious of the fact that the hansom cab had gone— belatedly, Rose realized she ought to have told it to wait, just in case—and of the fact that passersby on the sidewalk ogled her curiously, she forced herself to gather her courage.

Taking a deep breath and grabbing hold of the ornate brass door knocker, she rapped loudly on the imposing black door.

After a long moment, it was opened by a tall, dark Indian manservant. For what seemed an eternity to her, Rose stared up at him speechlessly, shocked and disbelieving.

Then she gasped out, "Mayur Singh...?" and, for the first time in her entire life, fainted.

Thirteen

> Virtue extends our days: he lives two lives
> who relives his past with pleasure.
>
> *Epigrams*
> —Martial [Marcus Valerius Martialis]

Harley Street, London, England, 1850

"*Sahib! Sahib!*" Mayur Singh shouted hoarsely, as he caught Rose just in time to prevent her from striking her head on the sidewalk.

Hearing the terrified cries of his manservant, Hugo rushed from his study to the foyer, where he drew up short at the sight of Mayur Singh reverently carrying Rose's unconscious body into the town house.

"I do not know why she came here, but seeing me was obviously a shock that she could not bear," the manservant explained quietly, his black eyes wordlessly accusing as he stared at his master.

Swearing softly, Hugo ran one hand raggedly through his jet-black hair. Then, tenderly, he took Rose's insensate body from Mayur Singh. Kicking open the French doors that led into the drawing room, Hugo bore her inside, laying her down gently upon the sofa. Minutes later, the manservant stood at his side, carrying a vial of smelling salts, a washcloth, and a basin of tepid water.

Uncorking the vinaigrette, Hugo waved it under Rose's nose. At first, she did not respond. But then the strong odor penetrated her nostrils, and she grimaced and jerked away, her eyes fluttering open slowly, evidencing her momentary disorientation. Dipping the folded washcloth into the basin, Hugo wet it, then wrung it out, pressing it upon her forehead.

"Do you know where you are, Rose?" he asked, his voice low, soothing. "No, don't try to rise just yet. Mahout has told me you suffered a shock."

Mutely, wonderingly, Rose gazed up at Hugo for what seemed to him forever. Then, hesitantly, she stretched out one trembling hand, laying it gently upon his dark cheek, her thumb tracing the angle of one dense black eyebrow above, the curve of the thickly lashed eye beneath, the plane of his cheekbone, the straightness of his aquiline nose, the sweep of his sensual mouth. Through the entire exploration, as light as the flutter of a butterfly's wings against his skin, Hugo sat very still, scarcely daring even to breathe. Sudden shame that he had ever doubted her, suspected her of conspiring with Lord Thornleigh against him, filled his being.

It was a very long time since he had known how to love.

"How…how can this be?" Rose shook her head slightly, as though to clear it of a dream. "All these years, I believed that you were dead. But you *are* my own dear Hugo, are you not, somehow come back to life again? That is why I sensed you watching me— because the bond we once shared as children is still there between us, as strong as ever. I marvel that I did not understand it, did not recognize you before. You were only a boy when last I saw you. But now, you are a man in his prime. Does Lord Thornleigh know? Is that the reason why he came to call on my family, and you did not?"

"No, Sir James Wormwood—for he is not truly and never has been Lord Thornleigh—has no clue that I am still alive. Does he call often, then, Rose?"

"No, in all these years since we came to England, he had never visited us even a single time until just a few days ago. Jasmine and I thought his unexpected visit must have something to do with the envelope and letter…. Oh, Hugo, I'm so confused, so inexplicably frightened. Ever since our childhood, I have feared your cousin, somehow. Now, since actually meeting him, I believe that fear was not misplaced. Will you please tell me what is going on? That is why I came to see you…to try to get some answers—not to pry into your affairs, but for my own peace of mind. Hugo, why didn't you let us know that you were alive? Why are you calling yourself Raj Khanna? And dear Mayur Singh...I should have guessed it was really you when I heard the name Mahout! Do you still handle elephants?"

"Now and again, *memsahib*—although not since we immigrated to England." Mayur Singh smiled, his swarthy, leathery old face crinkling with gladness.

"We do indeed have much to talk about." Hugo's hawkish visage was somber. "But first, are you feeling better now, Rose? Can we offer you some refreshment? Some tea to warm you? Some *sohanhalwa* to tempt your palate?"

"*Sohanhalwa!* Oh, I haven't tasted that since leaving India! I would adore some!"

"I thought that you might." For the first time, Hugo smiled, and happy to oblige, Mayur Singh disappeared toward the kitchen to prepare the tea and the *sohanhalwa*, the sticky sweetmeat made with dry fruits, sprouts and sugar, which Rose had loved as a child. "Come." Standing, Hugo held out his hand to her. "Let me take your cloak and gloves, and show you where I live. Then we shall talk."

After he had hung her cape on the hall tree in the foyer and laid her gloves on its marble top, he led her through the beautiful rooms of his tastefully decorated residence, pointing out this and that. Through it all, Rose felt as though everything were unreal, that, presently, she would awaken in her bed at the Winder-

OFFICIAL OPINION POLL

Dear Reader,

Since you are a book enthusiast, we would like to know what you think.

Inside you will find a short Opinion Poll. Please participate in our poll by sharing your opinion on 3 subjects that are very important to all of us.

To thank you for your participation, we would like to send you your choice of **2 FREE BOOKS** and a **FREE GIFT!**

Please enjoy them with our compliments.

Sincerely,

Pam Powers

Editor

P.S. Don't forget to indicate which books you prefer so we can send your FREE gifts today!

YOUR OPINION POLL
THANK-YOU FREE GIFTS INCLUDE

▶ **2 ROMANCE OR 2 SUSPENSE BOOKS**

▶ **A LOVELY SURPRISE GIFT**

DETACH AND MAIL CARD TODAY!

OFFICIAL OPINION POLL

YOUR OPINION COUNTS!

Please check TRUE or FALSE below to express your opinion about the following statements:

Q1 Do you believe in "true love"?

"TRUE LOVE HAPPENS ONLY ONCE IN A LIFETIME."
○ TRUE
○ FALSE

Q2 Do you think marriage has any value in today's world?

"YOU CAN BE TOTALLY COMMITTED TO SOMEONE WITHOUT BEING MARRIED."
○ TRUE
○ FALSE

Q3 What kind of books do you enjoy?

"A GREAT NOVEL MUST HAVE A HAPPY ENDING."
○ TRUE
○ FALSE

Place the sticker next to one of the selections below to receive your 2 FREE BOOKS and FREE GIFT. I understand that I am under no obligation to purchase anything as explained on the back of this card.

Romance

193 MDL EE6C

393 MDL EE37

Suspense

192 MDL EE3P

392 MDL EE4D

0074823 |||||||||||||| |||||||| |||||||| FREE GIFT CLAIM # **3622**

FIRST NAME

LAST NAME

ADDRESS

APT.#

CITY

STATE/PROV.

ZIP/POSTAL CODE

(TF-MI-06)

The Reader Service — Here's How It Works:

If offer card is missing write to: The Reader Service, 3010 Walden Ave., P.O. Box 1867, Buffalo NY 14240-1867

BUSINESS REPLY MAIL
FIRST-CLASS MAIL   PERMIT NO. 717-003   BUFFALO, NY

POSTAGE WILL BE PAID BY ADDRESSEE

THE READER SERVICE
3010 WALDEN AVE
PO BOX 1341
BUFFALO NY 14240-8571

NO POSTAGE
NECESSARY
IF MAILED
IN THE
UNITED STATES

meres' town house in Russell Square to discover it had all been only a dream. She could still scarcely believe that Hugo Drayton was alive, that he and Raj Khanna were one and the same man, that his manservant, Mahout, was none other than Mayur Singh. Yet she really could not doubt that it was so, for while Hugo had changed, grown to manhood in the past fifteen years, Mayur Singh was much the same as he had always been.

They ended their tour back in the drawing room, where Rose saw that during their absence, the manservant had lit a welcome fire in the hearth and had the tea and the *sohanhalwa* ready and waiting.

"Oh." Rose bit into one of the sweetmeats eagerly, closing her eyes, smiling with sheer joy at the taste of it and savoring the sugary fruit that seemed to melt on her tongue. "It tastes heavenly—just exactly as I remembered! How I have missed the taste of India!"

Even as a child, Hugo had thought Rose as lovely as the flower for which she had been named. Now that she was a woman grown, he saw the childhood promise of that beauty fulfilled.

How strange were the twists and turns of fate that had brought them together again. What were the odds that out of all the females in London, she would be the one whom he had nearly knocked down on High Holborn when making good his escape from Mrs. Squasher's town house in Lincoln's Inn Field? Hugo did not know, but he thought they must be as great as the number of stars in the night sky. So it could not be sheer coincidence.

Mayur Singh had once told him that destiny had bound him and Rose together. Now, Hugo knew that must indeed be true. Long ago, the gods had parted them; now, they had brought them together again. There must be a reason for that.

"In the future, whenever you miss the taste of India, you must come here, for here, you will always find a piece of India." And of my heart—the words crept unbidden into Hugo's mind, although he did not speak them aloud. There was still too much that must be said before then, too much that he must learn anew about Rose and she about him. "You will always be welcome in my home, Rose. I am glad you know the truth about me."

"But you were not going to tell me," she observed quietly, all her hurt at the coldly polite note that he had sent her suddenly returning. "You were not ever going to see me again. Oh, Hugo, why? Whatever did I do to cause that?"

"Nothing," he confessed, ashamed and angry at himself, for he could see that with his attempt to withdraw from her life he had so unexpectedly re-entered, he had wounded her. "I know that now. To be honest, I was actually on my way to call on you a few days ago, to return your father's cane, and to make my real identity known to you and your family, and to tell you about my past and why I have come to England. But when I arrived in Russell Square, I saw Sir James Wormwood's coach outside your father's town house. You said that my cousin frightened you, Rose. I am not afraid of him. But he is my mortal enemy."

"But...why? Is it...is it because he had something to do with the murders of your parents?"

"Why would you think that?" Hugo's voice was suddenly sharp.

"I—I don't know. During our childhood, I over-heard Mama say that he was a rakehell, a—a devil, and that she suspected him of having been involved somehow with the killing of your parents. She is afraid of him, too. Initially, Jasmine thought that perhaps Mama was merely overreacting—for she has a tendency toward the dramatic, you know—and that perhaps your cousin was only a wild profligate. But since meeting him, she is no longer so certain of that. I only know that during our childhood, I labeled him a monster in my mind, and that in order to try to make sense of what befell you and your parents when the dacoits attacked your *haveli* in Chandni Chowk, I laid all the blame for it at Sir James's doorstep, whether he was guilty or not, because I thought he was an ogre, and his visit to our town house only strengthened, rather than miti-gated, that opinion. Oh, Hugo, what really did happen that night? How did you manage to escape? Where have you been for the past fifteen years? How have you lived? How did you become Raj Khanna? What is so important about Sir James's envelope and its contents that you had to have them back? For, now, I take it that you were not acting as his messenger, that he is not bent on eloping, as Jasmine and I surmised upon reading the letter."

"No, to the best of my own knowledge—which is, however, unfortunately incomplete at the moment— Sir James is plotting to assassinate Queen Victoria."

Fourteen

Murder Most Foul

> Mordre wol out, certeyn, it wol nat faille.
> (Murder will out, certain, it will not fail.)
> *The Canterbury Tales, the Prioress's Tale* [1387]
> —Geoffrey Chaucer

Harley Street, London, England, 1850

For a long moment, Rose stared at Hugo incredulously, deeply shocked and thinking that she must not have heard him right.

"Murder the Queen! Are you...are you quite certain of that, Hugo?" she asked at last.

"Yes. As I said, there is much I still don't know, and as yet, I have little hard evidence that would convict him of the crime. Even so, I believe that's what he's planning, yes," Hugo reiterated grimly. "But...I get ahead of myself. So let me go back to the beginning, back to our childhood in Delhi—and to your mother's suspicions about him having had a hand in the murders of my parents." He paused for an instant to collect his thoughts, absently sipping from his teacup. Then he continued.

"Unlike you, Rose, my father had only a single sister, Louisa. She was younger than he—a shy, sweet creature, so much so that my father often said that he feared for her and what would become of her. She was just eighteen when she married Sir Philip Wormwood. But instead of helping her to gain maturity and confidence, as my father had hoped, the marriage seemed only to worsen her timid nature—for unfortunately, Sir Philip proved a cold, even cruel, autocratic man, and he caused her a great deal of unhappiness by treating her miserably instead of with kindness and understanding. Eventually, she died giving birth to Sir James."

"So Sir James never knew his mother?"

"No." Hugo shook his head. "Instead, he was left alone to be reared by his ruthless father. You yourself have seen the result, Rose. In virtually every respect, he is an exact copy of the deceased Sir Philip. As you know, my own father wed very late in life, so that for many years, Sir James was led to believe that he would be my father's heir—and naturally, an earldom was to be much preferred over a baronetcy. But then, whilst in India, my father met and married my mother, Anamitra. Among her tribe, the Khannas, she was a princess. So when I was a child, she used to tease me that whilst my father had named me Hugo, I would always be her little king—Raj."

"Raj Khanna," Rose said softly, smiling. "Now, I understand why you chose that name—but not why you could no longer be Hugo Drayton. Do you, too, suspect that Sir James had something to do with your parents' deaths, then?"

"Yes—for he had never reconciled himself to my birth and to the resulting loss of Thornleigh and my father's other estates. Adding insult to injury in Sir James's mind was the fact that I, my father's new heir, was not even pure English, but half Indian. Originally, of course, my dual heritage was of little significance, being relatively common in India, and in due course, like other such sons and daughters of English scions, I would have been sent to my father's homeland to be educated and to take my place in English society. Although dark-skinned, I am not, you see, so dark as Mayur Singh as to be found objectionable in polite circles, and of course, the rich son of a princess—even an Indian one—is welcomed even now among the *haut ton*. It was, of course, only with the advent of the steamers that made travel from England to India both safe and relatively swift that it became much easier for men of my father's ilk to bring their wives and families with them to India, rather than to choose an Indian bride and beget children with her. But still, it would not have mattered to Sir James what I was—for above all, I was my father's heir."

From where he sat beside Rose on the sofa, Hugo
abruptly stood to stretch his legs. Crossing to the fireplace with its richly carved mahogany mantel, he knelt,
adding more fuel from the brass coal bucket to the
flames, then took up the brass poker and stoked the fire.

"Do you mind if I smoke, Rose?"

"No, please do."

From a small, inlaid box on a nearby table, Hugo
withdrew a cheroot and lit up, inhaling deeply, then
blowing a cloud of smoke into the air. Restlessly, like
a Bengal tiger, he paced the room, then, after pouring
himself a drink from a crystal decanter that sat upon
a teacart, finally settled himself into one of the bergère
chairs across from the sofa.

"As you can doubtless imagine, that night the
dacoits attacked my parents' *haveli* was the worst night
of my entire young life. They killed my father and
mother first, of course, and whilst they were doing so,
one of them crept down the hall to my own bedroom,
where he would have murdered me, as well. But
because Mayur Singh was my manservant, he slept in
a small antechamber of my bedroom, rather than in
the servants' quarters. Fortunately, he was and still is
a light sleeper, and awakened by the intruder's ingress,
he fought momentarily with him, killing him. By this
time, my poor parents were dead, and the bandits had
set fire to their bedroom, too. Realizing then that the
entire household was under assault, Mayur Singh hurriedly dragged the dead man's body into my bedroom
and quickly roused me from my bed. After that,

placing the corpse into my bed, he covered it up, so that in the darkness, it might pass as my own body. Then he smuggled me down the back stairs and out into the night."

Briefly, Hugo paused again, puffing soberly on his cigar as he remembered that fatal night. Then he went on.

"The fire had spread with a frightening rapidity— no doubt aided by some accelerant employed by the intruders—so that by this time, wakened by the blaze, the servants had come running from their own quarters, and the outlaws, knowing my parents to be dead and believing me likewise, had looted whatever they could from the *haveli* and begun to make good their own escape. In all the confusion and panic, under the cover of the darkness and the clouds of billowing smoke, Mayur Singh was able to get me safely away. He left me but shortly, hidden amid a clump of crepe myrtle, whilst he slipped into my father's study to fetch the concealed strongbox before it was discovered. After that, fearing for my well-being, not understanding then why my family had been so brutally attacked—for the murderous, robbing dacoits do not usually pick such prominent targets for their vicious assaults as my father's *haveli* was—Mayur Singh, to protect me, took me away from Delhi, to the Punjab and my mother's people. There, as Raj Khanna, I grew to manhood.

"For some years, the true reason for the bandits' onslaught upon my father's *haveli* and their killing of my parents remained a mystery to us—although Mayur Singh had, like your mother, long suspected my cousin of being behind the evil deed. For of course, with all my family dead, my cousin was next in line to inherit. But unfortunately, we had no proof of his involvement, so could take no action against him. But then, quite by chance, Mayur Singh spotted one of the outlaws in the marketplace at Amritsar. He followed him into an alley, and there, he killed him—although not before learning that my father's *haveli* had not been chosen at random by the dacoits. Rather, they had been well paid in advance for their murderous work—by an Englishman whom the bandit referred to as "the Worm"—and, as a bonus, with whatever they could loot from the house in the process."

"Then, all these years, all of Mama's own suspicions about Sir James have been correct. He really *is* the devil that she called him—and I was right to fear him!" Inwardly, Rose grieved for Hugo, for the horror he had endured because of Sir James's greed, for the terrible deaths his parents had suffered, murdered in their beds.

"Yes. As you may know, in his younger days, he traveled widely, and although I understand that, these days, he claims to have visited India only briefly, I now know that to be a false tale. Because of my mother's standing among her tribe, I had—and still have— many resources at my disposal, and once I knew that it was indeed Sir James who had been behind the outlaws' attack, it was relatively easy for me to trace his movements during that time."

"So…why have you not exposed his perfidy, Hugo, and claimed your rightful place as the Earl of Thornleigh?" Rose inquired, deeply puzzled.

"For one thing, although, thanks to Mayur Singh's quick thinking in saving my father's strongbox, I have the documents necessary to prove my real identity, I do not likewise yet have any hard evidence of what Sir James did. Oh, over the years, after chancing upon the dacoit who initially betrayed Sir James's involvement, Mayur Singh and I managed to track down others of the band, as well, who, prior to their deaths, were happy to sign written confessions about the matter. But even were I to produce those, Sir James would merely claim that the papers were forged— most of the bandits could neither read nor write, of course, so made only their marks—or that the confessions were coerced and signed under duress."

"And were they?"

"The outlaws murdered my parents, Rose," Hugo declared quietly but fiercely. "Being a woman, you perhaps cannot fully understand my wish—my burning desire and need—to show the dacoits as little mercy as they themselves had shown my poor, sleeping father and mother. Whilst the God of all those Christian missionaries who poured into India may reserve vengeance for Himself, I was taught in the Punjab that it was my right—indeed, my *duty*—to seek revenge on my enemies!"

Rose shivered of a sudden, recognizing then that the Hugo Drayton she had known and loved as a child had not only grown to manhood in the intervening years, but also changed in ways that she could never have imagined. The Hugo she had known had been a gentle boy, who had rarely ever displayed anger and certainly never a desire for retribution.

"You've become harsh and forbidding, Hugo."

"And you think the less of me for that?"

"No, I do comprehend your reasons for it. It's just that it…it scares me a little."

"I would never hurt you Rose."

"You already did—by sending me that dreadfully courteous note!"

He had the good grace to flush guiltily at that.

"I apologize for that. When I spied Sir James's coach outside your father's town house, I thought that despite everything I had learnt about you and your family to the contrary, you were conspiring with him against me."

"No, as I explained, we had only just that day renewed our acquaintance with him—and I had far rather it had been you who called on us than Sir James—" Biting her lower lip at the inadvertent admission, Rose felt her cheeks flush with sudden heat. Embarrassed, she hastily changed the subject. "Oh, Hugo, are you quite certain that Sir James is plotting to assassinate the Queen? I can scarcely believe it! It all seems so…so unreal. Why would he want to kill such a good, kind lady as the Queen?"

"Ah, well, during his travels, Sir James fell in with all kinds of company, including many of those same revolutionaries and radicals who shaped the thinking of men like Karl Marx and Friedrich Engels."

"Oh—you mean the same sort of people whom so many in London are afraid will pour into the city during the Industry of All Nations Exhibition next year, fomenting rebellion, and—and killing Queen Victoria and Prince Albert, proclaiming a new republic! Yes, Papa has read us all about them from the *Times*. Do you mean to say that Sir James is one of those zealots, that he is actually planning to carry out such a scheme, when all of London is already on guard against it?" Rose was utterly astonished by the idea.

"No." Hugo shook his head. "Believe me, Sir James scarcely shares the sentiments of men like Marx and Engels, or else he would never have stooped to murder to gain my father's title and estates. However, Sir James *is* well aware of how those with such egalitarian ideals can be cleverly and ruthlessly employed as tools to further his own ambitions. He wants rid of the Queen, I think, because ever since her marriage to Prince Albert, she has grown more and more under his influence, burgeoning into a driving force for social reformation and equality. Should England continue down such a path, then, eventually, a day will come when those in the House of Commons, for example, are of more importance and wield more power than those in the House of Lords. Sir James would not wish anything like that to happen, of course, and he is both cunning and bold. The more loudly that such a notion as assassinating the Queen is debated, the more foolish it will seem to everyone that anybody would actually attempt it, and so, in the end, instead of becoming ever more vigilant, those who protect Queen Victoria and Prince Albert may grow smug and complacent."

"How did you learn of Sir James's involvement in the plot?"

"I've had him watched for some time, even before I myself journeyed to England," Hugo explained, grinding his cheroot out in a nearby ashtray. "I know everything about him, where he goes, whom he sees, what he does. I also have an informant who is a servant in Sir James's town house in Belgrave Square and one who is a servant at Drayton Hall, in Dartmoor, too. When I learnt of Sir James's relationship with one Mrs. Delphine Squasher, who lives in Lincoln's Inn Field, I deemed it prudent to set spies on her, as well. Since most of these are Indians, it proved relatively easy to ingratiate them into various households, where they are seen as exotic and therefore highly desirable servants.

"Recently, one of them reported to me that Mr. and Mrs. Blott had delivered a note to Mrs. Squasher. Since the missive had, in fact, been passed to her by the Blotts rather than sent by post, I judged that it was no doubt of some importance and must have something to do with the plan hatched by Sir James and his cohorts. So I myself broke into Mrs. Squasher's residence—not only to steal the note, but also to search for anything else that might prove useful to me.

"Unfortunately, since she had not retired until

nearly dawn the night before, I had counted on Mrs. Squasher sleeping much later than she actually did. She awakened during my ransacking of her bedroom and, naturally, began screaming and shouting for her servants. As a result, I barely made good my escape, with two of her hirelings hard on my heels. You know the rest."

"Yes, but what I still don't understand, Hugo, is why you don't simply take the envelope with the Thornleigh seal on it, and the letter it contains, to the Queen and tell her what is afoot."

"Because it's simply not enough to incriminate him, Rose. You and your sister read the letter. You both mistakenly believed that it described an elopement! If confronted and accused, Sir James himself would most certainly lie and say that it did, as well, that I had merely—or, perhaps more likely, deliberately—misconstrued its meaning to attempt to make trouble for him. As I've said, Sir James is very clever. Despite the fact that I am the true Earl of Thornleigh, he might be successful in convincing the Queen that I'm actually nothing more than an impostor or else that I irrationally thought that he had something to do with my parents' murders in order to gain my title and estates for himself, and that I was now trying to exact revenge on him not only through forged confessions signed by tortured dacoits, but also by an imaginary assassination plot! I could be made to appear a vindictive madman, and he could wind up getting away with everything, never being forced to pay for what he did!"

"Yes, now, I see the difficulties. What do you intend to do, then, Hugo?"

Lightly, he shrugged.

"I shall continue my observations and investigations, of course, until I am sure that I have enough to hang Sir James. Right now, I'm not even certain when or where the assassination attempt is to take place, except that it must be sometime in the spring—for that is when Sir James told Mrs. Squasher that he would come to London, and that on the day of the ceremony, they would be united in their celebration."

"Wouldn't that indeed seem to indicate May first, the day of the opening ceremony for the Industry of All Nations Exhibition, then?"

"Yes." Hugo nodded. "But I dare not take anything for granted. Sir James may be aware that he is being spied upon and so may have taken steps to misdirect me."

"Then he knows who you are?"

"No. He may indeed have heard of Raj Khanna. One hardly moves in the business circles I do and keeps oneself a secret. However, as yet, Sir James has no reason to suspect I am interested in him—and none at all to connect me with Hugo Drayton. At the moment, with the sole exception of Mayur Singh, only you can do that, Rose."

"Surely, you know that you can trust me, Hugo. I shall say nothing to anyone, of course," Rose insisted fervently.

"No, I know you will not. However, we must assume that since Sir James called upon your family, he has discovered that it was you whom I nearly knocked down that day in High Holborn. Because he may not believe that was an accident, but suspect that I passed the envelope to you, he may be having you watched. You might, in fact, have been followed here."

"I'm—I'm so sorry, Hugo. I didn't know." Rose was stricken with fear and remorse at the notion that she might somehow have endangered him, no matter how unwittingly. "However, since I made up my mind to come here alone, I—I wanted no one to know what I was about. So I left our town house by the back door and through the garden gate, into Keppel Street. I donned my old cloak that I wear when I work in the garden in, too. So even if someone *did* see me leave, I might have been mistaken for one of our housemaids, or even for Polly, our scullery maid. I had the hood drawn up around my face."

"Good. On this particular occasion, then, I would appreciate it if you would go back into the house the same way you exited it, if you don't mind."

"No, I don't. I shall. What else can I do to help you, Hugo?"

"Nothing at the moment. I truly don't want you any more mixed up in this than you already are, Rose. This is a hazardous game—and Sir James and his associates Mr. and Mrs. Blott play for keeps. I'm not certain that Mrs. Squasher actually grasps the true nature of the people she has got involved with. Mr. Blott's mother is a prostitute in Southwark, and he never knew his real father. Mrs. Blott's parents were a good deal more respectable, but her father went mad in the end and died in a private sanatorium for the insane. Afterward, she ran off with Mr. Blott, and upon learning his background, that he is not only the son of a whore, but is also a gigolo and a gambler, her mother disowned her."

"Meeting Mr. Blott was anything but a pleasure." Rose shuddered visibly at the memory. "He reminded me of a—a snake that had swallowed a rat! I cannot imagine what Mrs. Blott sees in him! What…what shall I do, Hugo, if Sir James calls on me and my family again? What if Mr. Blott should call, perhaps bringing Mrs. Blott with him? Sir James and Mr. Blott discussed business with my father. I am worried that they mean to try to swindle him somehow," she confessed. "Papa is not stupid, but he…he frets about me and my sisters."

"I understand—and I promise you I will do whatever I can to ensure he is not taken advantage of. In the meanwhile, you and your sister Jasmine must speak of the envelope and its contents to no one, Rose. If Sir James or Mr. Blott should return to Russell Square, either singly or together, you must behave as naturally as you can to avoid their becoming suspicious. Should you at any time feel yourself to be in danger, I trust that you will get in touch with me immediately. This is my battle to fight, Rose—not yours."

"Yes, all right." Rose swallowed hard, hoping that nothing would happen to Hugo, when she had only just found him again. Then, glancing at the small timepiece she wore pinned to her bodice, she gasped.

"Oh, good heavens! I meant to be away not more than an hour—and now, I've already been gone two. I must return home at once, before I am missed!"

She rose, as did Hugo, who walked her into the foyer and assisted her into her cloak and collected her umbrella from the stand in which Mayur Singh had earlier placed it. Then, after Rose, drawing on her gloves, had said goodbye to the manservant, Hugo led her through the town house to its back door and out into the small but well-tended garden beyond, where she observed that a narrow alley ran between his residence and the terrace house to the south. The passageway cut straight through from Harley Street to Mansfield Street, the latter of which fed into New Cavendish, Dutchess and Queen Ann Streets, so that there were several avenues of escape.

"Now, you undoubtedly see why I chose this particular town house, Rose. Its location has certain advantages, and it will be safer for you to leave this way, in case Sir James has somehow learnt that it was I who broke into Mrs. Squasher's residence, and has placed me under observation. I think not, but where you are concerned, I mean to take no chances."

Putting up her umbrella, holding it over the two of them to shield them from the drizzle that splattered from the leaden sky, Hugo pushed open the garden gate, escorting Rose down the short alley to Mansfield Street. There, he hailed a passing hansom cab. When it had drawn to a halt beside the curb, he assisted her inside, folding her umbrella and handing it to her. He gave the driver her address in Russell Square, along with the fare. Then, briefly, Hugo took one of Rose's hands in his, raising it to his lips and kissing it gently.

"Don't worry. Don't be afraid," he said. "When I'm certain that it's safe, I *will* see you again. Until then, have faith, my own dear Rose."

Then he rapped briskly on the box upon which the driver sat, and in response, the vehicle obediently rolled forward into the falling rain.

Fifteen

Some Advice Sought

Many receive advice, few profit by it.

Maxim 149
—Publilius Syrus

Russell Square and Belgrave Square,
London, England, 1850

As the vehicle that Hugo had hired for Rose conveyed her back to Russell Square, her mind raced furiously with all she had discovered that afternoon. Even now, she could scarcely credit it, still felt as though it must all somehow be a dream from which she would shortly awaken, tears of longing and grief streaking her cheeks. But the droplets that gently splashed her face were only the rain that now and again trickled beneath the bonnet of the hansom cab.

Hugo alive! It did not seem possible. But the lingering warmth of her hand, which he had held and kissed only moments ago, assured her that it was.

As previously instructed, the driver dropped Rose off in Keppel Street. From there, via the back gate, she let herself into the garden at the rear of the Windermeres' town house, hoping that she had not been missed. Hurriedly pushing open the back door, she stepped into the rear lobby, stripping off her mantle and gloves, returning the former to its peg on the wall and the latter to the pockets of her cloak. By means of a small mirror that hung near the door, she hastily smoothed her damp hair, tucking a few wispy, errant strands back into the simple snood that contained the heavy mass.

Then she went into the kitchen, where Mrs. Beasley and Polly were taking hot buns and loaves of fresh bread from the oven, setting them aside on metal racks to cool. There was also a delicate chicken soup simmering on the stove. Spread about the kitchen, in various stages of preparation, were a turbot with lobster sauce, an oyster paté, lamb cutlets with peas, a stewed beef with vegetables, a salad and plovers' eggs in aspic jelly, and a chocolate cream.

"Oh, there you are, Miss Windermere." From the cutting block where she was chopping carrots into generous slices, Polly glanced up without curiosity. "Mrs. Windermere 'as been lookin' for you, but she's gone away back upstairs again."

"I was outside in the garden." Even though the admission was not exactly a lie, Rose blushed slightly as she made it. "But as the rain is beginning to come harder now, I thought that I had best come inside."

"Aye, well, you're no doubt right, miss. Still, t' fresh air 'as put some color in your cheeks, so I imagine that it's done you good ta be outside for a while."

"Thank you, Polly. Everything looks and smells wonderful, Mrs. Beasley, as usual. Well, I had best go upstairs and see what Mama wanted."

Since neither the cook nor the scullery maid had questioned her absence from the town house, Rose correctly assumed that her mother had not been in search of her long enough for her to have been truly missed. For that, she was inordinately grateful, for although she was bursting to share her news about Hugo with somebody, she knew that she could tell no one. It was Hugo's secret to share, if and when he decided to make the rest of her family privy to it. Further, if Sir James were somehow to learn Hugo's true identity, that would prove disastrous to all of Hugo's plans, and Rose would never deliberately betray his trust. No, she must keep her newfound knowledge to herself—and try hard not to worry too much.

Raising one hand, Rose knocked lightly upon her mother's bedroom door.

"Come in. Oh, there you are, Rose!" Glancing up from the secretary at which she sat, responding to some correspondence, Mrs. Windermere sighed heavily, her brow knitted in an anxious frown. "As much as I would wish otherwise, Rose, having pondered the matter at some length, I see no way of avoiding paying a return visit to Lord Thornleigh without giving unbearable offense. I was thinking that tomorrow would be appropriate—not too soon, so as to seem overly eager to further the acquaintance, but also not too late, so as to appear unforgivably rude and insulting. What is your own opinion?"

"To be honest, I—I really hadn't given the idea any thought, Mama."

"No thought?" Shaking her head, Mrs. Windermere snorted with both annoyance and exasperation. "What a strange, fey child you've always been, Rose, to be sure! Why, when you were small, I sometimes wondered if you were a changeling from another world—for you've always seemed to have very little interest in this one! Do you not see how vexing and troublesome all this is? Lord Thornleigh is rich— Maria Penworthy said he is rumored to have seven thousand a year!—and he has no wife! Surely, it was not just business that drove him to seek your father's advice—for there are many others from whom he might have sought counsel—but that he had heard of your beauty and that of your sisters! Oh, if only any lord but the present Earl of Thornleigh would choose one of my daughters for a bride, I should be the happiest of mothers! You are the eldest, Rose. It is only right that you should marry first. But in truth, the notion that Lord Thornleigh should express any interest in you or any of my other daughters cannot help but make me shudder with apprehension and revulsion!

As I've told both you and your sisters—and your dear father, as well—I've never liked or trusted that terrible man! For all that he plays the part of a gentleman, there is really something...quite sinister about him, I fear. We must find some way to discourage him, without affronting him, lest he set out to ruin us all!"

"Mama, Lord Thornleigh must be at least thirty years older than I—and I—I do not like or trust him, either. So I beg you, please do not think of me having my head turned by him and setting my cap for him, for in all honesty, I would rather remain a spinster all my days than be wed to the likes of Lord Thornleigh!" Rose was so horrified by the prospect of marriage to Sir James that she was actually shaking.

"Why, Rose, my poor, dear girl. I had no intention of upsetting you this way. Truly, I had no idea that you found Lord Thornleigh as utterly disagreeable as I do. He appears to be a presentable and pleasant enough gentleman on the surface, does he not? Oh, he is not particularly handsome, of course...rather nondescript, in fact, I should have said, and it is a pity that he must wear such thick spectacles that make him resemble nothing so much as a fish or a toad. But still, beggars cannot be choosers, and I know that you cannot be unaware of what such a match would mean to us, Rose. And for your sisters to be launched into the company of the *haut ton,* as well. So I only wished to warn you that I had far rather you accepted Professor Prosser than Lord Thornleigh, no matter how much the latter might appeal."

"Indeed, I am not incognizant of what such a match would mean to us, Mama. But you simply must believe me when I tell you that there is nothing about Lord Thornleigh that holds any temptations for me, nothing on this earth that could possibly persuade me to wed him under any circumstances, even if he were to make me an offer, which I sincerely doubt is his aim, in any event!"

"Well, then, why do you think that he came here, Rose? For in truth, despite how much I love and respect your dear father, I cannot believe that it was genuinely to seek his advice about business affairs in India that prompted Lord Thornleigh and his associate Mr. Blott to call upon us. That is why I thought they must have some ulterior motive—and what else could it be but interest in attaining one of my daughters as a bride? I tell you, it has all been *most* worrisome to me!"

Hearing that, Rose actually had to bite her tongue to prevent herself from blurting out the whole truth about Sir James to her mother. Only loyalty to Hugo and the knowledge that the evil information about Sir James would only aggrieve Mrs. Windermere even further kept her silent.

"I do not know, any more than you do, Mama, why Lord Thornleigh should suddenly have taken it upon himself to visit us," Rose lied, although not without a sense of guilt at deceiving her mother. "However, you need not fret that either I or Jasmine will be prevailed upon to agree to a match with him. Of us all, it is Lily who will doubtless need dissuading from that direction, for she is the one of us who feels our situation in life most keenly." Silently, Rose berated herself for not recognizing sooner that, of course, regardless of how much Sir James repelled her mother, a deep sense of what constituted good manners would prompt Mrs. Windermere to pay him a return visit—and possibly Mr. Blott, too. The thought of calling upon the latter was even more disturbing to Rose.

"I suggest that, yes, we do return Sir James's—that is to say, Lord Thornleigh's—call tomorrow," she continued, "but that we keep our visit as brief as is politely possible, and that, whilst there, we do as little as we can toward encouraging him to have any further interest in us, but, rather, attempt to dampen any enthusiasm he may have where we are concerned. In that regard, it would be wise if you speak once more with Papa, Mama. For if ever he himself harbored any ill will toward Lord Thornleigh, I believe he has long forgotten it or else, more likely, suppressed it in his desire to try to better our fortunes."

"Yes, I think that you are right on that score, Rose." Mrs. Windermere sighed heavily again.

The matter thus settled, Rose exited her mother's bedroom to find her way to her own, relieved to discover that it was empty, that Jasmine must be elsewhere occupied. Firmly closing the door behind her, Rose took her jewelry box from atop the mahogany dresser and, after opening it, removed the treasured gold necklace with its Gupta coin. Unfolding the tissue paper in which it was wrapped, she slipped the chain over her head, tucking the necklace beneath the bodice of her gown, so that the half coin rested between her breasts. Now that she knew Hugo was alive, the necklace would no longer bring her sadness, but a world of hope.

Rose wondered if Hugo had kept his own half of the Gupta coin. They had had so much to discuss that she had forgotten to ask him.

Sixteen

Treason doth never prosper: what's the reason?
For if it prosper, none dare call it treason.
                    Epigrams. Of Treason
                    —Sir John Harington

Belgrave Square, London, England, 1850

It was difficult to believe that less than half a century ago, Belgravia had been known as "the Five Fields" and of such poor character that the area had been a positive terror to any person who must pass through it after nightfall, while traveling on foot between London and Chelsea. The clayish swamp had been a morass of stagnant water, weeds, and mud banks, occupied by only a few tumbledown sheds. But in 1824, a builder, Mr. Thomas Cubitt, discovering that the land at the Five Fields consisted not only of clay, but also of gravel, had extracted the former, turning it into bricks, which he had then laid upon the gravel, making the ground suitable for construction.

That same year, he had arranged with the landowners to cover great portions of the Five Fields and adjacent region in this manner, upon which Belgrave Square, Lowndes Square and Chesham Place had subsequently been built. Although still low-lying land (it had been determined that the ground floor of Westbourne Terrace, at Hyde Park Gardens, which was seventy feet above the high-water mark of the River Thames, was level with the attics of the houses at Belgrave and Eaton Squares), it was no longer an unhealthy mire. Rather, it was now one of the most fashionable and exclusive areas of London.

Like its poorer cousin, Bloomsbury, Belgravia was relatively quiet. But unlike Bloomsbury, the constant rattle of the endless stream of omnibuses, hackney coaches, hansom cabs and private carriages that filled the streets around Piccadilly and Knightsbridge gave way in Belgravia to grand, aristocratic houses whence exquisitely dressed gentlemen and ladies sallied forth on horseback for afternoon gallops along Rotten Row or leisurely carriage rides around Hyde Park, where they might see and be seen. When the sun shone and the inhabitants were out, the sidewalks were peopled with servants in wigs and livery, awaiting their masters' and mistresses' returns or walking overfed, temperamental little dogs who belonged to the *haut ton*; and the tranquil air itself was broken only by the sounds of door knockers rapping loudly upon stately doors, as well-to-do callers visited and left their calling cards for those who were either out or otherwise engaged.

This latter described Lord Thornleigh and his guests: Mr. and Mrs. Blott, Mrs. Squasher, Mr. Avery Ploughell, Mr. Douglas Delwyn and Mrs. Lynne Ambrose. Following a hearty luncheon, the seven had assembled in the small drawing room, there to indulge in several rounds of loo, while heatedly discussing their plan to assassinate Queen Victoria. Of them all, only Mr. Blott could be described as reasonably content. But as he was now on his third glass of whiskey, and it was not yet five o'clock, little else might be expected, for he had not yet reached that stage of inebriation that turned him mean and ugly.

Lord Thornleigh was annoyed because he had lost several hands of loo and a good deal of money to the pool, most of which had been won by Mr. Blott, whom he suspected of cheating, although he could not determine how. The earl did not like to lose, particularly when he could ill afford to do so. Although he had inherited Thornleigh and other estates, his gross mismanagement combined with his extravagant tastes had quickly served to deplete their revenues, and of course, there was the town house in Belgrave Square to be maintained, as well. That, like the Windermeres, he could have had one twice the size at half the price in Russell Square, he did not even consider.

Nobody who was anybody lived outside of the West End.

That none of his present company actually resided in the West End, he conveniently chose to overlook. One took one's comrades in arms where one found them, and Queen Victoria must be got rid of. She was not only, when it came to marriage and families, a relic, but also permitting her foreign-born husband, Prince Albert, to assume more and more power, instituting reforms that made life incommodious for those of the earl's ilk. He firmly believed in maintaining the various classes of society, that those who served never could and never should be the equal of those who ruled, and Queen Victoria and Prince Albert were clearly intent on blurring those boundaries. That Lord Thornleigh's reasons for wishing the Queen out of the way were thus vastly different from all those of his accomplices, he prudently kept to himself.

Unhappy because Mrs. Squasher and the others had been invited to Belgrave Square, Mrs. Blott paid little heed to the cards that she was dealt, making one stupid blunder after another. With the exception of her husband, she had hoped to have Lord Thornleigh all to herself, so that she could further her aim of detaching him from Mrs. Squasher and acquiring him for her own bed. She had no idea what the earl could possibly see in the aptly named Mrs. Squasher, who, in Mrs. Blott's estimation, resembled nothing so much as a grossly misshapen squash topped by a badly styled brown wig.

Further, Mrs. Squasher considered herself smarter than everyone else gathered in the room, and Mrs. Blott felt indignantly that that position should be accorded to her, despite the fact that she herself, while as crafty and conniving as her husband, was, in reality, as dumb as a fence post. Regardless of how many times it had been explained to her, she had no idea why the rest thought that the Queen needed to be killed. She simply accepted that it was so. Mrs. Blott was also jealous of Mrs. Squasher because prior to Mrs. Blott's having wed him, Mrs. Squasher had bedded Mr. Blott.

Mrs. Squasher was angry because her protests at the assignment of the actual shooting of the Queen to Mr. Blott had been soundly dismissed by the others. She had wanted Mr. Delwyn to pull the trigger. Next to herself, he was the most intelligent of their number, she thought, as he had been called to the Bar. But in addition to being the oldest of their group, he was also the biggest, standing well over six feet and weighing upward of seventeen stone, which would have made him not only slow, but also highly visible in a crowd. So the rest had vetoed him as the assassin, insisting that he would be unable to get anywhere near the Queen without being observed and almost certainly apprehended, thereby exposing them all.

Mrs. Squasher had then proposed herself as the shooter, but much to her fury, that had only resulted in howls of ribald laughter by the others at what they had deemed a good joke. Mrs. Squasher, however, had been quite serious. She lived for the day when women would be rightly recognized as the superior sex, and removing Queen Victoria and her antiquated ideas about marriage and family values was a large step in that direction.

A Member of Parliament, who sat in the House of Commons, Mr. Avery Ploughell was agitated because he worried constantly about his part in the plot to murder the Queen being revealed. He wished fervently that it were a better, more trustworthy class of people who now occupied Lord Thornleigh's small drawing room. That he himself was a fiery, arrogant, corrupt, Bible-thumping hypocrite who regularly accepted bribes from his constituents who operated gaming hells, brothels and pubs, Mr. Ploughell resolutely thrust from his mind. Due to the fact that his stature was diminutive—he stood only five feet tall—he had an extremely large, defensive chip on his shoulder, so that his political ambitions overrode even his religious zeal. He did not see why Parliament should continue to support such archaic systems as the monarchy and the House of Lords, to which admittance was based solely on one's having been born to the silver or having obtained a life peerage. That neither of these was his own lot in life secretly grieved him sorely, and he was thus determined to get even however he could with those whom he envied desperately and considered above him.

Mr. Douglas Delwyn, a judge, was offended because he had been voted against as the shooter by the others, except for Mrs. Squasher, of course. He hadn't particularly desired to be the one who actually shot the Queen. But still, he was resentful of the fact that much had been made of his great height and bulk, and adding insult to injury had been Mrs. Blott's tittered suggestion that he console himself with another sweetmeat. He had thought that rich, coming from a woman who must weigh over twelve stone herself and who had a prominent backside like that of an elephant he had seen at the zoo. Mr. Delwyn firmly believed social reforms were necessary so judges and barristers would henceforth not only interpret, but also institute the laws of the land— for who knew the Law better than they?

A peevish, nervous woman of indeterminate age, Mrs. Lynne Ambrose was a widow whose late husband had been a barrister. She was a longtime friend of both Mrs. Squasher and Mr. Delwyn, and as a result, she was upset because she had been compelled to cast her vote along with those of the rest who had said that Mr. Delwyn should not be the one to shoot the Queen. Now, she feared that both Mrs. Squasher and Mr. Delwyn were incensed at her, and Mrs. Ambrose could not bear discord of any kind. That was why she had gone along with the majority, in order to settle the quarrel that had appeared to brewing. She had become a part of the assassination plot because she ardently believed it was unfair that so many like herself should have so relatively little and that Queen Victoria, merely through an accident of birth, should have so much. Had she herself been the Queen, Mrs. Ambrose would have thought quite differently, however.

"I still don't understand why we can't just build a bomb and blow the Queen up!" Mrs. Blott carelessly laid another card upon the table, missing yet another opportunity to take a trick and thereby win at least a third of the pool. "Wouldn't that be easier than Mr. Blott having to get close enough to shoot her?"

"Possibly," Lord Thornleigh agreed dryly. "However, as we've explained to you previously, Mrs. Blott, there is concern about the iron girders that are to form the structural shell of the Crystal Palace. It seems likely that any kind of explosion within the building would create such vibrations that the girders would give way, causing the entire edifice to collapse. Our goal is to assassinate the Queen, not to murder thousands of innocent Exhibition attendees—this latter of which would most assuredly turn public opinion rabidly against us."

"I see." Mrs. Blott appeared to be satisfied at last.

"My lord," Eastlake, the earl's butler, intoned, as he entered the drawing room. "A Colonel Hilary Windermere, Mrs. Violet Windermere, and their daughters have called. Should I send them away, my lord, or do you desire me to show them in?"

"Show them in, Eastlake," Lord Thornleigh directed, abruptly casting down his cards. "The colonel is a twittering old fogy, and his wife is a flibbertigibbet with social aspirations that are quite beyond her. But as they are nonetheless a rather diverting couple, and their daughters are all beautiful and accomplished, they shall no doubt provide us all with much more amusement than this tedious game of loo!"

Moments later, the Windermeres were ushered by the butler, Eastlake, into Lord Thornleigh's small drawing room, and after being greeted by their host, they were presented to the rest of those who occupied the chamber. Rose thought she had never seen such a motley assembly as the earl's other guests, and because they were all his social inferiors, she immediately suspected they must comprise his fellow conspirators in the plot to kill Queen Victoria—for surely, he would not otherwise be entertaining them.

For that reason, although Rose had not wanted to come to Belgrave Square, she was now glad of the obligatory social call that had compelled her family's visit. With a great deal of interest, she surreptitiously studied the rest, carefully concealing her excitement at the thought of all she would have to relate to Hugo later.

What first attracted her attention was the sheer size of Mrs. Blott and Mrs. Squasher. Rose could not ever remember seeing two such huge women. Surely, Mrs. Squasher stood almost six feet tall, and Mrs. Blott was even larger, a veritable Amazon, several inches taller than her husband, Mr. Blott, whom she made resemble a dwarf in comparison. Was there ever a more incongruous pairing than the Blotts? Rose wondered. Mr. Delwyn was quite big, too, and waddled so when he walked that he reminded her of nothing so much as some monstrous, ponderous penguin. In sharp contrast, Mr. Ploughell was virtually a midget, standing just five feet tall, she estimated, and his skin was so swarthy that she knew that he must be half Italian or Spanish, for his was not the same kind of foreign blood exhibited by Hugo. Only Mrs. Ambrose was so unremarkable as to almost fade into the background.

They were all, Rose decided, extremely disagreeable people. Mr. Blott was obviously well on his way to being drunk and leered openly at her and her sisters, and both Mrs. Blott and Mrs. Squasher were so cheaply and vulgarly attired, practically bursting from their bodices, that Rose felt embarrassed even to be in their company. She knew from her entire family's demeanor that she was not the only one. Even Lily, who would normally have been positively triumphant at being ensconced in the small drawing room of the Earl of Thornleigh's grand house in Belgrave Square, was instead strangely cowed and subdued.

So, despite her morbid fascination with Lord Thornleigh and his companions, Rose could only be immensely relieved when, not one minute later than the appropriate length of time for a social call, Mrs. Windermere got to her feet and made her family's excuses, insisting that they dare not impose further on the earl and his guests.

Seventeen

Brooking No Competition

> O! beware, my lord, of jealousy;
> It is the green-eyed monster which doth mock
> The meat it feeds on; that cuckold lives in bliss
> Who, certain of his fate, loves not his wronger.
>   *Othello* [1604-1605]
>   —William Shakespeare

*Russell Square and Grosvenor Square, London,
England, 1850*

For the next several days, Hugo had his spies keep a
close eye on the Windermeres' town house in Russell
Square. It was not that he didn't trust Rose, for since
she had come to his lodgings in Harley Street, it had
been clear to him that she was still the same Rose that
he known and treasured as a boy in India. She had

been his best friend then, and she would never betray him now, for despite the fact that they had both grown to adulthood and, inevitably, changed, the bond that they had once shared as children together was still strong between them.

There were some things, it seemed, that one never lost.

But still, Hugo feared that Sir James suspected Rose of being in receipt of the envelope and its contents, and as long as that might be the case, he would do nothing to place her in any further jeopardy or to bring himself to his cousin's notice. So, although he wanted nothing more than to see her again and champed impatiently at the bit to do so, he forced himself to rein in his emotions, biding his time.

But at long last, after more than a fortnight, when his spies had reported naught untoward, Hugo determined that whatever suspicions Sir James might have harbored about Rose had been allayed, for he put in no reappearance at the Windermeres' town house. Nor did they visit him again at Belgrave Square—the latter of which Eastlake (ostensibly Sir James's butler, but, in reality, loyal to Hugo), had indicated to him had consisted of nothing more than an obligatory return visit.

"Trust me, m'lord," Eastlake had insisted to his true master, whom he had been overjoyed to learn was still alive. "I've never seen a family so uncomfortable as the Windermeres were—and rightly so. For 'tis bad company Sir James keeps in Belgrave Square, and no mistake! Your dear father—God rest his soul—is probably turning in his grave at the very thought of that wholly worthless lot darkening his doorstep!"

So Hugo had known that he need have no further worry that the Windermeres would conspire against him with Sir James, and his mind was at ease on that score. Much to his irritation, however, Professor Prosser continued to call at Russell Square, and from the updates regularly provided to Hugo by his spies, it was plain to him that the professor indeed harbored high hopes of marrying Rose. That she even possessed a prospective suitor annoyed Hugo no end, for during all the time he had spent in India, plotting, planning, and working endlessly toward the day when he would gain his revenge and reclaim his rightful heritage, it had never once occurred to him that Rose would not be there to share it with him.

Now, belatedly, Hugo recognized how very arrogant and unrealistic that had been. Of course, Rose would not remain a child forever. Of course, growing to womanhood and believing him long dead, she had moved on with her own life. Time had not stood still for her, in the peculiar way that it had seemed to do so for him. It was actually a wonder that she was not already wed, and he knew that were it not for her family's circumstances, she undoubtedly would have been. That would have proved a crushing blow to him, Hugo realized now.

As a boy, he had loved Rose—not in the way a man

loves a woman, of course, but, rather, with a child's simple faith and devotion, secretly believing her to be one of the fairies about which he had read in the books that had been his constant companions then, and still were. He had thought she was ethereal and magic, and when they had played together, he had often imagined himself as a prince, rescuing her from some darkly enchanted bower. In his mind, he had always associated her with fairy tales and living happily ever after.

Examining his emotions toward her now, Hugo understood that he had carefully locked his memories of Rose away in his heart because they had reminded him of all that had been good and sweet about the life he had lost when the dacoits had murdered his parents. If not for that horrible night, it would have been natural for him and Rose, having grown up together and been so close, to someday marry. Mayur Singh, a great believer in the gods and destiny, had hoped and thought that that day would eventually come to pass, Hugo knew. But although, like his manservant, he, too, believed in the gods and fate, his years in the Punjab had also taught Hugo much about free will, about seizing life by the throat and making of it what he could and would.

As a result, he was much changed from the boy that he had once been—and that fact had not escaped Rose's notice. She remained loyal to him for old times' sake, because of their childhood friendship that had forged the strong bond that they still shared. But could she ever care for him again, love the man whom he had become? Not as the child she had once been, but as a woman fully grown?

Hugo did not know, and there was only one way to find out.

"Mr. Raj Khanna," Miss Candlish announced to those assembled in the drawing room of the Windermeres' town house in Russell Square.

Following hard on the housekeeper's heels, Hugo momentarily drew up short at the sight that met his eyes. Belatedly, he wondered why he should ever have thought that he would find Rose alone, in a household that he knew to be bursting at the seams with her parents and sisters. Worse, it was not only they who were in attendance, but also Professor Prosser, who had proprietarily seated himself beside Rose on the sofa and who had evidently been prosing on at some length, as usual. For it was several minutes before the professor realized that Hugo had entered the chamber and finally sputtered into silence, scowling with such a great deal of annoyance at him that, under different circumstances, Hugo would have been highly tempted to laugh. As it was, his own emotions were such that he could only glower at Professor Prosser in return, so that Rose was quite taken aback by the fierce expression on his dark, hawkish visage.

Trembling a little with sudden fright and excitement, she stood.

"Mr.—Mr. Khanna, we weren't expecting you. But

still, how good of you to call. I trust that you are now fully recovered from your mishap in the park," she said.

"Yes…yes, quite, thank you, Miss Windermere. I'm afraid I must apologize for not visiting sooner. But unfortunately, the injuries I sustained, along with pressing business that was delayed as a result and could not therefore be put off any longer upon my recovery, combined to make it impossible for me to call before now," Hugo lied, knowing full well that she would understand why he did not immediately make his true identity known to her family and reveal why he had journeyed to England.

"Well, you're here now, sir, and we're delighted to have you," Colonel Windermere declared jovially, rising to shake Hugo's hand. "Mr. Khanna and I have some slight acquaintance through the East India United Service Club," he confided to those present, "and I, for one, shall be glad to further it."

"As shall I, sir," Hugo returned warmly.

Then, striding across the room, he took one of Rose's hands in his and, raising it to his lips, kissed it debonairly, causing her heart to flutter in her breast and the professor to frown even more sternly.

"It is a pleasure to see you again, Miss Windermere."

Hugo smiled, so that for an instant, Rose could almost believe that she had only imagined the savage look on his face just moments before. But still, his black eyes were sober as they lingered searchingly on her countenance, so that she blushed faintly under his intense scrutiny. She knew she looked tired, for the unaccustomed excitement of the past weeks and the revelation that Hugo Drayton was not only miraculously alive and well, but also had come back into her world, had made it virtually impossible for her to sleep. As a result, Rose had spent many long nights tossing and turning restlessly in the bed that she shared with Jasmine, and furtively prowling around their bedroom, often stroking her half of the solid-gold Gupta coin that she now wore daily, carefully concealed beneath her bodice.

Fervently, now, Rose wished that she had donned a finer gown earlier that day, and taken a good deal more care with her appearance.

"You remember Professor Prosser and my sister Jasmine, of course, Mr. Khanna, and it would seem that you have become acquainted with my father, as well. Won't you please allow me to present you to the rest of my family?"

The introductions were duly made, after which Hugo seated himself on the couch, squarely between the professor and Rose, completely dismaying the former and flustering the latter. It was surely too much to hope, she told herself firmly, that Hugo was actually jealous of the short, balding university teacher. But still, what else could satisfactorily account for his behavior? Her heart beat fast as she dwelled on the possibility, for it could only mean that Hugo still had feelings for her. But were they only the vestiges of their childhood friendship—or something more? Rose did not know. Nor was she at all certain of her own emotions toward him.

So much had happened so fast, she thought, that it was only natural that she should feel confused. Hugo was no longer the boy whom she had adored and idolized as a child, who had rescued her from more than one pretend tower, and whom she had dreamed of someday marrying. Rather, now, he was not only in so many ways a stranger to her, but also a virile man in his prime, bent on reclaiming his rightful heritage and gaining his revenge on his wicked cousin. From her father's own accounts, Rose knew that, as Raj Khanna, Hugo had acquired a reputation of being a dangerous man to cross, and now, she had seen first-hand that if he wanted something, he did not hesitate to take it.

Even the normally garrulous, long-winded Professor Prosser had apparently deemed it best to stifle any protest that he might otherwise have made at Hugo usurping center stage on the settee. For, after noisily clearing his throat, as though preparing to voice some complaint, the professor had, at Hugo's unblinking stare, reddened, closed his mouth, and swallowed hard, his owlish eyes blinking rapidly behind his round, horn-rimmed spectacles. Under other circumstances, Rose would have been hard put to conceal a smile at seeing the little university teacher so quelled into silence. As it was, however, she could only remember how respectful Hugo had always been of his elders during their childhood and be profoundly reminded of how much he had grown and changed in the intervening years.

Born and bred in India, Rose was not unaware of its hardships and cruelties, but still, she could only imagine the life that Hugo had lived in the Punjab— and wonder, not for the first time since learning his real identity, what it had done to him.

Oh, if only that terrible night when his parents had been murdered and their *haveli* set aflame had never happened! If only she and Hugo could travel back in time to that India they had known, loved, and shared in those all-too-fleeting halcyon days of their childhood!

But those days were gone forever—and their youth with them. She was a twenty-three-year-old spinster, longing desperately for a life that was swiftly passing her by. Five years older than she, Hugo was far nearer thirty than twenty, and of necessity, his experience of the world must be much greater than her own. Perhaps he had loved dozens of women, she mused sadly, while the only love of her life had been the boy whom she had lost that fatal night in India. For it was not the boy who had returned to her, Rose was old and wise enough to realize, but, rather, the man whom he had become; and while she could be sure of her feelings for the former, those for the latter were new, unfamiliar, and untested by time.

Certainly, she was physically attracted to him and had been from the moment when he had nearly knocked her down in High Holborn. Even without glancing at him, she was vividly aware of all the planes and angles of his handsome face, of the lean muscles that rippled gracefully with his every movement, and of the hardness of his thigh, pressed against her own soft one, as they sat close upon the sofa together. She had never before felt such a powerful attraction to a man. But, then, she had so very little experience of men, she reflected ruefully but honestly. Perhaps she would have been attracted to any man as handsome as Hugo was. But surely, she would not have felt the same emotional bond that she and Hugo shared from their childhood. No, of course, she would not. However, there was still a great deal of difference between children who were best friends and adults who loved as man and woman, she thought.

Rose knew that she was deeply shocked by and sorry for all that Hugo had suffered since that night in Delhi, when his entire world had been shattered, although she correctly sensed that he did not want her pity. And although she was frightened by it, still, she could understand the burning desire for justice and retribution that drove him now. Perhaps in his place, she would have felt the same. But beyond all that, she did not know what to think. At one point, Hugo had admitted to her that, mistakenly believing her to be in league with his cousin against him, he had never intended to see her again. If he had still loved her as a friend, would he have been so quick to judge her and find her lacking?

"You're a million miles away," Hugo murmured in Rose's ear, abruptly startling her from her reverie. "Have you slipped into some fairyland, wherein no mortal dare trespass?"

"No." Smiling faintly, she shook her head. "I was… just thinking about…you and me."

She bit her lower lip anxiously, for she had nearly said "us" instead of "you and me." But she could not be sure yet that there was an "us" to be spoken of.

"What about us?" Hugo asked softly, as though he had read her mind.

"We're…no longer children. We've grown up. We've…changed."

"What are you saying to me, Rose?" Hugo's brow knitted in a puzzled, vaguely troubled frown.

"I…don't know."

"Surely, you're not telling me that you mean to marry this prosy, overstuffed owl who has done his level best to bore us all to death this past quarter of an hour?"

"Hush!" Despite her mortification, Rose could not prevent the corners of her lips from twitching at his description of Professor Prosser, who, following the interruption engendered by Hugo's entrance, had as soon as possible resumed his one-sided discourse where he had left off. "He'll hear you!"

"So?" Hugo lifted one eyebrow demonically. "Maybe, then, he'll take the hint and wing his way home to his perch, where he belongs!"

Despite herself, hearing that, Rose was compelled to clap one hand over her mouth to stifle the laughter that threatened to bubble forth.

"Have I said something to amuse you, Miss Windermere?" the professor abruptly inquired.

"Who, you?" Hugo drawled, with seeming civility, but with his English, usually so precise, inexplicably suddenly so tinged with an Indian accent that the words came out sounding like "Whooooo, yooooou?" as though he were an owl hooting.

Glancing curiously at Hugo, the professor cocked his head a trifle, his eyes behind his spectacles blinking very rapidly again and the two tufts of white hair on either side of his balding head sticking up in such a way that he really did resemble nothing so much as a horned owl. Apparently, Rose was not the only one to whom this thought occurred, because without warning, Daisy was beset by such a fit of giggles that she was unable to suppress it.

"Oh, dear, I—I don't know what's got into me. I'm—I'm so sorry," she managed to gasp out.

"Yes, and so you should be," Mrs. Windermere observed reprovingly. Then she unwittingly added, "You'll feather no nest with that kind of foolish behavior, miss!"

At that, even Colonel Windermere whooped with mirth, only his wife and Professor Prosser still oblivious to the joke.

"I'm sure that I don't know what's got into all of you," Mrs. Windermere declared stoutly.

"Not what, m'dear. *Whooooo!*" The colonel slapped his knee, his belly shaking so hard that he nearly doubled over in his chair at his own humor.

"I'm afraid that I don't understand.... Who? Who?" the professor said, inadvertently causing them all, except Mrs. Windermere, to howl even louder. "My word, look at the time." Nervously flicking open the cover of his pocket watch, the little university instructor checked it cursorily. "I didn't realize that it was getting so late. I've really got to fly."

His unfortunate turn of phrase only provoked fresh gales of laughter. Shaking her head, Mrs. Windermere stood, politely escorting Professor Prosser from the drawing room, mumbling under her breath about Daisy being a silly, impertinent chit, to whom he should pay not the slightest bit of attention.

"Oh! Mr. Khanna! That was...that was really too bad of you!" Daisy cried indignantly, amid peals of amusement. "Now, Mama shall be so angry with me—when it was *you* who put such wicked thoughts into my head!"

"Whoooo, me?" Hugo queried, sending them all off again.

"Well, it's all well and good to laugh, I suppose, for Professor Prosy really *does* look like some molting old owl," Lily asserted carelessly, once all the frivolity had died down a little, "although I daresay that the poor fellow can't help it. But I do fear that he was much mortified by our behavior and has taken offense, and if that is indeed the case, then I very much doubt that he shall call upon you again, Rose."

"I thought that his name was Professor Prosser," Hugo said blithely.

"Oh, it is—and Daisy is right. That was really too bad of you, Mr. Khanna!" Rose insisted.

"I feel quite certain that you must have dozens of beaux, Miss Windermere, so that the loss of one can scarcely represent any real hardship."

"To the contrary, Mr. Khanna—" she spoke primly "—Professor Prosser was...one of a kind." Beneath his seemingly casual scrutiny, she blushed with both embarrassment at the admission and pleasure that Hugo should be interested in her number of suitors. For, surely, this last meant that he *was* jealous of the professor's attention to her, and that was what had prompted his misbehavior.

"In that case, it is undeniably incumbent upon me to make amends."

"Amends for what, Mr. Khanna, pray tell?" Mrs. Windermere asked, as she reentered the drawing room.

"I'm afraid that it was I who provoked such laughter at the unsuspecting professor's expense, Mrs. Windermere. Unfortunately, he bears an uncanny resemblance to an owl."

"Why, so he does, Mr. Khanna. Now, I understand the joke. I'm not normally so dull-witted. But I confess that ever since your arrival, I have been racking my brain to try to think who it is that *you* resemble—for your appearance is somehow familiar to me...."

"Indeed...? I...can't imagine why. However, I would be glad of a private word with you and Colonel Windermere, if you would be willing to spare me a few moments of your time. Miss Windermere, would you please be so kind as to join us, also?"

As she stood, Rose was aware of the fact that all her sisters were agog with interest and curiosity. But her parents, as her father led the way to his study, seemed more puzzled and thoughtful than anything else, so that she wondered if perhaps they already suspected who Hugo really was. However, once the colonel had closed the study door behind them and bade them be seated, she was quickly disabused of that notion. For once Hugo had finished recounting at some length his tragic tale, Mrs. Windermere cried out, clearly astonished by his revelations.

"Hugo Drayton! Of course, I should have known it at once! For there is the look of your father about you—that is who you reminded me of—except that you have your mother's eyes. But to think that you have been alive all this time…well, I'm sure I don't need to tell you that it hardly seems possible! Although the Colonel did say, at the time, that the—the bodies were burnt beyond all recognition… My dear Hugo— oh, I do hope that we need not stand on ceremony, for your parents were our best friends in India, you know— if only we'd known that you were still alive, we would have done whatever we could for you, I promise you."

"I know that you would have, Mrs. Windermere, and I appreciate it more than I can ever say," Hugo said gravely. "But even before we learnt for sure that Sir James was behind the murders of my parents, Mayur Singh suspected him and, so, feared to let it become known that I had survived. He felt that we could trust no one, that I would be safe only as long as my cousin believed that I was dead, and since I was, of course, just a thirteen-year-old lad, I did what Mayur Singh thought best and let him take me away to my mother's people in the Punjab."

"Understandable, my dear boy, entirely understandable." The colonel cleared his throat gruffly. "It was a terrible business, all the way around—and Mayur Singh wasn't the only one who had doubts about Sir James. Mrs. Windermere never liked or trusted him, either—and quite rightly, as it now turns out. But despite an extensive investigation, I was never able to locate any of the bandits who had been at your parents' *haveli* that night or any evidence that would have implicated your cousin, either. And quite frankly, the longer I tried, the more insistent he grew that I was just wasting my time. He became…rather threatening, Mrs. Windermere and I thought."

"I can imagine. I believe him to be a very dangerous man, Colonel," Hugo insisted grimly. "Perhaps he is even mad. That is one of the reasons why I hesitated to get in touch with you once I had come to England. I did not want to expose you or your family to any peril. But I'm very much afraid that in my resolve not to be captured with the envelope and its contents upon my person, I unwittingly drew Miss Windermere and Miss Jasmine into the situation that day in High Holborn. Now, I can only hope that Sir James, having called upon you and received a return visit, has dismissed any suspicions he might have had about their somehow being involved. As far as I have been able to determine, he has not set spies to watch your town house, in any event."

"Well, I'm most relieved to hear that." Colonel Windermere's normally jolly countenance was somber and anxious. "So, let us assume for the moment that Sir James indeed has no idea that you are not only still alive, but also in touch with us. What can we do to help? I cannot, in all good conscience, stand idly by whilst there is a possible plot afoot to assassinate the Queen! As you know, I was an officer in Her Majesty's Army for many years, and for that reason, I still have a number of connections who would prove quite useful to us…important men who will have access to information and resources that, for all those at your own disposal, Hugo, you will not. So I daresay that a word or two in the right quarters would result in at least Avery Ploughell and Douglas Delwyn being placed under examination and their papers and so forth being duly scrutinized by the Queen's agents."

"Yes, no doubt. The difficulty, Colonel, is in knowing whom to trust," Hugo pointed out logically. "Although I feel quite certain that Miss Windermere is correct in her assessment of Sir James's company the day of your visit to Belgrave Square, and that those companions comprise the core of those persons involved in the evil scheme, there may be others of whose identities we are as yet unaware, perhaps even some among the Queen's own ranks! Were they to be alerted…"

"Yes, yes, quite right. We don't want to put them on their guard."

Absently drumming his fingers on his desktop, the colonel narrowed his eyes thoughtfully, and for the first time that she could clearly remember, Rose caught a glimpse of her father as he had been in his prime. In that moment, it struck her most forcibly that he was not really the slightly befuddled, dear old gentleman whom she had always perceived him as being, but, rather, that the post he had held in Delhi had actually been quite a valuable one, which he had earned through his own intelligence and competence. In military matters, he was in his milieu, as he demonstrated when he continued.

"Nevertheless, discreet inquiries may still be made here and there. With all the news being reported in the *Times*, it is only natural that the idea that Queen Victoria and Prince Albert might be the target of an assassination attempt should be discussed in the clubs and elsewhere, and much may be learnt from a man's reaction to same. For sooner or later, both liars and fanatics invariably trip themselves up in some fashion. There is also another avenue we might employ—the street lads and lasses with whom my daughters have become acquainted over the years. After all, those boys were not only able to spot you, but also to take you by surprise, Hugo—and judging from what I have seen and learnt about you, I suspect that was not easy. Having survived on the mean streets of London and its surrounding districts, they are all sharp customers, who know how to keep their eyes and ears open, and their mouths shut, when necessary. Rose can tell them that she dislikes Sir James and that his call upon us has made her uneasy— which is no less than the truth, after all—and that, as a result, she wishes to be apprised of anything concerning him. That should do the trick—and without revealing your own true identity or what you believe that Sir James is planning."

"Yes, I agree." Hugo nodded slowly. "For it may be that as matters unfold, my own spies will fall under suspicion and observation, due to the fact that they are most all Indians by birth. The only thing that I cannot like is the notion that either you or your family should be placed in any jeopardy, Colonel. Please believe me when I say I would never forgive myself if something should happen to any of you because of me."

"I understand and am most appreciative of that, Hugo," Colonel Windermere remarked gratefully. "But it was my duty, in Delhi, to ferret out the culprits responsible for the murders of your parents and the burning of their *haveli*. I deeply regret to say that I failed miserably, and that is a circumstance that has long haunted me and for which I am glad to be given the chance to make amends—not only because it was my job, but also because, as Mrs. Windermere noted earlier, Lord and Lady Thornleigh were our closest friends in Delhi. I wanted justice for them then—and I still do."

"Exactly so, dear Colonel." Mrs. Windermere spoke soberly, much subdued by all that she had heard. "What was done to Lord and Lady Thornleigh was horrific—a plot devised by a complete monster! Sir James must, as you say, Hugo, be a madman! But thankfully, forewarned is forearmed, and it is we who shall be on our guard. Further, please rest assured that when the time comes, you will not stand alone to make your case before the Queen. There are others who were in India, in Delhi, at the time of your parents' murder, who have now returned to England, and I believe that they, too, will remember young Master Hugo and Mayur Singh, and so can be persuaded to vouch for you, if necessary."

"Thank you, Mrs. Windermere. You are most kind." Hugo paused for a moment. Then he went on. "Now, I have taken up more than enough of your time, so will bid you good day. I leave it for you to decide whether to make my real identity known to the remainder of your daughters."

"Jasmine is a sensible lass, with a good head on her shoulders. So she will bear telling," the colonel declared. "But as for the rest, I think that it is best if they know as little as possible of this affair."

"Very well."

His business concluded, Hugo stood, and after he had made his farewells to her parents, Rose walked him to the front door.

"I hope that I have done the right thing," he confided, frowning slightly.

"Don't worry, Hugo. For I'm certain that you have," she reassured him. "You have been too long alone, I fear. But as you have seen, you are among friends now."

"Yes." Taking one of her hands in his, Hugo kissed it gently, lingeringly, his dark eyes smoldering with a light that sent a sudden shiver of mingled fright and excitement through her. "Did you mean to marry Professor Prosser?" he asked abruptly.

"No," she answered quietly, shaking her head.

"Then I have done us both a great service," he said.

Book Three

The Crystal Rose

> Come live with me, and be my love,
> And we will some new pleasures prove
> Of golden sands, and crystal brooks,
> With silken lines, and silver hooks.

The Bait
—John Donne

Eighteen

A Great Service

> So long as we love we serve; so long as we are
> loved by others, I would almost say that we are
> indispensable.
>
> Across the Plains [1892]
> Lay Morals
> —Robert Louis Stevenson

Russell Square, London, England, 1850

Then I have done us both a great service.

Long after she had closed the front door behind
Hugo, Rose felt that his words echoed in her heart,
causing such a tumult within it that she could scarcely
contain it. Yet even as her heart soared, her mind
urged caution and restraint, telling her that she was

perhaps reading more into his words than he had ever intended. Still, it was difficult to remember that when even her family appeared convinced that Hugo was bent on courting her.

"Is that why Mr. Khanna wanted a private word with you and Mama, Papa?" Lily inquired archly, unable to repress an envious sigh. "To obtain your permission to pay his addresses to Rose?"

"Well, and why should he not?" Mrs. Windermere queried, flitting nervously around the drawing room, not only upset, but also excited by all she had learned.

To think that the rich, handsome, mysterious Mr. Khanna was actually Hugo Drayton, the true and rightful Lord Thornleigh! Surely, it was the answer to all of her prayers, all that she had ever dreamed of for her eldest daughter—for Mrs. Windermere, beneath all of her perpetual fluster, was really quite astute about human nature, and she had not missed the way that Hugo had looked at Rose, nor she at him. In their minds, they had placed each other on pedestals born of their childhood friendship, Mrs. Windermere felt sure, perhaps even read a great deal more into the relationship than had ever truly been. Children possessed such vivid imaginations, shared such secrets, and made such pledges that the overwhelming importance of all that at the time frequently persisted into adulthood, overriding the common sense even of those who ought to know better. Perhaps that was the case with Hugo and Rose, and they would gradually learn that what each saw in the other was only a fantasy, a mirage born of naïveté and fond memories. On the other hand, there were those rare childhood sweethearts who, no matter what, never outgrew their attachment to each other, Mrs. Windermere also knew, so that over the years, their innocent, young love only deepened and grew, evolving into a lifelong bond so strong and lasting that even death would never break it. She rather fancied that this last was how it would eventually prove between Hugo and Rose, if only they were given time and the opportunity to discover it.

"Any man would be fortunate to gain one of my daughters for his wife," Mrs. Windermere continued, "including Mr. Khanna. Rose is very beautiful, and yes, I believe that Mr. Khanna is most taken with her!"

"Oh, he must be indeed." Daisy grinned impishly. "For he certainly sent that old hoot owl Professor Prosy packing!"

"By Jove! In all the excitement, I'd forgotten all about *him*." Colonel Windermere's eyes twinkled merrily. "Still, it's a pity that he most likely shan't be putting in a reappearance here at Russell Square, for I feel quite certain that *he* could have been persuaded to overlook all of your freckles, Daisy, and to set his cap for you instead of Rose."

"Oh, Papa! As though I could ever care a fig for Professor Prosy!"

Observing her family happily occupied, surprised but relieved to see how cleverly and easily her parents had explained Hugo's private conservation with them,

Rose quietly slipped away to the bedroom she shared with her sister Jasmine. There, despite all of her attempts to restrain herself, Rose discovered she felt as giddy as a schoolgirl and that her feet appeared to have developed not only a mind of their own, but also wings. For after closing the door behind her, she found herself dancing and spinning around the floor, her hands clutching tightly the gold half coin she wore around her neck.

"Well, I can see that I don't need to ask you how you feel about Mr. Khanna's attentions toward you." Jasmine smiled widely as she entered the bedroom and observed Rose skipping and pirouetting around. "What's that you're holding?"

"My half of a Gupta coin, which was given to me during our childhood by Mayur Singh." Rose blushed to be caught dancing with an imaginary partner. But still, she felt she must confide in someone or burst. "Oh, Jasmine, now that I am released from keeping Mr. Khanna's secret from you, I can tell you all!"

Clasping her sister's hands in her own, Rose led her to the bed, where they sat down together companionably and Rose told her tale. Hearing it, Jasmine was as astounded as her parents had been.

"Hugo Drayton! Oh, Rose, no wonder you are so happy—and I am so happy for you! For I know how close you and he were during our childhood. Surely, it is a miracle that he is still alive, and surely, now that you have found each other again, that is a sign that your relationship was always meant to be!"

"I would like to think so. But still...Hugo is... much changed, Jasmine. I care deeply for him, yes. I always have and always will. But now that he has come back to me, I realize that he is in many ways a stranger to me now."

"Do you believe that you could not love him, then?"

"No. But I think that in my mind, I must be sure that that is what I truly feel for him, and he for me."

"Time and your own heart will tell you that, Rose, just as they will Hugo."

Nineteen

Love Comes Softly

Equal to the gods seems to me that man
who sits facing you and hears you nearby sweetly
speaking and softly laughing. This sets my heart
to fluttering in my breast, for when I look on you
a moment, then can I speak no more, but my
tongue falls silent, and at once a delicate flame
courses beneath my skin, and with my eyes, I
see nothing, and my ears hum, and a cold sweat
bathes me, and a trembling seizes me all over,
and I am paler than grass, and I feel that I am near
to death.

Fragment 2
—Sappho

Russell Street, London, England, 1850

In the days that passed, Rose sometimes felt as though
she were living in a dream, or perhaps even the fairy-

land that Hugo had more than once claimed during their childhood was her true demesne. For as often as he could, he came to the Windermeres' town house at Russell Square, and she discovered that the old rapport they had once shared was still there, that she could talk to him as easily as she had of old, in Delhi. Frequently, once she had ascertained that it did not cause him pain, she asked him about their homeland and how it had changed in the past fifteen years since she had seen it. At those times, they reminisced at length about their childhood, and played "Do you remember…?" laughing over some memories and saddened by others, and it was especially then that Rose observed the deepest changes in Hugo.

Once, he had been open and forthright about his thoughts and emotions. Now, she saw just how grievously that fateful night in Delhi had scarred him, so that he had built a very high wall around his heart and vigilantly guarded himself against all further hurt. Sometimes, his eyelids would sweep down to veil his black eyes enigmatically, so that she could not guess his thoughts, and when she inadvertently trod too near old wounds, he passed the moment off with some lightly spoken but bitterly cynical joke or else fell into a brooding silence, retreating to a place where she could not reach him.

In her heart, Rose ached dearly for him then, yearning to stretch out her hand and gently, soothingly, smooth back the jet-black hair from his brow, to turn back the clock to those carefree days of their youth, before their world had been so brutally shattered. But more than anything, she recognized that Hugo did not want pity, not anyone's—but especially not hers. So instead, at such times, she would carefully steer the conversation in a different direction, still not quite certain where it was that they were going, knowing only, ever more strongly and surely, that wherever it was, they were indeed going together.

For the more time that she spent with him, the more certain Rose knew in her own heart and mind that she loved him—that she always had and always would—and that it was not just the love of a child for her best friend, but, now, that of a woman for a man. Had she never known Hugo before in that other, long-ago life in Delhi, she would still have loved him now, she thought.

Among other things, all of her family liked and respected him, and already, he had done so much for them that Rose did not know how she could ever repay his many kindnesses. The business and investment advice alone that he frequently gave her father had resulted in financial dividends that she was aware her father could never have achieved on his own. She was deeply appreciative of the fact that, these days, the colonel fretted a good deal less, that his naturally cheerful disposition was no longer occasionally dampened by the saddening notion that he wished he could do more for his wife and daughters. Slowly but steadily, little niceties began to trickle into the town house at Russell Square, and Rose felt her heart swell with love and gratitude for Hugo at the simple pleasure that her father derived from being able now to afford a few of the finer things in life for his family.

Her mother and sisters were completely won over the day the invitation to the ball arrived.

"Oh, my dear daughters, you won't believe what has happened!" Mrs. Windermere's face was flushed with overwhelming excitement as she rushed into the drawing room of their town house in Russell Square. "Oh, I just knew that becoming acquainted with Mr. Khanna would prove the making of us all! How very fortunate, it was, that Rose thought to bring him to our town house that day when the poor man was set upon in the park! We have now been invited to a ball to be held in Grosvenor Square—by no less than the Marquess of Highmoor himself!" With a hand that trembled victoriously, Mrs. Windermere held out the elegant, expensive invitation.

"The Marquess of Highmoor! But, Mama, we don't even know him!" Rose frowned slightly with puzzlement.

"Oh, good grief, Rose! Who cares a fig about that!" Leaping from her chair, Lily ran to their mother's side, enthusiastically snatching the invitation from her and reading it herself. "It's true! It really *is* from the Marquess of Highmoor! Lord, whatever shall I wear? For surely, I've nothing grand enough for such an occasion! Papa! *Papa!*" Lily dashed from the drawing room, obviously bent on finding their father and wheedling a new ball gown out of him.

The rest of the sisters, including Rose, gathered around Mrs. Windermere to examine the invitation she had only just managed to retrieve from Lily in the nick of time.

"Mama, I'm sure that we'll all very flattered, but really, I cannot think why the Marquess of Highmoor should have invited us to his ball." Rose continued to be curious as to what had prompted the unexpected invitation, although, like her mother, she felt that it must indeed be Hugo's hand at work. But still, a niggling doubt assailed her.

"I don't know why you are fretting over that, Rose," Mrs. Windermere said, "for what else could it be but Mr. Khanna's influence?"

In truth, Rose did not know, and in the end, she was glad to discover that the highly coveted invitation could, in fact, be laid squarely at Hugo's door, as she learned during his next visit to the Windermeres' town house.

"I am so relieved to hear that, Hugo, because although I did believe that to be the most likely case, there was always the chance that it was some evil trick of Sir James's."

"No." He shook his head. "And I'm so sorry that you were given even a moment's fright on that score, Rose. I should have realized that you might have some faint suspicion and told you beforehand, but I wanted to surprise you. Lord Highmoor and I became acquainted through mutual business interests, and we have since grown to be friends. So, of course, when he mentioned the ball, I did not hesitate to put your family's name forward."

"I don't how I can ever thank you enough, Hugo."

"Please. Think nothing of it." With a casual wave of one hand, he dismissed her gratitude as though it were more than what he deserved, although she knew that was not true. "It is I who am in debt to you and your family. Your father has actually been of great assistance in ferreting out information from all of his cronies at the East India United Service Club, and those street lads and lasses of yours truly are sharp customers who have provided more than one snippet of interesting news, as well."

"I'm so glad."

Twenty

No Wallflowers

> Thou wast that all to me, love,
> For which my soul did pine—
> A green isle in the sea, love,
> A fountain and a shrine,
> All wreathed with fairy fruits and flowers,
> And all the flowers were mine.
>
> *To One in Paradise* [1834]
> —Edgar Allan Poe

Russell Square and Grosvenor Square,
London, England, 1850

In the three weeks that passed prior to the Marquess of Highmoor's ball, the Windermeres' town house was such a flurry of anticipation and activity that Rose often felt as though she could scarcely even think.

Although she was not acquainted with Lord Highmoor, she thought that any friend of Hugo's must be a friend of hers, as well, and so she was looking forward to the gala and to meeting the marquess. In fact, were it not for her fear for Hugo and what might happen to him, Queen Victoria, and perhaps others, too, as the result of all of Sir James's evil plotting, Rose knew that she could not have been happier than at any other time since leaving India fifteen years ago.

She wished fervently she could do more to help Hugo, but was at a loss as to what she could actually do. She and her family did not move in the same circles as the dubious company in which they had found themselves at Sir James's town house in Belgrave Square the afternoon when they had called upon him. So, even learning more about those whom she suspected of being a part of Sir James's terrible scheme had proved difficult.

Despite everything, Rose still found it hard to grasp that a Member of Parliament, a judge and two widows of barristers should have mixed themselves up in such a treasonous plan. Until now, she had always believed that politics and the law were undertaken by just men whose honesty, integrity and fairness were above reproach. Now, she recognized that those two professions were instead riddled with deception, corruption and bias. It was surely an extremely sad commentary on the state of society and human affairs, she thought.

"You're very far away, Rose," her father observed, as he entered the dining room, where she stood at the sideboard, absently arranging a crystal vase of autumn flowers. "Are you not as happy and excited as your dear mother and sisters to be attending Lord Highmoor's ball?"

"Yes, of course, I am, Papa." She smiled brightly, trying to shake off her glum mood and apprehensions. "It's just that I can't help worrying about Hugo and whether Sir James can be exposed in time."

"Indeed. It is a thorny thicket, is it not? As the Earl of Thornleigh, Sir James is a powerful man, and even though we now know him to be a fraud and a murderer, such accusations cannot be made lightly, without any hard proof. But still, never you fear, Rose. For from what I have seen of Hugo, he is not a man to be easily beaten. So I have complete faith that matters will come aright in the end. Now," he abruptly changed the subject, "are you not going to beg me for a new ball gown, like your mother and all of the rest of your sisters? I am advised by Miss Candlish that they have all gathered in the drawing room, with the dressmaker, and that your presence is therefore required posthaste!"

"But...the expense, Papa. Are you quite certain that we can afford it?"

"Now, Rose, you're not to fret about that, I promise you." The colonel patted her arm awkwardly, as he always did when displaying affection. "For in truth, Hugo has been more than generous with his knowledge and advice, you know, so that I have been able to increase our income in ways that I had never previously anticipated. Thus, among other things, I have enjoyed some modest gains on the stock exchange, and I hope to do even better in the future."

"I'm glad. You're a good man, Papa." Gently, affectionately, Rose kissed his cheek.

Then, with a much lighter heart, she headed to the drawing room, where her mother and sisters had gathered to pore over fashion books and, with the seamstress, Mrs. Leclerc and her assistants, to discuss fabrics for ball gowns.

"Rose, what do you think about our dresses all being done in materials that match our names?" Jasmine queried, glancing up from a copy of *Godey's Lady's Book*, which, in addition to many other articles and beautiful plates, contained a fashion section. "Daisy suggested it, and I have to admit that the idea does have a certain charm and appeal. It's bound to get us noticed—and if there's one flower that I'm determined *not* to be at the ball, it's a wallflower!"

"I think that it's a wonderful suggestion!" Rose agreed, laughing, her spirits rising even higher at the sight of her family's happiness and at the thought that this, too, was Hugo's doing. Picking up a bolt of dusky-rose fabric, she draped it about her, dancing and whirling with an imaginary partner around the room. "What do you think? Shall I be the perfect Rose?"

"Yes, you will, dear." Mrs. Windermere nodded with approval. "All my sweet daughters shall be the belles of the ball!"

Fortunately, the astute Mrs. Leclerc and her assistants had brought bolts of tulles, silks, satins and velvets in a number of different colors, along with a wide assortment of artificial flowers, festive feathers, trailing ribands and other elaborate trims to match. For Jasmine, there was a watery yellow, and for Lily, a gorgeous white. Heather selected a soft lavender, while Angelica settled on a pale chartreuse. Observing that she had the widest range of shades from which to choose, since her sunny flower came in so many different hues, Daisy finally decided on a sky blue. Mrs. Windermere, in keeping with her own name, Violet, and matronly status, picked a vibrant purple. Measurements were taken and recorded; styles for the dresses were decided on; and cloaks, headpieces, gloves, fans, reticules, and Morocco slippers were all ordered, as well.

In the days that followed before the Marquess's ball, Rose found that despite the fact that Hugo's well-being and Sir James's plotting were always at the back of her mind, she still felt that her feet scarcely touched the ground. Her mother and sisters, too, were giddy with anticipation. Even the two housemaids, Hannah and Nancy, were filled with unaccustomed excitement, for they were to accompany the sisters and act as their ladies' maids for the evening.

"Good Lord," Colonel Windermere frequently said, shaking his head at all the activity taking place in his household. "I confess that I don't know how the *haut ton* endure such an endless round of routs, parties, assemblies, and balls myself—for only look at the uproar just a single ball has caused us!" But his blue eyes twinkled all the same, and in truth, he was as pleased as punch to see his wife and all of his daughters so merry and gay.

For all the Windermeres, the night of the ball could not come fast enough. But at last, it did arrive, and garbed in all their new finery, they piled into the two coaches necessary to convey the entire party to the Marquess's town house in Grosvenor Square.

Grosvenor Square was located in the district of Mayfair, where from the late seventeenth century to the middle of the eighteenth century, an annual fair had been held during the month of May, upon the one hundred acres of rolling fields north of Piccadilly. Eventually, however, its two largest land owners, the Grosvenors and the Berkleys, had developed the area, laying out elegant squares with magnificent houses set amid harmonious landscapes punctuated by well-arranged walkways. Grosvenor Square itself was situated around a large oval park and home to a gilt equestrian statue of King George I, which had been erected in 1726 and was famous for having been mutilated not long afterward and having a seditious paper affixed to its pedestal.

As the coaches finally turned in to the square, Rose observed through the windows of the vehicle she shared with her parents and Jasmine that street lamps glowed all around, softly illuminating the substantial plaza and the beautiful park at its heart. Drizzle fell from the night sky to dapple the sidewalks and the heavy old paving stones of the street, the raindrops sparkling like thousands of diamonds in the lamplight.

With the coming of autumn, the deciduous trees that dotted the park had turned red and gold; some of the spreading branches had already lost their leaves, which whorled like strange brown fairies across the damp ground, whispering and rustling with each sough of the wind across the square. Ghostly wisps of mist blown inland from the sea and the River Thames billowed and drifted over the plaza and its park, flitting among the trees and the obscuring long shadows they cast beneath the hazy, silver-ringed moon.

In conspicuous contrast, the splendid town house of the Marquess of Highmoor was ablaze with hundreds of lights, whose bright luminescence spilled through the front windows, making the residence shine like a welcoming beacon in the darkness, and liveried footmen standing like soldiers in ranks lined either side of the front door, holding umbrellas to protect the marquess's guests from the mizzle as they disembarked from their coaches and hurried across the sidewalk to the town house. After passing beneath this artificial canopy, the Windermeres were admitted into the reception hall, with its gleaming checkerboard of black and white marble tiles and its imposing, sweeping staircase. There, the butler greeted them courteously, taking their cloaks, then conducting them to the glorious, mirrored ballroom, where he formally announced them.

At the unarguably stunning picture presented by

the six sisters decked out in the finest gowns they had ever owned, a buzz of excitement hummed through the room. Who were the Windermeres? Everyone wanted to know. As he greeted his guests, Saxon St. Giles, the Marquess of Highmoor, smiled with great delight at the sensation that had been created. His friend Raj Khanna had proved correct, as usual. The production of the Windermere daughters was bound to ensure the success of the marquess's ball and to have the *haut ton* talking about it for weeks afterward. It would be judged one of the triumphs of the Season!

Rose found Lord Highmoor an attractive, charming man—even more so when he told her that there was someone at the ball who had been longing to further his acquaintance with her.

"Ah, and here he is now, as a matter of fact. Miss Windermere, I believe that you've already met Mr. Raj Khanna…?"

"Yes, I have." Brightly, Rose smiled up at Hugo, her heart beating fast in her breast. "Good evening, Mr. Khanna. You are looking very well."

In fact, if anything, Hugo appeared more handsome than ever, she thought, in formal dress, for the rich black color suited his dark good looks, emphasizing his piercing black eyes and the hawkish cast of his features. His white gloves were spotless, and he wore a dusky-rose rosebud in his lapel.

"Thank you, Miss Windermere." He bowed low over her hand, his lips just brushing its back. Then, lowering his voice, he observed, "And you yourself look ravishing! Your proud father and I shall be reduced to beating the gentlemen away with canes!"

"You will turn my head with such flattery, Hugo," she teased softly, her breath coming shallowly and her heart still thrumming fast as he tucked her arm possessively into his, strolling a little away with her from the reception line. "I owe you my deepest thanks. As you can see, your endeavors on my family's behalf have made us all very happy."

"I'm glad. But as I've told you before, Rose, it is I who am indebted to you and your family, and truly, it is little enough that I have done. A bit of sound advice to your father, a word to the marquess. And in all honesty, my motives have not been entirely altruistic, but, rather, selfishly designed to ensure my own pleasure. Even as the reclusive Raj Khanna, I do not go entirely unnoticed, and this seemed one of the safest courses of action in accounting for our relationship without arousing Sir James's suspicions. A public introduction to the Windermeres by my friend the marquess...my own interest obviously immediately piqued by the beautiful Rose...it would be completely understandable if I were to be deemed by those in the know to be as smitten as though I had been struck by a thunderbolt."

"Would it, indeed?"

"Yes, it would—and it would not be a lie, in truth. For you are even more beautiful now than you were in our childhood, when I used to think that you were a fairy come to India from some faraway, magical place." Momentarily, Hugo's arm tightened around hers, and his hooded dark eyes smoldered as he gazed down at her. "But already, I see that my competition is descending upon us. So, quick, give me your programme, Rose, so that I may place my name upon it for all of the best dances. Then we can talk."

"Yes, I would like that very much. But...must you truly fling me to the wolves, Hugo?" Rose asked, half in entreaty.

"Alas, yes. Already, I can feel the daggers in my back for monopolizing you as swiftly and as long as I have. But here is your sister Jasmine. So you need not brave the pack alone. Good evening, Miss Jasmine. How nice to see you again, as always."

Within moments, Hugo had disappeared into the crowd, and Rose and Jasmine were surrounded by a bevy of admirers, all angling for proper introductions from Lord Highmoor, then, having got those, vying for attention and begging for dances. Soon, the programmes of both sisters were filled, and as the small orchestra in the gallery commenced to play, Rose and Jasmine were led by their partners to the dance floor, where they saw that none of the Windermere daughters was to be a wallflower at the ball. Indeed, Lily had been claimed for the first dance by none other than the marquess himself. If Mrs. Windermere, now seated to one side in the cane-work "rout seats," with a fashionable group of inquisitive matrons, had beamed any harder, she would have blinded someone.

For Rose, however, the only dances that mattered

were the ones that she shared with Hugo, especially the waltzes, when he might hold her near and speak to her without the constant partings that formed a portion of the quadrilles and other dances. Now, as he elegantly swept her around the ballroom, she was aware of little besides Hugo himself, how tall and dark he was, how strong, how his black eyes seemed to drink in every detail of her appearance. Despite the fact that she was not vain, Rose knew that she had never looked better than she did this evening, with her silver-blond hair swept back in a mass of cascading curls ornamented with tiny flowers; the décolletage of her dusky-rose gown displaying her graceful throat, shoulders, and the full curve of her bosom; and the trailing ribands at her waist emphasizing its slenderness.

"Are you having a good time, Rose?" he asked.

"Yes, but still, I—I fret, Hugo. Perhaps it would have been better to keep our connection private, for what if Sir James should learn of it? Surely, in that case, he would put two and two together, and realize that it was you whom Delphine Squasher's hirelings pursued that day in High Holborn."

"I can trust Lord Highmoor not to reveal that it was at my own urging that you and your family were invited to his ball, and I am, of course, perfectly willing for him to take credit for having 'discovered' the Windermere sisters. As for the rest, I do not believe that there is currently any reason for Raj Khanna to be associated with the thief who broke into Delphine

Squasher's town house. So I think it most unlikely that Sir James will uncover my true identity because of our relationship, Rose."

"I hope that you are right, Hugo." Her face was grave. "Have you learnt anything more about what Sir James is plotting?"

"No, unfortunately, I have made little progress since discovering that he and his cohorts are planning to shoot the Queen. As you already know, from what my informant in Sir James's town house told me, they considered several other alternatives, such as a bomb. But after much discussion, they discarded them all in favor of shooting the Queen, and Mr. Blott was assigned the task of actually assassinating her, as it was felt that he has the best chance of disappearing into the crowd and escaping afterward. But more than that, I do not yet know."

"Oh, I don't understand why you do not just go to the Queen with what you do know, Hugo!"

"Because whilst I now have considerable information about Sir James and what he and his associates are scheming, I still have little hard proof of their intentions. They would simply deny everything, and I myself would be made to look either foolish or mad or both!"

"But then…how will you obtain any proof of what they are up to? Whilst I did not like any of them and was truly shocked to discover that Mr. Ploughell, a Member of Parliament, and Mr. Delwyn, a judge, are in on their plot, none of them except for Mrs. Blott and Mrs. Squasher struck me as being particularly stupid—although Mrs. Ambrose was certainly very peevish! Indeed, a more fretful, complaining woman, I hope never to meet!"

"I'm not yet sure how I shall get the evidence that I need." Hugo shook his head. "Sir James and his fellow conspirators have been a great deal more careful than I had hoped and expected, which is why there has been so little real proof with which to incriminate them. I can only continue my observations and investigations, and try to turn up something that will eventually assist me in convincing the Queen that she is in danger." He paused. Then he continued.

"My primary concern is that time is growing short. Once we are through all the holidays and the Little Season starts, there will be barely three months remaining before the opening ceremony for the Industry of All Nations Exhibition on the first of May—and of course, there is always the chance that in the meanwhile, Sir James and the others will alter their plans, choosing a different time and place for their assassination attempt. But you must not worry, Rose—especially tonight. Tonight, let us imagine that we have somehow been transported back to our childhood, before that horrible night, and that you are a fairy queen, the belle of the ball. For in truth, there is no woman here who outshines you."

She blushed, unable to repress a smile of pleasure at his compliments.

"You flatter me, I fear."

"No, for at this moment, I am the envy of every

man present. Tomorrow, you shall have all of London at your feet."

"I do not want all of London at my feet."

"How do you know? You have so little experience of men and the world."

"And you believe that I should have more, Hugo?"

"I believe that where I am concerned, I want you to be sure, Rose. Right now, I cannot even offer you my real name. You deserve a great deal more than that."

"But I ask for nothing more than you, Hugo, if you'll have me."

"In your heart, you must already know that I will, Rose."

"I do not take anything for granted."

"Nor do I—for I know how easily one's whole world can be wiped out in a heartbeat. But now, I am a man, and for the sake of our future, I will—I *must*—bury the ghosts that haunt my past."

No more was said just then, for the strains of music died away, and the dance ended. But as Hugo had possessed the foresight to put his name down, on Rose's programme, beside the last dance prior to supper, which was served at midnight, he was accorded the privilege of escorting her downstairs to the dining room. There, long buffet tables groaning with an array of food such as cold joints, beef and ham tongues, chickens and lobster salads were set out, and chairs and round tables covered with tablecloths had been placed wherever there was room. As the seating was not arranged, guests were free to come and go, and to sit where they pleased. So the Windermere sisters and their companions found two tables together, making up a merry party.

All were sorry when the evening had ended.

Twenty-One

Sweet Surrender

> Now sleeps the crimson petal, now the white;
> Nor waves the cypress in the palace walk;
> Nor winks the gold fin in the porphyry font:
> The firefly wakens: waken thou with me.
>
> > *The Princess* [1847]
> > —Alfred, Lord Tennyson

Russell Square and Harley Street,
London, England, 1850

In the days that followed the Marquess of Highmoor's highly successful ball, dozens of callers paid visits to the Windermeres' town house in Russell Square. Many went away again, thinking that while there was nothing objectionable in either the family's breeding or manners, and while the six marriageable sisters were undoubtedly beautiful, their Bloomsbury address was most unfortunate and would continue to prove a hindrance to their acceptance into polite circles. But others, who had no need to acquire either titles or wealth, were more than willing to overlook the sisters' lack of either and to become regular visitors to Russell Square.

Hugo—still known to everyone, save Rose and her parents, as Raj Khanna—continued to be one of these. Sometimes, he came alone, as he had before the ball. At others, however, he was accompanied by Lord Highmoor or some other gentleman with whom he was apparently engaged in various business ventures. Often, these men would be closeted with Colonel Windermere in his study for an hour or two before joining the ladies in the drawing room. But still, it was clear to all that although Hugo might spend time with the colonel, it was really Rose who drew him to the town house.

If the weather, which had turned even colder and rainier with the coming of winter, were not too bad, they would walk together in the park at the heart of Russell Square, where they could talk privately about the near future and what might be done to stop Sir James and his cohorts from succeeding in their plot to assassinate Queen Victoria.

About their own future, however, little more was said, and Rose feared to ask, to press for more than she already had the night of the ball. She knew only that if she were honest with herself, she must admit that somewhere along the way, she had fallen in love with Hugo, the man, and that she loved him more deeply with every passing day. In her heart, she hoped and believed that he felt the same way toward her, and she thought that were it not for the existence of his cousin, Sir James, they would have been happy together. But instead, Hugo remained fiercely determined to reclaim his inheritance and see Sir James punished for his many crimes, and from his words to her at the ball, Rose suspected that until that happened, he was reluctant to speak further to her of the future, that if and when he did so, he wanted it to be as Hugo Drayton, the true Earl of Thornleigh, and not as Raj Khanna, an immigrant from India.

In addition to receiving callers and paying visits themselves, as the holidays approached, Rose and her sisters spent many hours creating little gifts for all the neighborhood lads and lasses they had come to know over the years, which they would distribute following Christmas, on Boxing Day. They had decided to knit warm woolen stocking hats and mittens for all the boys and mufflers and gloves for their two favorite flower girls, Ashley and Jolette.

Now and then, Rose continued to find odd jobs around the house for Bobby, the pickpocket, to perform, although these had become fewer with the onslaught of winter. Still, she knew that he and the rest of the lads continued to keep a sharp eye out for her, for she had told them of her dislike and distrust of Sir James, the counterfeit Lord Thornleigh, and how she wished heartily that he had never called upon her family.

Now, as, baskets in hand, she and Jasmine made their way through Covent Garden Market on their usual marketing day, Rose smiled as Ashley and Jolette spotted them in the crowd and waved, insistently beckoning them over. During the winter months, from their flower cart, the girls sold posies fashioned of blossoms that were grown in large greenhouses and brought to market by railway and wagon. But as she and Jasmine approached the flower cart, Rose's smile slowly faded, for the girls' pretty young faces were unaccustomedly serious, and their eyes were filled with fear.

"What is it, Ashley, Jolette? What's wrong?" Rose asked, concerned.

"We didn't know if you'd 'eard yet, Miss Windermere, or not. But Leddy and Bobby told us all that you wanted us all ta keep an eye out in case Lord Thornleigh came 'round ta Russell Square again," Ashley whispered, glancing around to be certain no one else was listening.

"Have you seen him, then?" Rose's voice was sharper than she had intended.

The flower girls shook their heads.

"No, but Chandon came by earlier this mornin'," Jolette explained softly, twisting ribbon around a nosegay and deftly tying it into a bow. "You know 'e works on t' docks, unloadin' all t' barges an' such. But sometimes, 'e does other odd jobs when 'e can get them, unpackin' t' produce an' flowers from t' boxcars an' lorries, an' once in a while, if 'e can get away, 'e 'elps Jordan an' 'is dad bring their fruits an' vegetables ta market."

"I see." Puzzled now, Rose wondered where all this was leading.

"Anyway, it was Chandon who told us about t' body." Ashley's dark eyes were huge.

"Body? What body?" Jasmine queried, shocked and appalled.

"T' one some lighter men pulled out o' t' Thames early this mornin'!" Jolette announced, shivering.

"Good Lord, are you trying to tell us that Lord Thornleigh has drowned?" Rose was aghast at what she thought was the flower girls' news.

"No, miss, not Lord Thornleigh 'imself," Ashley corrected. "But it was 'is butler's corpse that was found—an' no mistake, 'coz some o' them who were down at t' river when 'is body was 'auled out recognized 'im from when they'd made deliveries ta 'is lordship's town 'ouse in Belgrave Square."

"At first, it was thought t' butler—Eastlake was 'is name—might o' been drinkin' an' toppled into t' Thames. But then it was seen that 'e'd been beaten, miss, an' 'is throat 'ad been slit!" Jolette's eyes were filled with horror at the notion.

"Are you saying that someone *murdered* Lord Thornleigh's butler?" Rose's mind raced. She knew that the butler, Eastlake, had been Hugo's informant inside of Sir James's town house in Belgrave Square. Now, she feared that Sir James had somehow learned that the butler was betraying him, and had tortured and killed him.

"Aye, miss. We thought…we thought you'd like ta know," Ashley said.

"Yes...yes, thank you, girls—and thank Chandon for me, too. I deeply appreciate your telling me about all this." Opening her reticule, Rose paid for twice the number of bouquets that she usually bought. Then, after tucking them into her basket, she told her sister, "Jasmine, you must finish the shopping by yourself today. I don't know whether Hugo is yet aware of what has befallen the butler, Eastlake, and if not, his own life could be in grave danger. I must go to him at once and warn him."

"Why? I don't understand the connection between the butler, Eastlake, and Hugo." Jasmine's brow was knitted in a frown of puzzled concern.

"Eastlake was Hugo's informant inside of Sir James's town house. I believe that his murder means that Sir James somehow discovered that Eastlake was spying on him—and if Sir James did, in fact, torture the poor man before killing him, then it's possible that Eastlake revealed Hugo's true identity to Sir James!"

"Oh, my! Of course, Hugo must be warned immediately, then! What shall I say to our family to explain your absence?"

"Tell them...tell them Ashley or Jolette was suddenly taken ill and that I stayed to help—for I don't want to worry Papa and Mama needlessly. I'll be home just as soon as I can. But, Jasmine, if I haven't returned by nightfall, then you must inform Papa, at least, about what has occurred, for it will mean that something has happened to Hugo and me."

"I will. Oh, Rose! Do take care!"

"Don't worry. I shall."

Handing her market basket to her sister, Rose hurried away, pushing her way through the crowded square, practically running across Covent Garden Market to Long Acre, where she hailed a hansom cab. Giving the driver Hugo's address in Harley Street, she settled back into the vehicle, the wheels of her mind churning faster than those of the cab. She was not only shocked and horrified about Eastlake's murder, but also terrified for Hugo. For if the butler's corpse had been discovered only this morning, then Hugo was probably unaware that Eastlake was dead—and the fact that the butler had been beaten prior to being killed led Rose to think he must undoubtedly have been brutally tortured.

As the vehicle neared Harley Street, she instructed the driver to drop her off in Mansfield Street. Then she found her way down the narrow alley to Hugo's rear gate. Pushing it open, she wound through his garden to the back door, which she knocked on lightly.

"*Memsahib!*" Mayur Singh was obviously surprised to see her. "What has happened? Is something wrong?"

"I don't know. Is Hugo home, Mayur Singh?"

"Yes, in the study. This way, *memsahib*."

When the manservant rapped upon, then, at his master's command, opened the study door and entered to announce Rose, Hugo sprang instantly to his feet, coming around from behind his desk to take her hands in his.

"Rose! What's wrong? Why have you come?"

"I was very careful, Hugo. I had the driver set me down in Mansfield Street." Breathlessly, Rose divested herself of her bonnet, cloak, and gloves, handing them to Mayur Singh. "So I don't believe that I was followed. But I had to see you right away. I was so worried that you—that you might be in imminent peril!"

"I see. Then you shall tell me all, of course. But first, come into the fire, Rose," Hugo insisted. "You are shivering from the cold and wet. Mayur Singh, some tea for our guest, if you please."

"Yes, of course, *sahib*. I shall go prepare it at once."

Leading Rose to one of the two leather wing chairs that sat before the cheerfully blazing hearth, Hugo bade her be seated. Gratefully, she held out her hands to the warmth of the crepitant flames, for in truth, she was chilled to the bone, although not just from the chilly, rainy weather, but also from fear. Picking up a small, fringed cashmere blanket that lay upon the other wing chair, Hugo gently wrapped it around her, his slender but strong hands lingering tenderly and reassuringly upon her shoulders.

"My poor Rose. You are still trembling. Do you want to tell me now what has happened to upset you so?" Hugo's dark, hawkish visage was filled with concern. "I hope that there is nothing the matter at Russell Square. Your parents...your sisters, they are all well?"

"Yes, it's nothing like that—and in fact, you may already know what has occurred. But I—I couldn't take the chance that you didn't." Rose paused for a moment, gathering breath. Then she continued.

"Hugo, do you remember when you told me that the butler, Eastlake, was loyal to you and serving as your informant inside of Sir James's household?"

"Yes, why?"

"His corpse was dragged from the Thames this morning, by some lighter men. He had been badly beaten, and his throat had been cut."

"The devil you say!" Suddenly springing like a tiger from his chair, Hugo loomed over her, his face bent very near to hers and upon it such a fierce expression that it frightened her. He supported his weight with his hands on either armrest of her chair, trapping her in it. "How do you know this, Rose?"

"Ashley and Jolette, two of the flower girls in Covent Garden Market, told me so only a little while ago whilst Jasmine and I were shopping. Chandon— he's the lad who works on the docks—is sweet on Jolette, and he's the one who, early this morning, informed her and Ashley about Eastlake. Chandon was present, I think, when some passing lighter men spied the poor man's body and hauled it from the Thames."

Hugo's lips thinned grimly.

"Rose, I earnestly hope that this news isn't true. But since I can't think of any reason why Chandon or either of the two flower girls would lie, I'm afraid that it probably is. Damn it!" His voice was low and filled with anger. "Eastlake had been with my family for years! He loathed Sir James, and he was the one person in that household whom I trusted, besides."

"Did Eastlake know your true identity?"

"Yes—and if he were tortured before he died, as would indeed seem the case if he was as badly beaten as you say, then he might have given it away to Sir James."

"Oh, Hugo, that is what worried me so. That is why I came here! I couldn't bear the thought that you might be in jeopardy and not even know!"

"Yes, Rose, and I appreciate the warning more than I can say. I was not scheduled to meet again with Eastlake until later this week, and it would have taken me a great deal of time to discover what had befallen him when he did not show up for our rendezvous, either. I owe that lad Chandon a debt—and the two flower girls, also. But you've not told them who I am or that Sir James is plotting to assassinate Queen Victoria, have you?"

"No." Rose shook her head. "For that would not only have betrayed your trust, but also endangered them. So, no, I merely told them of my distaste for Sir James, that I feared he might be a threat to me somehow."

"Good. Ah, here is Mayur Singh with the tea," Hugo observed, straightening from where he bent over her and moving to stand before the hearth. "Mayur Singh, Rose has brought me very distressing news, and now, I have an errand for you. I wish you to discover whether Eastlake was murdered last night and his body dumped into the Thames and fished out this morning by some lighter men."

"If this is true, it is indeed terrible news, *sahib*, and we must be even more on our guard," the manservant said soberly, his dark, weathered face grave. "For it may be that Eastlake made your real identity known to Sir James."

"Yes, I know."

"I will go right away to see what I can learn, *sahib*." Bowing, the manservant left them, and a few minutes later, they heard the back door close and knew that he had left the house.

"What will you do, Hugo, if Sir James has learnt your true identity?"

Lightly, he shrugged.

"Obviously, there is very little that I can do. If confronted by Sir James, I can deny it, of course, although to do so would, I believe, only complicate my own claim to the title and estates later on. However, I do not think that will prove Sir James's course of action, for he himself has a great deal to lose by it, not the least of which is exposure as a fraud and a murderer. No, my guess is that he will tell no one. Even if he is aware of my real identity, he doesn't yet know what, if anything, I know about the murders of my parents or about his plot to assassinate the Queen, either.

"But he shall certainly perceive me as a threat and will therefore attempt to kill me—and the worst part of it is that you and your family may be in danger, as well, Rose, for Sir James will not know whether you are cognizant of my real identity or not. I shall never forgive myself if anything happens to you or your family. I should have followed my first instincts and never seen you again until all of this was finished!"

"No, oh, no, Hugo!" Rising from her chair, Rose

went to his side, laying one hand on his arm and gazing up at him earnestly. "After finding out that you lived—were not dead and buried in your grave all these long years as I had thought—I don't believe that I could have borne not seeing you again!

"Mayur Singh was right. Since that day in Chandni Chowk when you saved my life, you have always been a part of me, and I of you, I think. Why else should it have been I whom you nearly knocked down that day in High Holborn? Was that not the hand of fate, bringing us together once more for some purpose, however unknown to us at the time?"

With fingers that quivered now with emotion rather than with cold, Rose suddenly reached beneath her bodice to withdraw her gold necklace with its half of the Gupta coin.

"Look, Hugo. I've never forgotten, but kept this always."

He was humbled by her faith and trust in him, by the deep, abiding love for him that now shone nakedly and unashamedly in her wide green eyes, glistening abruptly with unshed tears, as she looked up at him. Wonderingly, he closed his hands around the half coin that hung from the gold chain around her neck. It was warm from the heat of her body, of her breasts between which it had lain so tenderly and securely, and smelled fragrantly of the attar-of-roses scent that she always used. Had she worn the necklace since their childhood, in remembrance of him? Hugo did not know, for strangely, she had never spoken of the coin before.

He knew only that he wanted her with a sudden, fierce possessiveness that he had never before felt for another woman, that he could have drowned in the soft, seemingly limitless depths of the verdant pools that were her entreating eyes, and never even have struggled for air. Relinquishing their hold on the half coin, his hands crept up to cup her beautiful oval face; his thumbs brushed her high cheekbones gently. It was the lull before the storm, but Rose, who'd had so little experience with men, did not know that.

She knew only that his touch seemed to steal away her very breath, leaving her feeling as though she had run an exceedingly long way, and that she suddenly ached at the very core of her being, in some peculiar, indefinable way that she had never before felt. She yearned for something as yet unknown and inexplicable, as though seen through a glass, darkly, but that, if found, would become light and clear, carrying her to some glorious new state of being.

"Rose. Oh, Rose…"

Without warning, Hugo's mouth descended on hers, kissing her deeply, hungrily, as though all of the high walls he had over the years built around his heart had suddenly crumbled to free all his pent-up emotions, and that, now, there was no turning back for him—or for her.

But although frightened as she stood poised for what seemed an eternity on that threshold between girlhood and womanhood, Rose did not want to turn back. What lay beyond the door that Hugo had flung open wide beckoned too strongly, too passionately, to be left unexplored. Trembling from the force of her own wild emotions, she passed through the doorway and into a place that she had unwittingly searched for all of her life—and at long last, she knew that she would never again question whether the heart that she had given to him all those many years ago in their childhood had been treasured and loved, and still was.

In Hugo's bedroom, he and Rose lay quietly, basking in the afterglow of their lovemaking, talking quietly, in the way that lovers do.

"This wasn't the way that I meant for things to happen between us," Hugo told her, as he cradled her close, stroking her head, which lay against his shoulder.

"And now that it has, do you regret it?" Rose glanced up at him a trifle anxiously, worried that perhaps he felt that he had taken advantage of her, when she had wanted him as much as he had her.

"No." He shook his head gently. "It is only that I am so afraid for you, Rose. Sir James is truly an evil, dangerous man, and if Eastlake is really dead, as you say, Sir James may indeed have learnt my true identity. He may try to strike out at me through you. In all honesty, I know that I should have waited until I was restored to my rightful title and estates before seeing you again. But you were, I confess, a temptation that I have found most difficult to resist."

He paused, then rose from the bed, unashamed of his nakedness as he strode across the room. Opening an ornately carved wooden box on the dresser, he drew forth an object that she could not see. Then he returned to the bed, once more slipping in beside her.

"I want to show you something," he said. Unclutching his fist, he revealed a fine gold chain, a duplicate of the one she wore around her slender neck. From it hung his own half of the gold Gupta coin that Mayur Singh had cut in two so many long years ago. "Like you, I have kept mine always, to remind me of you, Rose, of how happy we were together in those halcyon days of our childhood, before the lives that we knew were changed forever."

Picking up her own coin that lay upon her breast, he pressed the two halves together to form a whole.

"Years ago, we were broken apart by Sir James. I will not let that happen again, Rose." Both Hugo's dark visage and his tone were so grim and determined that she felt a momentary chill run down her spine, causing her to shiver. "You are cold…? Come. Let me help you dress, and we will sit again before the fire in my study. No doubt, Mayur Singh will be returning presently, as well."

"Yes, I know. But I cannot wait for him. I've already been gone from home far too long as it is—and Jasmine cannot cover for my absence forever, and she will worry about what has become of me, besides. She knows what has happened and where I am, and if I do not return home before nightfall, she is to tell Papa everything. I— I did not want to worry him and Mama before then."

"Yes, all right. I understand. As reluctant as I am to let you go, then, I know that I must—but, still, only for the moment."

After they had dressed, he walked with her to Mansfield Street, where he hailed a hansom cab for her, paying the driver and giving him her direction. Then he kissed her tenderly.

"You must be even more careful now, Rose—and if Sir James should call again upon you and your family, you must send word to me at once."

"I shall. But it is not myself for whom I fear, Hugo, but for you."

"I'll be all right. I spent many long years in the Punjab, learning how to take care of myself. Go now, and I'll see you when I can."

So saying, he rapped on the box, and as the driver slapped the long leather reins against the back of the single black gelding harnessed to the vehicle, the hansom cab rolled forward, carrying her away from Hugo.

The ride home was short, but between the time she left his lodgings in Harley Street and reached the Windermeres' town house in Russell Square, Rose was abruptly struck by the enormity of her actions. She had lain with a man, given herself to him unreservedly, and although she could no longer doubt his abiding love for her, still, she experienced a momentary maidenly fright at what she had done. But overriding her fear was her deep love for Hugo and her newly wakened awareness as a woman fully grown. Of a sudden, a strange exhilaration filled her, for she knew that she would never again be the same.

Twenty-Two

The Abduction

> As in the cold season their wings bear the
> starlings along in a broad, dense flock, so does
> that blast the wicked spirits. Hither, thither,
> downward, upward, it drives them.
>
> > *The Divine Comedy* [1310-1320]
> > > —Dante Alighieri

Russell Square and High Holborn,
London, England, 1850

The holidays drew near, but for Rose, the preparations
were marred by the fact that Mayur Singh had discovered that the butler Eastlake was indeed dead—had
been tortured and murdered just the way Chandon, the
dock worker, had described to the two flower girls,
Ashley and Jolette, in Covent Garden Market.

Somberly, Hugo gave Rose the grim news when he arrived a few days later to visit her. In a household such as the Windermeres' own, it was difficult to find any privacy. But fortunately, Mrs. Windermere had decided that even if he never regained his rightful title and estates (although she felt sure that he would), Hugo was still the only man for her eldest daughter, and she had arranged that the two should be left alone together in the drawing room, in order to further her daughter's future.

At any other time, Rose would have been ruefully disconcerted by her mother's painfully obvious tactics. But at the moment, she could only be grateful for them.

"I feel as though I should speak to your father—to assure him that my intentions toward his daughter are indeed most honorable," Hugo remarked, as Mrs. Windermere firmly closed the drawing-room doors behind her.

Rose felt her heart soar at his words.

"Are they, then, Hugo?"

"Of course. You must know that they are, Rose."

"I did. I—I suppose that I wanted only to hear it from you. We have…never really spoken much about our future together."

"No, I guess not. But you must be fully aware that I have been…hesitant in the face of such uncertainty as my life currently holds. When I marry you, Rose, I want it to be as Hugo Drayton, the rightful Earl of Thornleigh, and not as the mysterious Mr. Raj

Khanna—however much he, too, is a part of me. I want you to be able to take your proper place in society as my wife and countess."

"I don't care about any of that, Hugo. I would be both happy and honored to be Mrs. Raj Khanna."

"I know. But...if Sir James did manage to learn my real identity from Eastlake, you would be in even worse danger than perhaps you already are now, Rose."

"Then...Eastlake is, in fact, dead...?"

"Yes, I'm afraid so. That's one of the reasons why I called today, to let you know what Mayur Singh had learnt."

"I'm so sorry."

"Yes, so am I. Eastlake was a good man and, as I told you, had served my family for many years. He understood the risk that he assumed in spying upon Sir James, but still, I never thought that he would be found out and killed. Most people—particularly those of Sir James's ilk—tend to ignore servants. I can only suppose that in his desire to assist me, Eastlake somehow attracted a fatal attention to himself. Further, under the circumstances, it is unlikely that I could cultivate anyone else as an ally at Belgrave Square, even were there somebody I could trust, which there isn't."

"Then there's no way for you to learn whether Eastlake actually revealed your true identity to Sir James, is there?"

"No. But still, I dare not make the mistake of presuming that he didn't, but must proceed from here on as though Sir James knows who I really am."

"Then your life is surely in jeopardy, Hugo!"

"Not if Sir James is still ignorant of my real identity. But yes, I must be on my guard at all times, as must you, Rose. You must promise me that you'll do nothing to involve yourself in this matter any more than you already have and that you'll take every precaution in the coming weeks. For I could not bear it if anything should happen to you because of me!"

"Yes, yes, of course, I promise."

After a moment, as though to dwell no longer on the unpleasant subject, Hugo noted the mistletoe that hung from the chandelier above them, and he drew her into his warm embrace, kissing her deeply. When he finally released her, Rose was breathless and blushing.

"Mama will most certainly ask me a barrage of questions once you have gone. Whatever shall I tell her?"

"Tell her…tell her that I am a very reserved suitor who has not yet proposed, but that you are…hopeful." Hugo smiled at her gently, teasingly, so that he suddenly seemed far younger and less forbidding than he normally did, and Rose caught a glimpse of the boy whom she had once known in India in what seemed a lifetime ago.

Tenderly, she reached up and brushed a strand of jet-black hair from his forehead.

"I've been longing to do that for ages. That is the Hugo I remember. I am glad he is still a part of you."

"As you are a part of me, Rose, and always have been. I've loved you ever since I was that boy. Once, I thought that I had lost you forever, that I would never see you again. But you were always there in a special place in my heart, and now that I've found you once more, I don't intend to lose you ever again."

The holidays came and went, and as nothing untoward happened, Rose began to breathe a little easier, believing that despite having been hideously tortured, Eastlake must somehow have been able to remain loyal to Hugo and had not given away his real identity, after all.

From the small sum of money that she had saved over the years, Rose had bought Hugo a beautiful leather-bound book for Christmas, a novel that she had thought might interest him. She had agonized over the purchase, but had not known what else she could afford that he did not already possess. But she need not have worried, for when she presented him with the gift, he was delighted. In return, he gave her a solid-gold bracelet with tiny gold charms upon it, each one a replica of something indigenous to India, including an elephant and a tiger. She was deeply touched by the present and knew that she would wear it always, just as she did the fine chain with her half of the gold Gupta coin.

It was some weeks after the holidays, when Rose and Jasmine were returning home from Covent Garden Market, that Bobby, the pickpocket, approached them. As usual, their last stops were the bakery, the butchery, the fishmonger's and Chris the young pie man's pie cart. They were standing at this latter, in front of the three shops, eating their pies and admiring the new velocipede that Joey, whose father owned The Hobby Horse, was showing off to his friends, when Bobby appeared.

"Mornin', Miss Windermere, Miss Jasmine," he greeted them politely. "Miss Windermere, see that coach o'er there? There's a gentleman an' a couple o' ladies inside what say that they know you, an' they paid me a shillin' ta come o'er here an' ask if you'd mind steppin' o'er there for just a moment, as they'd like ta 'ave a private word with you."

"Oh, all right. Thank you, Bobby, for letting me know."

Still, Rose was slightly puzzled, as she did not recognize the carriage. It did not belong to Sir James, for his had his despicably and fraudulently acquired coat-of-arms emblazoned on the side panels, and those of this vehicle were plain. Maybe it had been hired by some of her mother's friends, she speculated—Mrs. Collingwood and Mrs. Penworthy, perhaps. Yes, that was probably it, she thought with some relief.

Handing her marketing basket to Jasmine, Rose made her way to the equipage, where the coachman stood waiting. He seemed vaguely familiar to her, so that for a moment, she was reassured, and she smiled at him as, at her approach, he opened the coach door for her. But then Rose was brought up short at the sight of Mr. and Mrs. Blott and Mrs. Squasher inside.

"Well, for God's sake, don't just stand there, Miss Windermere! It's freezing outside, and you're letting all of the cold air in," Mrs. Blott said petulantly.

"Come in, come in! Onslow, assist Miss Windermere inside, then close the door!"

Rose was at a complete loss. Good manners dictated that she ascend into the vehicle and greet its occupants. But it was with the gravest of misgivings that she did so, and she was not at all comfortable when the coachman put up the steps and shut up the door behind her afterward.

"Good morning, Mr. and Mrs. Blott, Mrs. Squasher," she managed to say calmly enough, however. "I understand that you wanted a private word with me...?"

"Drive on, Lombard!" Mrs. Squasher rapped imperiously on the box above them. "Quickly, you fool! Quickly!"

Before Rose realized what was happening, the carriage lurched away from the curb so abruptly that she was thrown back violently against the squabs.

"What are you doing? What is the meaning of this?" she cried, as she clutched the safety strap at hand, in order to keep from being flung about the equipage as it began to pick up speed. "Where are you taking me? Stop the coach at once!"

"Oh, do be quiet, Miss Windermere!" Mrs. Squasher ordered coldly, her fat cheeks quivering. "For if you don't, Mr. Blott will be compelled to drug you—and I'm sure that you don't want that!"

As Rose gazed, stricken, at Mr. Blott, sitting on the seat across from her and Mrs. Squasher, he looked at her with seeming innocence and smiled as pleasantly as though they were on a friendly, planned outing together before pulling a bottle of what she recognized as chloroform from his jacket, along with a handkerchief.

"Well, go on, Mr. Blott." Beside him on the seat, Mrs. Blott giggled like a silly schoolgirl. "I've never seen someone chloroformed before. How long does it take to work, do you think? Will Miss Windermere pass out right away, do you suppose? Or will it be a while before she loses consciousness?"

Rose was horrified. She was being brazenly kidnapped in broad daylight—and threatened with drugging at the hands of three people who must surely be mad!

Twenty-Three

In Hot Pursuit

> Mad in pursuit, and in possession so;
> Had, having, and in quest to have, extreme;
> A bliss in proof-and proved, a very woe;
> Before, a joy proposed; behind, a dream.
> All this the world well knows; yet none
>   knows well
> To shun the heaven that leads men to this hell.
>   *Sonnet 129*
>   —William Shakespeare

High Holborn and Nine Elms Road,
London, England, 1851

"Rose has got inside that carriage—and now, it's pulling away from the curb!" Jasmine observed worriedly, as she stared at the departing vehicle. "Something…something must be wrong! She wouldn't go off like that without telling me."

"Gor, she's bein' abducted, do you mean?" Chris's mouth dropped open.

"Bobby, who was inside that coach? Describe them to me!" Jasmine demanded. Apprised of their appearances by the pickpocket, she recognized the carriage's occupants as Mr. and Mrs. Blott and Mrs. Squasher, and she grew even more frightened. "Oh, no! I'm terribly afraid that they mean to do Rose some harm!"

Hearing that, Brock, the butcher boy, abruptly raced after the equipage, his bloodstained apron flapping wildly in the wintry air as he dodged passersby on the sidewalk. As Jasmine and the rest watched, astonished, he jumped the curb into the street, deftly weaving his way through horses and vehicles before managing to leap onto the back of the coach, which was starting to pick up speed.

"Well, don't just stand there with your mouth 'angin' open, Joey!" Nick, the baker boy, commanded. "Hop on that new contraption of yours, get down to Covent Garden Market, and fetch the rest of the lads!"

"Once you've got them rounded up, meet us at Jake's father's livery stable! We've got to save Señorita Windermere!" Victor insisted.

"Right!" Climbing onto the velocipede, Joey peddled away furiously.

"Don't worry, Miss Jasmine. When that rum cur gimme that shillin', I picked 'is pocket! So they won't get too far!" Bobby yelled over his shoulder, as he,

Nick, Victor and Chris began to run down High Holborn toward Long Acre, where Jake's father's livery stable was located.

"Brock, Brock, where is that lazy rascal?" Mr. Cox, to whom Brock was apprenticed, suddenly stepped irately out of the butchery on to the sidewalk. "I spied him out here a minute ago, talking to you, Miss Jasmine, and whilst I appreciate your custom, miss, I'm not paying that bone-idle young scamp to stand around chitchatting! He's always taking advantage, that one is!"

"Oh, Mr. Cox, I'm so sorry, but my—my sister's just been kidnapped! Brock ran after the coach to try to save her, and the other lads took off after them, too."

"Good Lord!" The butcher was momentarily shocked speechless. Then, recovering his wits, he urged gruffly, "Come inside, Miss Jasmine. Sit down, sit down, whilst I go next door to the bakery and the fishmonger's. Nick's or Victor's father can send for a constable, and then we'll get to the bottom of this, I promise you!"

Inside the coach, Rose sat mutely, angry and frightened. But at least with her silence and apparent compliance, she had succeeded in preventing Mr. Blott from drugging her with the chloroform. So she still had her wits about her.

She did not know where the Blotts and Mrs. Squasher were taking her, but as the carriage hurriedly headed toward Long Acre and Covent Garden

Market, she feared that the intent was to carry her across the Waterloo Bridge, into the unsavory districts of Lambeth, Southwark and Bermondsey south of the River Thames. At that realization, her heart sank, for she did not know how anyone, even Hugo, could hope to find her in those crowded, sprawling slums.

Like the Blotts and Mrs. Squasher, Rose was unaware that Brock, the butcher boy, clung to his perch at the rear of the vehicle, wondering what he should do now that he had actually got a foothold on the equipage. There was no doubt in his mind that he could climb up on top of the coach, taking the driver and the coachman by surprise. But he did not know whether they were armed with pistols, while he himself had only his meat cleaver from the butchery, and if he were flung off the carriage or even killed, what would happen to poor Miss Windermere?

The vehicle clattered on southward and, from The Strand, swung on to Waterloo Bridge, which spanned the River Thames. The equipage was nearly across when, much to his vast relief and sudden glee, Brock spied a coach behind him, just turning from the street on to the bridge. Jake held the reins, and Brock could see some of the rest of his mates atop the carriage. He correctly surmised that when Miss Windermere had been kidnapped, Joey and the others present had run to the livery stable for transport and had spotted the vehicle bearing Miss Windermere when it had passed by Long Acre and Covent Garden Market.

Now, grabbing one corner of the long apron he

wore at the butchery, Brock flapped it wildly to signal to his chums that they were on the right track, and a wide grin split his face when, beside Jake on the driver's box, Joey stood up precariously, shouting and waving, before, abruptly losing his balance, he toppled back down on the seat.

Entering Lambeth, the equipage carrying Rose and her three captors wound its way along the south bank of the river, toward Battersea Fields, dampening her low spirits even more. For now, she believed that the Blotts and Mrs. Squasher were bent on taking her away from London entirely, and in that case, she did not know what would become of her—for how would anyone, even Hugo, know where to look for her then?

Past that curve of the river known as the Lambeth Reach, the coach wended, finally jolting on to Nine Elms Road amid the wide expanse of Battersea Fields. Nine Elms Road was a long, isolated stretch, relatively free of traffic, and much to Rose's dismay, reaching it, the surly driver, Lombard, shouted to the four horses harnessed to the carriage, and his whip cracked, so that the vehicle began to travel along at breakneck pace, roughly jostling its occupants about inside. Mrs. Blott complained bitterly to Mrs. Squasher about the inadequacy of the equipage's springs and squabs, instigating an argument between the two women, as the coach had been hired by Mrs. Squasher. Taking a whiskey flask from inside his jacket, Mr. Blott swallowed a long draft, ignoring the quarrel. Biting her lower lip tremulously, Rose clung to the safety strap and wondered if she dared risk opening the door and jumping from the carriage.

It was not the first time the thought had occurred to her, but she had been afraid that in the traffic of the city, she would be crushed to death. Now, with despair, she decided that the speed of the vehicle was currently such that even though Nine Elms Road was deserted, she would almost certainly still be killed if she were to attempt to leap from the equipage.

Between her breasts, her prized Gupta coin lay securely and comfortingly, but still, her heart pounded frantically beneath it as she wondered if she would ever see Hugo again. For the fact that the Blotts and Mrs. Squasher had abducted her surely meant that Sir James had indeed discovered Hugo's true identity from the murdered butler, Eastlake, she surmised, and that they were bent on holding her prisoner to gain some sort of leverage over Hugo. Even more chilling was the notion that perhaps Hugo was already dead, and that she had been kidnapped merely to learn what she knew about the assassination plot before she, too, would be mercilessly killed. For in her racing mind, she had now placed both the driver and the coachman, and she had realized that they were the two brawny thugs who had chased Hugo that day in High Holborn, when he had given her the envelope and its contents.

She was surely lost, Rose thought.

But then, suddenly, a coach appeared from nowhere, pulling alongside the one in which she sat, lost in terrified reverie, and as she recognized Jake and Joey on the driver's box, she felt hope burgeon within her breast. She was not alone! The lads had come to help!

"Pull over! Pull over!" Joey yelled furiously at Lombard, shaking his fist threateningly.

But the demand only spurred the driver to push the four horses harnessed to the carriage to an even more rapid pace. At that, the rest of the boys, who clung to the top of the other vehicle and filled its interior, started shouting, as well, and in a manner that would have been comical in any other circumstances, Burke, the street artist, who was clearly the worse for drink, waved a heavy glass tankard brimming with ale out the open window of the equipage.

"Pull over, or you'll be sorry!" he hollered.

"Faster, Lombard! Pay them no heed!" Mrs. Squasher ordered unnecessarily, beating on the box. "They're just a bunch of drunken louts!"

"No." Mr. Blott spoke, abruptly snarling an oath. "It's those brats from High Holburn! I recognize the one whom I paid a shilling to fetch Miss Windermere." Reaching into his jacket, Mr. Blott withdrew a small, deadly Derringer and, lowering one window of their own coach, aimed the gleaming silver barrel toward the lads.

"He's got a pistol! He's got a pistol!" Chandon, who sat atop the other carriage, warned excitedly.

At that, Burke suddenly heaved the tankard wildly toward Mr. Blott, and it smashed like a bomb through one of the closed windows of the vehicle, sending shards of broken glass and a gush of ale exploding into the interior. Everything happened so fast that, initially, Rose mistakenly believed that Mr. Blott had discharged his weapon before she could act to try to prevent him from doing so and that it had somehow backfired. As the splinters of glass and the shower of ale struck her, she was afraid that it was bullets—for she knew nothing about pistols—and blood that sprayed her, and she screamed and screamed, and tried to shield herself from the barrage. The panicked shrieks of Mrs. Blott and Mrs. Squasher, and the curses of Mr. Blott, also rended the air, adding to the confusion and pandemonium.

Then, terribly, Jake's equipage bashed their own, and from atop the box above them, Onslow's bloodied body tumbled into the road, unbeknown to Rose at the time, a victim of Brock, the butcher boy, and his meat cleaver. The impetus of the other coach swiping theirs caused their own to career wildly before, in the end, it toppled heavily to one side, its shaft snapping in two and the horses pulling free of their traces and galloping away.

Inside, Mr. Blott was the first of them to recover, and groaning with the effort, he flung open the door of the carriage, which now lay on its side in the road, its wheels still spinning slowly, and, with difficulty, climbed out. The other vehicle was halfway down the road, its driver clearly having trouble hauling its team to a halt. A few feet away from the fallen equipage,

Lombard lay dead, his neck broken, and an obviously dazed, husky lad whom Mr. Blott did not recognize was struggling to rise from the ditch. Mr. Blott did not wait to see any more, but took to his heels, fleeing across Battersea Fields to make good his escape while he still could.

Moments later, recovering his senses, Brock staggered toward the downed coach.

"Miss Windermere! Miss Windermere!" he cried anxiously. "Are you all right?"

"Yes...yes, I think so..." Rose replied unsteadily, as she attempted desperately to collect her wits. "My— My head hurts." Placing one hand on her forehead, she felt a large bump and blood.

"Let me help you out of there!"

By this time, Jake had got his own carriage slowed and turned around in the road, and after he had pulled to a stop alongside them and set the brake, he and the other boys leaped from their perches, rushing to assist Brock in getting Rose out of the toppled vehicle. Beneath her, Mrs. Blott moaned and whimpered, but Mrs. Squasher made no sound, and Rose thought that the wholly unpleasant woman must be dead. As Brock and the rest helped her from the equipage, Rose knew that there was little or no way that she could have freed herself from it, hampered as she was by her crinoline and petticoats, so she was grateful for the lads' assistance.

"Get me out of here! Get me out of here!" Mrs. Blott whined peevishly.

Because she was so tall and heavy, it was only

through the combined efforts of Joey, Burke, Nick, and Victor that Mrs. Blott was finally hauled roughly from the coach. Like Rose herself, she was thoroughly shaken up, displaying several cuts and bruises, but otherwise largely uninjured.

"We better tie 'er up," Leddy insisted, glaring at Mrs. Blott, "so that she doesn't try ta run away."

"Aye." Bobby nodded. "You got any rope, Jake?"

"In the coach," Jake said.

"I'll get it," Chris offered.

In moments, despite Rose's weak protests and Mrs. Blott's shrilly voiced outrage, some of the boys had bound her securely and hustled her into Jake's carriage. In the meanwhile, the others had discovered that Mrs. Squasher was, in fact, dead. A long, fatal shard of glass from one of the windows broken during the accident had pierced her eye and driven into her brain.

"Even so, we—we just can't leave her here like this," Rose declared. "I mean it—it just wouldn't be decent."

"It'd be a lot more decent than what she tried ta do ta you, Mam'selle Windermere," Jordan pointed out grimly.

But in the end, Rose prevailed, and the lads pulled Mrs. Squasher's considerable corpse from the vehicle and loaded it on the top of Jake's own. They had nothing to cover her with, however, and as they headed back toward London, Rose thought how extremely angry Mrs. Squasher would be at having her body publicly exposed to every gaping passerby in the city streets.

Twenty-Four

Bound for Trial

The fiery trial through which we pass will light us down in honor or dishonor to the last generation.

Second Annual Message to Congress [1862]
—Abraham Lincoln

Russell Square, London, England, 1851

It was not to be supposed that something so serious as her having been kidnapped could be kept from Rose's family—or from Hugo, either, who, mercifully, she quickly learned was still alive, although an attempt had been made on his own life, too, perhaps by Sir James himself, or, at the very least, by Avery Ploughell and Douglas Delwyn.

Not knowing what else to do, Rose instructed the

lads to take her, Mrs. Blott, and Mrs. Squasher's corpse to the Windermeres' town house in Russell Square, where she dispatched Joey to fetch Constable Dreiling. There, she also discovered that her entire family was already aware of her abduction, Jasmine having sent word from High Holborn to Russell Square and also to Hugo, in Harley Street.

"He is even now searching all of London for you, Rose," her father informed her, as he embraced her emotionally, with obvious relief that she was safe. "We must get in touch with him right away, if we can, and with your sister Jasmine, as well, for she is still at the butchery, in case the boys should have returned there empty-handed. Oh, thank God, you are safe!"

Eventually, Constable Dreiling arrived at the town house, and after taking Rose's and all of the lads' statements, he sent Joey to summon an undertaker, as well as additional constables and a police wagon, into this last of which Mrs. Blott was shortly thereafter imprisoned, to be driven away to gaol.

"What will become of her?" Rose asked the constable quietly.

"At t' very least, she'll be charged with kidnappin', Miss Windermere."

"I'm afraid that that is just the tip of the iceberg, Constable!" Hugo announced grimly, as he entered the drawing room. "Rose!" He strode across the floor, clasping her hands tightly in his own, his black eyes scrutinizing her face searchingly. "I came as soon as I received word of your rescue. Are you all right? Did they hurt you? Your head's gashed—"

"From the carriage accident," she explained, deeply relieved to see him alive and well as she recounted at some length what had occurred.

"Thank God, that is the worst of it—for I've no doubt that they would have killed you!" Hugo stated soberly, when she had finished. "And I want to thank all of you lads, too, for your quick thinking and your brave, noble action in coming to Miss Windermere's aid. You shall all be handsomely rewarded for it, I promise you."

"Gor, we didn't do it for any reward, guv'nor," Brock observed gravely, "although I won't deny as how a bit o' coin wouldn't be welcome ta all o' us... might even be enough for me ta marry Ashley, which I've been tryin' ta save up ta do. That is, if I ain't arrested first for killin' that bloke what were ridin' as coachman on t' carriage that Miss Windermere was abducted in."

"No, Brock, I won't permit that to happen." Hugo's voice was firm. "For you were trying to save Miss Windermere's life, and so your behavior was entirely justified. Wouldn't you agree, Constable?"

"Ahem...why, aye, sir, most assuredly—besides which, who's ta say whether it was Brock's meat cleaver or t' vehicle's accident that actually brought about t' culprit's demise?" the constable pointed out shrewdly, reasoning that Hugo must be a man of some means and importance, and not wishing to be caused any trouble. "In reality, Brock may 'ave only wounded 'im."

"Either way, I am very glad to hear that Brock will

not be arrested and charged, Constable. There are, however, several more charges besides kidnapping that should be brought against Mrs. Blott." Turning to Colonel Windermere, Hugo continued. "Now is the time, sir, to employ all of your most trusted contacts in both the military and the government. For, from what I have learnt of her, Mrs. Blott would appear to be an inordinately stupid and self-serving woman. So I believe that if she is properly interrogated, she will not hesitate—in order to save her own skin—to reveal the whole of Sir James's plot to assassinate Queen Victoria. That, coupled with all of the information that I myself have now collected, as well as the letter that Sir James sent to Mrs. Squasher, and along with the desperate attempt to kidnap your daughter, should provide enough evidence to demonstrate to the authorities that such an evil scheme as to murder the Queen actually *is* in motion."

"Murder the Queen!" Constable Dreiling cried, stricken and dumbfounded. "Lud, guv'nor, surely, you're not serious!"

"Constable, I assure you that I have never been more serious in my life," Hugo declared dryly. "And I feel quite certain that any assistance you can give us in this matter will result in your being generously promoted."

"You don't say…? You don't say, guv'nor?" The constable stroked his muttonchops and mustache thoughtfully. "Well, o' course, whatever I can do ta help—"

"Will be very much appreciated," Hugo reiterated. In due course, the undertaker arrived, and Mrs.

Squasher's body was finally removed from the vehicle belonging to Jake's father. Mrs. Windermere, although she was astonished and slightly discomfitted to have several street lads ensconced in her drawing room, could not help but be more than grateful to them for so courageously saving her daughter's life, and with that thought in mind, seeing that their presence was no longer required, she led them away into the dining room, where she insisted on feeding them all.

Meantime, Hugo, Colonel Windermere, and Constable Dreiling closeted themselves in the library, where they devised a plan for notifying the necessary authorities about dealing with Mrs. Blott and extracting a confession from her. Rose and her sisters remained in the drawing room, where they treated her injuries, reassured themselves of her well-being, and speculated about what would happen next.

"What horrible people!" Angelica shuddered involuntarily. "I know that it's undoubtedly terrible of me, but I'm glad that Mrs. Squasher was killed—and I hope that they hang Mrs. Blott by the neck until she is dead, too!"

"What a fiery creature you've always been, Angelica," Heather remarked solemnly. "But in this particular instance, I fear that I cannot help but agree with you. Those dreadful people surely meant to kill Rose, and I, for one, will not rest easy until Mr. Blott, also, is captured and imprisoned. Where do you suppose he is?"

"I don't know." Rose shook her injured head

gingerly. "After the coach had overturned, he was able to pull himself from the wreckage, and before Jake could get his own team reined to a halt and his carriage turned around to come to our assistance, Mr. Blott had run off. The last that we saw of him, he was disappearing across Battersea Fields."

"How awful!" Daisy's normally sunny face was glum and appalled. "I mean, he left his own wife there, obviously not caring if she were dead or alive, but bent only on making good his own escape!"

"Yes, quite." Jasmine's own countenance was filled with revulsion and disapproval. "Mr. Blott is clearly insane, a complete monster devoid of any natural feelings whatsoever. When I think of poor Rose in his hands…well, the thought is simply not to be borne!"

"No, but I'm safe now, thank goodness," Rose said, "and I shall always be grateful to all of the lads who rescued me."

"As shall we all," Jasmine observed softly. "I'm glad, now, that I never pressed charges against Bobby for trying to steal my reticule…. Oh! I've just now thought! Before you got into the coach, Bobby picked Mr. Blott's pocket, so surely, the man will not be able to get very far!"

Twenty-Five

The Slums of Southwark

> He's tough, ma'am, tough, is J. B. Tough
> and devilish sly.
>
> > *Dombey and Son* [1848]
> > —Charles Dickens

Russell Square, High Holborn, and Nine Elms Road,
London, England, 1851

Gerald Blott was angrier than he had ever before been in his life. Despite the fact that he had picked plenty of pockets himself, to discover that his own had been so violated and his wallet absconded with by a mere street urchin enraged him no end. Not to mention the fact that there had been a considerable amount of money in his purse, which he had only just got off his old, slovenly mother the day before, in Southwark.

Despite the fact that his mother had truly never cared one whit about him, farming him out to be raised by his maternal grandmother, still, whenever Mr. Blott was in need of funds, he hurried home to his mother's rat-infested hovel, there to flatter her outrageously and seduce her. And since Charlotte Blott did not wish to admit, even to herself, that she was a wholly unnatural mother, lacking any maternal instinct for her son, with whom she had had an incestuous relationship ever since he was a lad, she invariably appeased what little poor conscience she possessed by giving him whatever cash he desired.

"I don't know 'ow some light-fingered young clapper-dudgeon got t' better o' you, Gerry. I thought that you was smarter 'n that. I teached you all o' t' tricks o' t' trades, didn't I?" Charlotte's words were slurred, for like her son, she was an inveterate drinker, addicted to gin, the "blue ruin" that was the bane of many an old bawd such as herself. She arranged her tattered, soiled wrapper in a way that she imagined was more attractive about her, then ran one spotted, clawlike hand through the thin, dry tufts of her hair, which was not only a totally unnatural platinum color from the concoctions that she used upon it, but always looked as though it had not been combed in months. " 'Sides, I gave you a whole wad o' blunt jest t' other day—an' it ain't so easy fer me ta git more these days. I ain't as young as I used ta be, you know."

Actually, Charlotte was even a great deal older than

she ever let on, having lied for years about her true age—a fact of which her son, however, was not unaware.

"So? I know that you're into a lot of other stuff besides drunken old bastards, Mum. You've got mumper's brass stashed all over the place, and I need it, I tell you! Don't you ever read the newspapers? No, of course not, for you've never learnt to read! Do you know? I frequently marvel at my pitifully crude, ignorant beginnings—and how I was able by hook and by crook to overcome them! Dora has been arrested—and naturally, in order to try to save her own neck, the big-butted cow has sung like a canary to the authorities. As a result, Ploughell, Delwyn and Ambrose have also been taken into custody, and Lord Thornleigh has vanished, flown the coop—the old scum bucket! I've got to have funds for bribes and such, so that I don't get caught myself. You don't want me to go to the gallows, do you?"

"Nay, but what'd you come here fer, then? That dumb Dora 'as prob'ly tole t' all o' them flat-footed city bull-dogs an' 'our-grunters where I live! They might be watchin' t' place right now, jest waitin' ta cotch you!"

"No." Mr. Blott shook his head. "The silly lump of dough might be stupid, but she knows which side her bread is buttered on. She'll not give this location away."

"'Ow can you be so sure, Gerry?"

"She loves me. You'll see. In the end, she'll recant everything that she's blabbed to the authorities and throw them off balance by telling them a bundle of lies instead."

"Well, I know that I ain't t' sharpest person around, but still, that don't make much sense at all ta me,

Gerry. Them as what sit in judgment at t' Ole Bailey ain't goin' ta be fooled by anythin' like that!"

"Either way, it's not my problem, because the authorities aren't going to apprehend me, anyway. Now, give us a kiss and some cash, Mum. The only way out of this mess is to carry out the original plan and get rid of the Queen. Once she's no longer around, those who are waiting in the wings to step in and seize the reins of the government will pin a medal on my chest—not hang me! But I've got to lie low until then."

"Dora's got plenty o' blunt. That's why you married 'er, ain't it?"

"Yes, but at the moment, I can't lay my hands on any of it. Do you think that I'd be risking my neck here, otherwise? For there is always the slim possibility that she has indeed betrayed us both."

"Then what are you standin' around 'ere fer, you fool?" Kneeling, Charlotte pulled up a loose floorboard, hauling a small sack from beneath it. "'Ere. Take it. It's all I got left right now. But you're right. I can always git more." She grinned broadly, showing bad teeth and rotting gums. "Me latest bloke is goin' downhill purty fast, an' I can git a copper or two fer 'is clothes an' such when 'e's finally gone—an' good riddance ta him!"

"When I've killed the Queen, Mum, I'll make you one," Mr. Blott declared, flashing his mother a brilliant smile, disposed to be pleasant and charming, now that he had got what he had come for.

"Aw, go on with you." Charlotte snorted. "Me? A queen?"

"You ought to have a little more faith in me, Mum. After all, I got myself out of Southwark, didn't I?"

"Aye, that, you did, Gerry. That, you did."

"I can do anything, you know. I'm invincible. No one can touch me."

"Aye, well, you always was a sharp 'un, Gerry, even from t' time that you was jest a lad, an' no mistake. But mind you take care—an' don't you dare let Dora's mumper's brass git away from you! What luck 'twas that 'er dad put a bit by afore 'e turned into such a nutter, eh, Gerry?"

"Yes. In fact, I shouldn't be at all surprised to find out that poor Dora is as loony as he was. Maybe, instead of hanging her, they'll lock her away in Bedlam, do you think?"

Both mother and son laughed raucously at the notion, suddenly companionably swilling from the gin bottle and dancing a jig.

Twenty-Six

The Morning News

> That proverbial saying, "Bad news travels
> fast and far."
>
> *Morals. Of Inquisitiveness*
> —Plutarch

Russell Square, London, England, 1851

"Good morning, Leddy."

"Mornin', Miss Windermere. 'Ow are you this fine spring day?"

"I've quite recovered now from my ordeal, thank you. Truly, I shall never forget what you and the other lads did for me that day! I don't know how I can ever repay you."

Leddy colored with pleasure.

"Gor, Miss Windermere, you don't need ta worry

none about that. Mr. Khanna—er, 'is lordship—
rewarded us all most generously." Taking a copy of the
Times from the canvas bag that he carried, Leddy neatly
folded it in half, as he always did, and handed it to her.
"You won't want ta miss this edition, Miss Windermere," he declared. "The trial is front-page news!"

"Oh! I shall be most anxious to read the report!
Thank you for letting me know, Leddy!"

Hurrying inside, Rose called for her father, and presently, the entire family was gathered around the
breakfast table in the morning room.

"What does the *Times* say, Papa?" Rose asked
eagerly, for in the end, she had been unable to bring
herself to read the article, lest it reveal that Mrs. Blott
was to be released—besides which, it would have
spoiled the Windermeres' morning ritual.

"Yes, Colonel, don't leave us in suspense! Is that
horrible woman to be convicted or not?" Mrs. Windermere queried, indignant at the thought of the part
that Mrs. Blott had played in Rose's abduction.

"Well, let us see," Colonel Windermere said,
opening the newspaper. "Good Lord. What a singu-
larly humongous, ugly female Mrs. Blott is!"

"How do you know, Papa?" Daisy spoke up curiously.

"There is a sketch." The colonel turned the front
page of the newspaper around, so that his wife and
daughters could view the large, unflattering image of
Mrs. Blott ensconced in the accused's box at the
Old Bailey, along with Mr. Ploughell, Mr. Delwyn
and Mrs. Ambrose. "Now, on to how the trial is pro-

gressing." Reading from the *Times* article, he informed his family that the trial, which, following the capture of most of the conspirators, had swiftly ensued, had been pronounced a "shocking spectacle," in that it involved both a Member of Parliament and a judge.

"Mr. Ploughell has insisted that the documents discovered in his office by the authorities and that his signature attached thereto are forgeries, that they must have been planted there prior to his arrest by either Sir James, Mr. Delwyn, or Mrs. Ambrose to frame him. But of course, no one on the tribunal believes him. Mr. Delwyn is thought to be suicidal, but he has insisted that that is only a lie put forth by Mrs. Blott to cause him even more embarrassment and distress than he is already suffering. Good heavens! It seems that since the conception of the assassination plot, Mrs. Ambrose and Mrs. Squasher had foolishly engaged in quite a bit of private correspondence between them, and some of that, too, having been seized by the authorities, is now being made public— despite the apparent salacious nature of several of the letters, detailing Mrs. Squasher's intimate relationship not only with her late husband, Jeffrey, but also with Sir James and Mr. Blott. But according to the report, perhaps those particular letters will not be published."

"And what of the equally despicable Mrs. Blott, Papa? Is she to hang or not?" Angelica queried impatiently, determined that the awful woman should not escape from being made to pay for kidnapping Rose.

"Well, she has now changed her story, claiming that it was the police who came up with the notion of the assassination plot, and that she is completely innocent of any wrongdoing."

"Why, the very nerve of that woman!" Heather cried, outraged. "How does she account for abducting Rose?"

"Mrs. Blott is asserting that it was simply all a big misunderstanding, that 'the lady, one Miss W—' as the newspaper identifies Rose, had agreed to accompany the party to Battersea Fields."

"Oh, how truly mortifying to be mentioned in connection with all of this in the *Times*, even if I am only referred to as 'Miss W—.' For surely, people will learn that it is I who is meant." Rose was visibly upset at the discovery. "Papa, do you believe that I will now be compelled to testify at the trial? For I could not bear that, to become any more a part of such a public scandal than I already am."

"No, for the barristers involved in the case have assured us that you will not have to appear," Colonel Windermere insisted. "We have all, including the street lads, given our statements to Constable Dreiling, as well as to various other authorities, and the focus of the case is on the plot to assassinate the Queen, besides, rather than your kidnapping, Rose."

"Is there any news about Hugo's own case?" she inquired anxiously.

"Yes." The colonel nodded. "In light of all of the events surrounding all of the evidence that Hugo has presented, it is judged quite likely that the Court of

Chancery will indeed confirm his true identity, authenticate his father's last will and testament, and transfer the Thornleigh title and estates to him."

"I'm so glad," Rose said, with heartfelt sincerity. "How fortunate that Mayur Singh thought to rescue Lord Thornleigh's strongbox that night in Delhi, when Hugo's house was attacked by the dacoits and set afire! Have Sir James and Mr. Blott yet been located? For I shall not rest easy until they, too, are captured, since I am quite certain that it must have been Sir James who fired those shots at Hugo, attempting to kill him, the day of my own abduction. Thank goodness, Hugo was on his guard!"

"Yes, for no doubt, you are right that it was Sir James who wielded the pistol. Unfortunately, however, despite the fact that all of London is searching for them, neither Sir James nor Mr. Blott has yet been apprehended. But still, you are not to worry, Rose." Having now finished relating all of the latest news to his family, Colonel Windermere folded up the *Times*, laying it neatly beside his plate on the table. "I feel very strongly that it is only a matter of days before they are, in fact, caught."

But in this notion, the colonel's stalwart faith soon proved sadly misplaced. For despite the extraordinarily large manhunt that had ensued for them, in the days ahead, neither Sir James nor Mr. Blott was located.

Twenty-Seven

At the Crystal Palace

A very stately palace before him, the name
of which was Beautiful.

The Pilgrim's Progress [1678]
—John Bunyan

Hyde Park and the Crystal Palace,
London, England, 1851

May 1, 1851, the day of the grand opening
ceremony for Prince Albert's Industry of All Nations
Exhibition, dawned bright and clear, so that it
seemed that even the weather favored the event.
But still, Rose felt that even had the day proved
chilly and raining, it would not have dampened the
enthusiasm of those who flocked in droves to the
Crystal Palace that had ultimately been erected in

Hyde Park to house all of the exhibits from nations far and wide.

Hugo and Colonel Windermere had arranged for two coaches to convey all of them to Hyde Park, and Mrs. Beasley had prepared an al fresco luncheon for them to enjoy. Mrs. Windermere and her daughters all had new hats and frocks for the event, and all of them except for Rose chattered excitedly among themselves as, carrying their parasols and reticules, they piled into the two carriages that waited outside the Windermeres' town house in Russell Square.

"Are you not as happy as your sisters to be attending the exhibition, Rose?" Hugo asked, as he assisted her into one of the vehicles, then climbed in himself to sit beside her.

"Yes, of course. But, oh, Hugo! I cannot help but worry, to wonder if despite everything that has taken place these past several weeks, either Sir James or Mr. Blott or both still mean to attempt to assassinate Queen Victoria today!"

"I agree that I, too, believe that to be a possibility, Rose. But even so, you may rest assured that in light of all that has transpired, neither the Queen nor any of those responsible for her safety is now discounting the chance that an assassination attempt might be made—and not only on Queen Victoria's life, but also on Prince Albert's. So security will be very strict, and I myself do not think that even should one or more persons try to kill either the Queen or the Prince or both, the attempt will prove successful."

Resolutely, Rose forced herself to smile.

"I know that you are right, Hugo. So I must try to put my fears behind me, so that I will not spoil this outing for my parents and my sisters. Lily, especially, has been so looking forward to being present at the exhibition."

"Indeed, I have, Rose!" Lily, overhearing, chimed in eagerly. "Oh, I do hope that we have left early enough that we will not be caught in the horrendous traffic that is bound to ensue!"

But in fact, the occupants of the two equipages quickly discovered that once they had left Bloomsbury behind by reaching the intersection of Tottenham Court Road and Oxford Street, navigating the remaining straight shot down the latter to Hyde Park and the Crystal Palace was not going to prove at all an easy task. Oxford Street was positively clogged with horses, coaches, and tens of thousands of persons on foot, as well, some bent on making their way to the exhibition, but most others hoping to catch a glimpse of the Queen, the Prince, and their entourage as they wound through the streets to the park.

"Perhaps we would be better off to get out and walk," Jasmine mused aloud.

"What? And have our new gowns crushed and dirtied by that mob?" Clearly, as anxious as she was to get to their destination, Lily was aghast at her sister's notion.

"I'm certain that constables are about, directing traffic, Jasmine," Hugo pointed out logically, and indeed, the shrilling of police whistles could be heard all along the street. "Besides which, I'm not sure that walking would be any faster. All of London must have tickets for the exhibition, it seems!"

Rose thought that must be right, and almost, she wished that the traffic would prevent them from reaching the park altogether. But then, gradually, thanks to the direction of the constables, the horses, carriages, and people on Oxford Street pressed forward, and eventually, she, Hugo, and her family were deposited at their destination.

As they left their two vehicles behind, Rose had to admit that despite all of her misgivings, she still could not repress her excitement as the party followed the serpentine paths through the park to the place where the huge Crystal Palace had been erected.

"Oh!" Daisy cried, enraptured. "Even the pictures in all of the newspapers did not do it justice! Truly, it is magnificent!"

Rose thought that it was, too, and she marveled at the wholly impressive feat of engineering and construction that the building represented. Towering over the treetops, it was over eighteen hundred feet long and over four hundred feet wide. As a result, it covered approximately twenty acres of the park and boasted the largest roof ever made, as well as 293,655 panes that amounted to just under nine hundred feet of glass in total. In addition, it utilized over three thousand tons of cast iron, 330 colossal iron columns, nearly thirty miles of gutters and over 600,000 feet of wooden flooring.

Inside, it was separated into a series of courts right and left, where the history of art and architecture throughout the world was on show. The enormous, arched Center Transept housed the planet's largest organ and was host to the many concerts that would be performed during the exhibition, as well as to a circus complete with tightrope walkers and other performers who engaged in amazing feats of daring. The three-tiered wings were composed of galleries filled with the displays of the nearly 14,000 exhibitors from all over the globe. To guard against fire, twelve fire engines, along with their brigades, were on duty at all times within.

But what astounded and pleased Rose most of all was the way in which the big trees—mostly elms—in the park had indeed been preserved, rising from the ground inside of the Crystal Palace to loom over the street lamps, wrought-iron fences, and gazebos that populated the interior of the structure.

It had been estimated that the edifice could hold between forty and sixty thousand visitors, and today, for the opening ceremony, twenty-five thousand people had paid four pounds apiece for seating in the Center Transept to witness Queen Victoria's dedication of the new building. Finally, after making their way to that spot, Rose, Hugo, and her family discovered that a dais had been set up for the ceremony. Because of their assistance in exposing Sir James's plot to assassinate the Queen, they had been assigned special seating near the dais, so that when the ceremony actually ensued, they had a bird's-eye view of the proceedings.

Initially, it was Prince Albert who addressed the large crowd gathered in the Center Transept before presenting to his wife, Queen Victoria, a copy of the illustrated catalogue of the items contained in the exhibition. After that, both the Queen and the Prince, accompanied by their entourage, toured the entire building to see the wide variety of displays before Queen Victoria once more began slowly to make her way back to the dais to officially proclaim the exhibition open.

It was while those seated in the Center Transept waited for the Queen's return that Rose was shocked and horrified to spy Mr. Blott.

"Oh, my God, Hugo!" She grabbed his arm frantically. "There is Mr. Blott!"

"Where?"

"Standing over there, near the dais! He's dressed as a constable! Surely, he is mad and is going to try to shoot the Queen!"

"Not if I can prevent it!" As he stood, Hugo's dark, hawkish visage was grim with fear. "Colonel, that policeman over there is Mr. Blott. I'm very much afraid that he intends to attempt to assassinate the Queen!"

"Good Lord!"

Colonel Windermere shot to his feet, and both men scanned the Center Transept desperately, well aware of the nearly insurmountable obstacles that they faced. To accommodate the crowd, the seats had been set up extremely close together, so that there was very little room to maneuver. Hollering to alert one or more of the real constables milling about would doubtless prove fruitless, as both men realized, for the cacophony currently being made by the thousands of spectators present echoed loudly throughout the arched Center Transept.

"You go that way, Colonel! I'll take this other side!"

Muttering their apologies to the onlookers, Hugo and Colonel Windermere pushed their ways along the rows of seats, both terribly afraid that they would not get through in time. Already, Queen Victoria, escorted by her husband, Prince Albert, was nearing the dais, where she would again step forward alone to address the crowd and thus become a prime target. Much to Hugo's terror, he could see that Mr. Blott's disguise had proved an inspired stroke, for it never even occurred to anyone to question the fake policeman who edged ever closer to the dais, smiling charmingly—oilily! Hugo thought—at a number of the spectators along his path, pretending to inspect them to be certain that they did not block the Queen's route.

Even though the seats that Hugo and the Windermeres had been assigned were relatively near the dais, Hugo grasped the fact that neither he nor the colonel was going to reach Mr. Blott in time to halt the attempted assassination.

"Mr. Blott!" Hugo cried out desperately, reaching into his pocket for the pistol that he had brought with him this day, just in case. "Mr. Blott!"

Hearing his name above the noise of the onlookers, who had started to quiet down at Queen Victoria's reappearance, the fraudulent constable turned instinctively toward Hugo, suddenly hauling his own weapon from beneath his jacket and firing at him. As the shot reverberated wildly through the Center Transept, terrified screams erupted. The people seated up front, abruptly realizing what was happening, panicked, adding to the fright of those farther back, who, only hearing the loud echo of the bullet ricocheting, erroneously believed that the iron girders of the Crystal Palace had begun to give way, as so many in London had feared. Rose watched, horrified, as a stampede started, not only afraid that she and her parents and sisters might be trampled in the pandemonium, but also that the other policeman now hurrying to the scene would mistake Hugo for the assassin and kill him.

"Mr. Blott!" Hugo shouted again, scrambling over empty seats, shoving resolutely through the fleeing crowd, and then running toward the dais. "Mr. Blott!"

More shots were fired, but Rose could not tell whether they came from Hugo's gun or Mr. Blott's. As she fought to gain the dais amid the press of the confused and frightened crowd, she was dimly aware of Prince Albert moving to protect Queen Victoria, and of her family calling her name. But her only clear thought was for Hugo's safety and well-being.

Then, without warning, a strong, ruthless hand gripped her arm hurtfully, viciously dragging her through the mass of spectators, and as she spied her captor, she realized that it was none other than Sir James.

"Let me go! Let me go!" she spat, furious and

fearful, and began to struggle wildly against him, trying frantically to free herself.

But to her utter horror, instead of releasing her, he suddenly slapped her hard across the face, stunning her and nearly knocking her unconscious. Then he grabbed her up and unceremoniously flung her over one shoulder, brutally forcing a path through the onlookers and carrying her swiftly through the Crystal Palace.

"Help! Help!" Rose cried—or thought that she did. In reality, she was shocked to hear that her voice was instead so faint and tremulous that no one could possibly have heard her.

Recognizing, then, that she must attempt to save herself, she started once more to try to escape, pummeling and kicking Sir James unmercifully, thinking that if only people observed her terrified struggle, they would surely grasp the fact that she was being kidnapped and come to her aid. But instead, because of the panic that had ensued in the Center Transept, those who saw her simply assumed that she was hysterical and being borne to safety by her escort, and no one offered to assist her, too concerned about their own well-being to give hers a second thought.

Several long minutes later, Sir James had got her out of the Crystal Palace and bundled into a nondescript coach that he had waiting nearby. Roughly throwing her into the seat opposite his own, he beat on the box above, and the carriage lurched forward so abruptly and quickly that Rose, attempting to right herself, was instead violently pitched back against the squabs again. Before she could regain her balance, Sir James savagely pressed a sickly sweet-smelling handkerchief over her face, and as she felt a terrible darkness swirl up to engulf her, her last clear thought was that she did not even know whether Hugo was dead or alive.

Twenty-Eight

Drayton Hall

The bride hath paced into the hall.
Red as a rose is she.
> *The Rime of the Ancient Mariner* [1798]
> —Samuel Taylor Coleridge

Drayton Hall, Dartmoor, England, 1851

When Rose finally swam up from the depths of her subconscious, it was to discover that dusk had fallen and that the vehicle in which she traveled had long ago left London far behind. Her head ached, throbbing dully with the aftermath of the chloroform that Sir James had employed to subdue her, and she felt as impotent as a newborn kitten, as though all of her strength had been drained from her. Although she had not eaten since early that morning, she was not hungry, but, rather, hideously sick to her stomach, as though she were going to retch, a sensation that was only badly heightened by the jolting of the speeding equipage. Softly, she moaned, pressing one hand to her pulsing temple and trying to sit up.

"You may as well stay where you are, my dear Miss Windermere," Sir James told her, in a voice that reminded her chillingly of a sinuous, insidious snake. "For we've a ways yet to journey, and you shall not escape in the meantime, I promise you."

"You're…insane," she gasped out weakly. "For you cannot possibly think that you will get away with this!"

"I already have."

"Hugo will come after me."

"If he's still alive. But I do believe that Mr. Blott killed him, for I'm quite certain that I saw Hugo fall."

"No! You're wrong! You're lying to me!" Rose protested desperately.

"Am I? Well, believe whatever you wish, then. It matters not one way or the other to me, I do assure you."

"Why have you abducted me? Of what possible use can I be to you now? For you must know from the newspapers, if nothing else, that your plot to assassinate the Queen was exposed to the authorities by your fellow conspirator Mrs. Blott, that Mr. Ploughell, Mr. Delwyn, and Mrs. Ambrose were taken into custody, as well and that Mrs. Squasher was killed during the previous attempt to kidnap me!"

"Yes, indeed…all too true, unfortunately. I knew that I should never have trusted that fat-arsed sow

Mrs. Blott. Was there ever a more stupid, conniving wench? Not that her silly about-face saved her own skin in the end, for she is to hang right along with the rest, is she not? Still, I was compelled to take her into our confidence, for she would have wheedled all knowledge of our scheme from Mr. Blott, anyway. It was he whom I needed. A man of many talents is Mr. Blott, not the least of which is his own sadly misplaced but unshakable belief in his own omnipotence. Such hubris! But still, I knew that it would serve me well, for he would do anything to further our plan, thinking quite arrogantly that he would never be caught. It quite amused me, you know, to observe how he, Mrs. Blott, and Mrs. Squasher used to compete among themselves, each believing whole-heartedly that he or she was smarter than all of the rest of us."

"In truth, none of you has any real intelligence at all," Rose pointed out coldly. "You are merely mad, puffed up like odious toads with your overbearing pride and presumption, and devoid of any sane, caring human emotion. To gain your evil ends, you stooped to abducting me, to torturing and murdering poor Eastlake, the butler, and you would have killed even the Queen, too. You are all wholly despicable!"

"That is only your opinion, my dear. And the fact is that you are as pathetically idealistic as the rest of your ilk! In the history of the world, real change has more often than not always been brought about by violence. Even a single assassination can alter the entire course of history! Had we succeeded in our plot, we would eventually have been judged as heroes—for with all of their social reforms, Queen Victoria and Prince Albert are setting England on a dangerous path, one upon which the lowliest chimney sweep shall soon think himself the equal of a lord!"

Rose stared hard at her captor.

"Hugo was right, then. The aims that you personally hoped to achieve were far different from those of your wicked cohorts. Do they know how you used and deceived them? I wonder."

Sir James smiled superciliously.

"As you yourself remarked, Miss Windermere, they are scarcely intellectual giants. Still, one takes one's conspirators where one finds them, and as I said, I felt sure that Mr. Blott, especially, despite his great and unpredictable volatility, would prove extremely beneficial."

"Still, I cannot believe that despite the arrest and trial of the others, you somehow managed to persuade him to carry out your dreadful scheme."

"To be honest, I actually had nothing to do with that, my dear. For I've neither seen nor heard from Mr. Blott since the day that he and the rest made such a bungle of your abduction. I am simply an astute judge of human nature, and I know that above all, Mr. Blott cannot bear to be bested. Such is his obsession in that regard, in fact, that he even cheats at cards. He is not, you see, a gentleman, but, rather, a lowlife scoundrel who managed by hook and by crook to haul himself from the putrid muck of Southwark, aping his betters to acquire his speech and manner—although, in reality, he frequently unwittingly exposes his true, distasteful antecedents by some incorrect word or gesture, as did Mrs. Blott. For despite all of her grandiose pretensions, her own birth was to relatively humble parents. Her father was a mere tutor, and he acquired what funds he left Mrs. Blott by shamelessly robbing the family for whom he worked prior to his decamping from their household. He managed to get away—the police are so tiresomely plodding, you understand—and was never caught. But ultimately, his theft did him little good, for he died in a lunatic asylum."

Although she had known that the conspirators were a motley bunch, still, she was shocked and deeply repulsed by all of these so casually spoken revelations, and involuntarily, she shuddered. By now, she had managed to drag herself into a seated position, so that she could gaze out the windows of the coach, and her heart sank as she viewed the increasingly desolate landscape beyond, where the twilight was even now fading into darkness.

"Where are you taking me? And why?" she asked, swallowing hard. "For you've still not answered the last, and under the circumstances, I believe that I have a right to know."

"To the contrary, Miss Windermere, under the circumstances, you have no rights at all, but are my prisoner, to do with whatever I wish," Sir James insisted softly, in a way that sent an icy shiver up Rose's spine. Then, lightly, he shrugged. "However, since there is no harm in it, I will tell you that we are currently en route to Dartmoor, to Drayton Hall, where I have some staff who, unlike that foolish butler, Eastlake, are loyal to me, not to Hugo. There, you and I will be speedily married—I've obtained a special license for that. Then we shall journey to the Continent, where I've prudently transferred much of my money, where we will reside until I am quite certain that Hugo is dead. At that time, all of this will have blown over, and I shall once more take my rightful place in society as the Earl of Thornleigh. My title and wealth will go a long way in convincing the authorities that it was really Hugo who was a part of the plot to murder Queen Victoria all along, not I, and that Mrs. Blott never betrayed him, for she still hoped that he would manage to complete the task. As for you, my dear, I'm very much afraid that after your family and you, in particular, have been properly punished for interfering with all of my plans, you shall go quietly mad and expire in a lunatic asylum, just as Mrs. Blott's father did."

"You will never get away with all of that!" Rose declared stoutly, with a courage that she did not feel.

Inwardly, she quaked with fear at the idea that perhaps Hugo really was dead, that Mr. Blott had killed him, and that Sir James might actually succeed with his awful scheme. He was, she now realized, much cleverer than she had previously credited him with being. And when, shortly thereafter, the carriage swung off the main road that stretched across the isolated moors that had given Dartmoor its name, turning onto a long, serpentine drive paved with crushed seashells, and she at last spied Drayton Hall, she felt that she had sunk to the depths of despair, that she would never be able to escape from the place.

With the falling of darkness, it had started to drizzle, so that the windows of the vehicle were occluded by not only the shower, but also by the mist that swept in from the distant sea to blanket the land ghostily and lie low in its secret hollows. Still, now, ahead, Rose could by the hazy light of the full, silver moon high above and the dim glow cast by the brass lanterns bolted to the sides of the equipage, glimpse the manor, and unwitting, as she did so, she felt her breath catch in her throat.

Perhaps had she come here in broad daylight, as a young bride on the arm of her loving husband, Hugo, she would have loved Drayton Hall. But now, she could only think that it looked as grim and forbidding as its wild, desolate setting. It was three stories high— four if one counted the attic revealed by the row of dormers protruding from the steeply gabled roof—and built wholly of dark-gray granite, solid and daunting. At its fore rose looming twin towers and the facades of the wings on either side. Along the front, tall, narrow, mullioned casement windows with lozenged, lead-glass panes peered out at her like eyes behind the slits of a mask in the brume and rain, and the oriels were covered with creeping, clinging ivy that, in the diffuse, eerie half light, resembled some fantastic, distorted brier in a nightmare.

Past the spike-topped, wrought-iron gates and the dark, crumbling lodge, the coach rolled thunderously. Then, finally, it drew to a halt before the ponderous oak front door. Descending from the carriage, the coachman opened the vehicle's door, letting down its steps, and Sir James roughly half carried, half hauled her from the equipage, gripping her tightly to prevent her from falling as she swayed on unsteady legs. In some dark corner of her mind, she realized that the four horses harnessed to the coach were wet with the drizzle and frothy with sweat from their exertion, and that she, too, was now being showered with rain and perspiring as though she had been bodily and brutally whipped to a speed as fast as that of the steeds had been.

But Rose had no time to assimilate these idle thoughts, for just then, the front door creaked open wide on rusted iron hinges, and Sir James strode into the grand foyer beyond, dragging her along behind him. As the butler greeted him, she understood that she would get no help from that quarter, as she would have done from poor Eastlake, and she knew that her fate would prove very bleak, indeed, if she did not somehow find a way to escape.

The rooms through which she and Sir James quickly passed made only dim impressions upon her, of being closed up and long neglected. For all the furniture was swathed in sheets turned yellow with age and grime; intricate cobwebs spanned all of the corners, nooks, and crannies; and dust that was lightly stirred by their traversing layered the carpets and the wooden floors. Upon at last reaching a tiny cubicle in the attic, Sir James unlocked the door, then shoved Rose inside, turning the key in the lock behind him.

For some time afterward, she pounded vainly upon the door and called for help. But either no one heard her in the immense house, or else they ignored her. Finally, once more swallowing hard, she forced herself to gather her wits, realizing that her current actions were not only exhausting her, but also futile.

By the dim luminescence of the moonbeams that streamed in through the dormer window, she saw upon a small table a candle and the means to light it, and after she had got it burning, Rose was able to take far better stock of her surroundings. She was imprisoned in what was one of the servants' rooms, she surmised, for there was a narrow bed, a short dresser and a chamberpot. Moving to the window, she attempted to open it, but much to her dismay, it was rusted shut. Still, it seemed her only avenue of escape, and spying a hairbrush lying abandoned on the dresser, she took it up and began to prize desperately with its handle at the window.

Rose had some wild notion that if she succeeded in opening the window, she could climb out onto the roof and somehow get away. That, instead, she would most likely slip on the slick shingles that covered the roof and fall horribly to her death, she determinedly thrust from her mind.

She would far rather be dead, she thought, than at Sir James's mercy.

Twenty-Nine

The Rescue

> Rescue my soul from their destructions,
> my darling from the lions.
> > *The Book of Psalms, Chapter 35, Verse 17*
> > *—The Holy Bible*

Hyde Park, London, and Drayton Hall,
Dartmoor, England, 1851

In Rose's panic at the Crystal Palace, she had quite forgotten that the constables carried only billies and were not armed with pistols, so that when Mr. Blott produced his weapon, the policemen right away recognized the fact that he was not truly one of their own. That, combined with Prince Albert shouting instructions as he moved to protect his wife, Queen Victoria, let them know that it was Mr. Blott who was the assassin, not Hugo.

To avoid Mr. Blott's wild shots, Hugo himself dived onto the floor, employing one of the abandoned seats as a shield, and ultimately, taking careful aim and at last certain that he would not hit anyone else by accident, he fired, shooting Mr. Blott right between the eyes. As the lethal bullet drilled into his forehead, Mr. Blott stood still for what seemed an eternity to both him and Hugo. Upon the former's swarthy, bloated visage was an expression of incredulity, as though he could not believe that his death was imminent. He had thought himself invincible, that he would live forever, and to realize in that moment that he was not only mortal, but also that death was but a heartbeat away stunned him even more than the bullet itself had done.

Then, as though in slow motion, Mr. Blott crumpled to the ground, his eyes still filled with surprise as they stared sightlessly up at the arched glass ceiling that towered over him.

"Lord Thornleigh, we owe you a great debt of gratitude," Queen Victoria announced, as she recognized that her would-be assailant was dead.

By this time, the constables, the firemen, and other authorities were managing to restore order, reassuring the crowd that the iron girders that supported the immense Crystal Palace were not in the process of collapsing, but, rather, that an attempt had been made upon the Queen's life. Under Prince Albert's direction, Mr. Blott's corpse was being swiftly removed from the premises, and with her inestimable courage, the Queen was declaring to all present that the opening ceremony for the exhibition would continue if they would only calm themselves and resume their seats. Some terrified persons, of course, had already run from the building. But most had been restrained by the seats and the close confines, so Queen Victoria's instructions were obeyed, and in her stalwart manner, she went on with the ceremony as though it had never been so disastrously interrupted.

But Hugo, having been given leave by the Queen and the Prince, did not stay to see the remainder of the ceremony, being frantically informed by Colonel Windermere that during the assassination attempt and the resulting chaos, Rose had been abducted by Sir James.

"I'm so ashamed!" Wringing his hands, the colonel nearly wept. "For although I saw what was happening, I could not save her. He—he slapped her, Hugo! Then he threw her over his shoulder and bore her away. Oh, my poor daughter!"

Hugo's jaw set grimly.

"Do not despair, Colonel, for I believe that I know where he is taking her: to Drayton Hall. He has allies there, and from there, he can arrange for a boat to ferry him across the Channel to the Continent, besides. But he has not got that much of a head start on us, and if we hurry, we will catch him, I swear!"

Quickly arranging for the Marquess of Highmoor, who was also present, to take charge of Mrs. Windermere and the remainder of her daughters, Hugo and

Colonel Windermere immediately set out for Dartmoor, accompanied by Constable Dreiling, who was on duty at the Crystal Palace and whom they happened to spy as they were hurrying from the edifice. Apprised of what had befallen Rose and of their destination, he instantly offered to go with them, and shortly thereafter, they were all three en route, aided by the fact that by now, many of the people who had previously thronged the surrounding streets had gone home, consoling themselves with the thought that in the coming days, they would be able to view the Crystal Palace for only five shillings apiece, which was to be the standard price of admission after today. So, the crowd having thinned, Hugo, the colonel, and the constable got rather more speedily away than they estimated that Sir James might have managed, and this gave them hope that they could make up for lost time.

Each time that they stopped to change horses, they inquired about Sir James, relieved to learn that he had indeed passed that way, so that they knew that they were on the right track, and they also obtained directions to Drayton Hall, to ensure that their driver did not take a wrong turn in the dusk that fast seeped over the moors and thereby delay their progress.

Still, by the time that Hugo's inheritance at last came into view, darkness had long since descended; rain was showering down upon their coach; and a thick, eerie mist had drifted across the land, intermittently obscuring the manor. Nevertheless, at any other time, Hugo would have wanted to stop the carriage, so that he could take it all in. But now, his fear for Rose overrode any other emotion, and he ordered the driver to press on, completely downcast when they reached the heavy, wrought-iron gates to discover that they were shut and locked tight, barring their path.

"Colonel, you and Constable Dreiling must go and find the nearest authorities, to get help," Hugo said, his voice low, lest it should somehow carry on the wings of the night wind that soughed over the moors. "For it may be that we shall require it. I will go on alone, on foot, over the wall, and try to locate Rose. Return as swiftly as you can—and break those damnable gates down, if necessary!"

This plan thus decided, Hugo disappeared into the darkness, hauling himself with some slight difficulty up the gates and over the dangerous spikes that topped them, then dropping down the other side to the ground below.

Silently and furtively, he slipped along the edge of the winding drive, taking care not to tread upon the crushed seashells, which would have crunched beneath the soles of his shoes. Then, suddenly, he drew to a halt, transported for a seemingly interminable moment back to his childhood and the night of the fire at his parents' *haveli*. For at the window of one of the dormers that lined the steeply gabled roof, he could see Rose. As it had in distant Delhi so many long years ago, his heart lodged in his throat. But this time, it was because his fear for her had never been greater than it was in that instant. Somehow, she had managed to pry open the window, and now, even as he watched, utterly stricken, she began to climb through it, out onto the viciously slick shingles.

"Oh, God!" Hugo gasped out, before his breath caught in his throat with horror, for without warning, she suddenly slipped and slid, and was only saved from falling by clawing for purchase at the windowsill and succeeding in catching hold of it. He didn't want to startle her, causing her to lose her grip. But neither did he want her to continue her desperate attempt to escape. "Rose! Rose!" he called softly. "Can you hear me?"

"H-H-Hugo?"

"No, for God's sake, don't look down! Can you pull yourself up and get back inside?"

"I—I think so."

At the realization that Hugo was not only alive, but had come for her, was actually here at Drayton Hall, Rose felt her heart soar in her breast, even as it pounded hideously at her current predicament. Wisely, she had earlier removed all of her crinolines and even torn away part of her gown so that she would be free to maneuver across the roof. But even so, her skirt still tangled about her legs, and for a terrible moment, she was afraid that she would not, in fact, be able to climb back into the tiny room that was her cell. Then, slowly, she somehow managed to inch her way up, and finally, she lay across the windowsill, panting heavily for breath. With a last, determined effort, she then crawled forward, tumbling headlong onto the floor.

Hugo, knowing that she was safe, did not wait any

longer, but hastened to the manor, gaining admittance by breaking open a set of French doors, through whose panes he spied Sir James.

As Hugo brutally kicked in the doors, sending shards of wood and glass flying, Sir James sprang to his feet, momentarily startled out of his wits. Then he began fumbling wildly through the drawers of the desk behind which he had been seated in his study. Whipping out a pistol, he fired it at Hugo. Dropping and rolling across the carpet to avoid being struck, Hugo withdrew his own weapon, returning fire.

"It's over, James! Give it up!" he shouted, from behind the cover of a sofa. "The colonel's outside with the authorities, smashing down the gates! You and anyone who helps you will be placed under arrest!"

Much to Hugo's surprise, instead of shooting at him again, Sir James instead snarled a vicious oath, then leaped through the broken French doors, running across the sweeping lawn toward the stables. Swearing hotly himself, Hugo gave chase, using the strangely twisted, gnarled old trees that dotted the yard as protection against the two shots that Sir James now turned and loosed upon him before once more fleeing. But Hugo knew that he had the advantage, for he was not yet thirty, and Sir James was not only over fifty, but also heavier and unfit from the dissolute life that he had led. He gasped loudly for breath as he staggered on toward the stables, his legs like lead beneath him, and at last, Hugo flung himself upon him, violently knocking him to the ground.

From the dormer window far above, Rose watched, terrified, as the two men fought and struggled savagely together, and then, to her everlasting horror, another shot rang out, and one of the two combatants fell, blood spreading in a gruesome puddle upon his chest, darkly staining his white linen shirt.

Epilogue

A Bond Everlasting

Happy, thrice happy and more, are they whom
an unbroken bond unites and whose love shall
know no sundering quarrels so long as they live.
Satires [35 B.C.]
—Horace (Quntus Horatius Flaccus)

The Honeymoon

Weave a circle around him thrice,
And close your eyes with holy dread,
For he on honeydew hath fed
And drunk the milk of Paradise.

Kubla Khan [1798]
—Samuel Taylor Coleridge

Chandni Chowk, Delhi, India, 1851

The *haveli* that had so long ago burned upon that fatal night had at some point during the intervening years been rebuilt, rising like a phoenix from the ashes—as he himself had risen, Hugo thought, as he gazed at the spot where his life had taken such a drastic turn.

Beside him, Rose stood silently, her arm tucked lovingly in his as she waited patiently for him to absorb all of the alterations that had taken place since she and he had lived as children in Chandni Chowk. For although much was still familiar to them, time had not, of course, stood still in their absence; change had proved inevitable, as it always did.

"I thought…I thought that there would be ghosts here," Hugo said quietly, at last. "But my parents are long gone—I know that now, finally and forever. But still, I think that they would be happy to see that a new *haveli* has been constructed where their own once stood."

"Do you want to go inside, Hugo, and view the

place?" Rose asked. "I'm sure that whoever owns it, hearing your tale, would be glad to let us in."

"No." He shook his head, smiling tenderly at her. "Whatever was once there for me is now in the past. You are my future, Rose—you and all of the children that we will make together. You are blushing terribly, do you know? Have I said aught amiss? No, I think not, for it is but the truth that I speak to you, and after all, you *are* my bride, my wife!"

"Yes, that, I am—but still, what if Mayur Singh should hear you?" Rose glanced covertly at the manservant, who waited respectfully for them a short distance away.

"He will only be delighted that the Gupta that he cut in two for us all of those years ago is now once more whole—as is my heart. I love you, Rose. I have always loved you."

"As I do and have you. Oh, Hugo! How very happy I am that it was here to Delhi that you suggested that we come for our honeymoon! Perhaps it was cowardly of me, but I—I did not want to be in London for the executions." She bit her lower lip gently, for despite everything, she could find no joy in the fact that those who had persecuted her—Mrs. Blott, Mr. Ploughell, Mr. Delwyn and Mrs. Ambrose—had been condemned to hang.

"I know," he observed softly, understanding. "Once we have returned to England, it will all be over and in the past, as well. Do you think that after all that has happened, you can ever call Drayton Hall home?"

"Yes…yes. It is a sad place at the moment. But just like the *haveli*, something can rise from its ruin. It is your heritage, Hugo, and yes, that of our future children, too. We cannot abandon it, but must restore it to all of its former glory."

"Thank you for that, Rose." Briefly, he paused, his heart overflowing with his deep, abiding love for her. Then he continued. "Now, would you like some *sohanhalwa* from Ghantewala?"

"Indeed, yes!" She smiled up at him brightly, so that for a moment, he glimpsed the child that she had once been.

"Come, Mahout!" Hugo called to Mayur Singh. "For we are bound for Ghantewala, in hot pursuit of *sohanhalwa*, and it may be that we shall require your services in the event of passing elephants!"

"I am ready, *sahib*."

The old manservant grinned broadly, deftly catching the ancient, gold Gupta coin that Hugo suddenly tossed to him. As his palm closed around it, felt the smoothness and warmth of its newfound wholeness, Mayur Singh did not even have to glance at it to know what it was. Carefully, he tucked it into his pocket.

The gods gave, and the gods took away, he thought. But true love was not destined, as he had once believed. It was simply forged of such a strong, everlasting bond that even the gods themselves could never break it.

Two classic romances from
New York Times **bestselling author**

DEBBIE MACOMBER

Damian Dryden. *Ready for romance?* At the age of fourteen, Jessica was wildly infatuated with Evan Dryden. But that was just a teenage crush and now, almost ten years later, she's in love—truly in love—with his older brother, Damian. But everyone, including Damian, believes she's still carrying a torch for Evan.

Evan Dryden. *Ready for marriage?* Mary Jo is the woman in love with Evan. But her background's blue collar, while Evan's is blue blood. So three years ago, she got out of his life—and broke his heart. Now she needs his help. More than that, she wants his love.

The Dryden brothers—bachelors no longer. Not if these women have anything to say about it!

Ready for Love

Debbie Macomber "has a gift for evoking the emotions that are at the heart of the [romance] genre's popularity."
—*Publishers Weekly*

MIRA®

Don't miss this
Aurora Teagarden mystery
by *New York Times*
bestselling author

Charlaine Harris

Aurora Teagarden never forgot
her first case: a serial killer
who terrorized suburban
Lawrencetown. Now that
story is about to hit the small
screen, and Aurora can't help
getting involved. Her ex, Robin,
wrote the screenplay and her
stepson, Barrett, has a starring
role. Then there's Celia, the
catty actress portraying
Roe—who also happens to be
Robin's latest squeeze.

But when Celia is murdered
and Barrett is accused, the real-
life script takes a deadly turn.
Between threatening letters,
deranged fans and renewed
feelings for Robin, Aurora has
one goal: catch a killer and
make it to the final scene alive.

Last Scene Alive

"Best of the series to date."
—*Publishers Weekly*

*Available the first week of
December 2006, wherever
paperbacks are sold!*

MIRA®

REQUEST YOUR FREE BOOKS!

2 FREE NOVELS
FROM THE ROMANCE/SUSPENSE
COLLECTION PLUS 2 FREE GIFTS!

YES! Please send me 2 FREE novels from the Romance/Suspense Collection and my 2 FREE gifts. After receiving them, if I don't wish to receive any more books, I can return the shipping statement marked "cancel." If I don't cancel, I will receive 4 brand-new novels every month and be billed just $5.24 per book in the U.S., or $5.74 per book in Canada, plus 25¢ shipping and handling per book plus applicable taxes, if any*. That's a savings of at least 10% off the cover price! I understand that accepting the 2 free books and gifts places me under no obligation to buy anything. I can always return a shipment and cancel at any time. Even if I never buy another book from the Reader Service, the two free books and gifts are mine to keep forever.

185 MDN EF3H   385 MDN EF3J

Name _____ (PLEASE PRINT) _____

Address _____ Apt. # _____

City _____ State/Prov. _____ Zip/Postal Code _____

Signature (if under 18, a parent or guardian must sign)

Mail to The Reader Service:

IN U.S.A.
P.O. Box 1867
Buffalo, NY
14240-1867

IN CANADA
P.O. Box 609
Fort Erie, Ontario
L2A 5X3

Not valid to current subscribers to the Romance Collection,
the Suspense Collection or the Romance/Suspense Collection.

Want to try two free books from another line?
Call 1-800-873-8635 or visit www.morefreebooks.com.

* Terms and prices subject to change without notice. NY residents add applicable sales tax. Canadian residents will be charged applicable provincial taxes and GST. This offer is limited to one order per household. All orders subject to approval. Credit or debit balances in a customer's account(s) may be offset by any other outstanding balance owed by or to the customer. Please allow 4 to 6 weeks for delivery.

BOB206